CAN'T WALK AWAY

T0352093

CAN'T WALK AWAY

Nashville Dreams

Book One

Sandy James

FOREVER
YOURS

New York   Boston

Copyright © 2017 by Sandy James
Preview of *Can't Let Her Go* copyright © 2018 by Sandy James
Cover design by Brian Lemus.
Cover images © Shutterstock.
Cover copyright © 2017 by Hachette Book Group, Inc.

Forever Yours
Hachette Book Group
1290 Avenue of the Americas, New York, NY 10104
forever-romance.com
twitter.com/foreverromance

First published as an ebook and as a print on demand: October 2017

Forever Yours is an imprint of Grand Central Publishing. The Forever Yours name and logo are trademarks of Hachette Book Group, Inc.

The publisher is not responsible for websites (or their content) that are not owned by the publisher.

The Hachette Speakers Bureau provides a wide range of authors for speaking events. To find out more, go to www.hachettespeakersbureau.com or call (866) 376-6591.

ISBNs: 978-1-4555-9559-4 (ebook), 978-1-4555-9558-7 (print on demand)

This book is for my new granddaughter,
Rosaline Emma.
Grandma loves you to the moon and back,
Bunny!

ACKNOWLEDGMENTS

This book would've gone nowhere without the help of editor Lexi Smail. Thanks for all the insight and encouragement!

As always, thanks to my agent, Danielle Egan-Miller. You're amazing.

I can never sing enough praises to honor my critique partners, Cheryl Books, Nan Reinhardt, and Leanna Kay. Love you, ladies!

CHAPTER ONE

My joint is jumpin'.

Brad Maxwell smiled to himself, wondering if other people's thoughts often reduced experiences to familiar song lyrics. Trying to ignore the old song that was now stuck in his head, he wiped a bar towel across the already clean wooden surface just as a blonde and a brunette made themselves comfortable right in front of him at the only two seats left open at the bar.

Dressed in jeans and a tight red top, the blonde locked her gaze on him and smiled in invitation—a smile he knew very well. How many times had he accepted one of those promising grins?

Too many.

Instead of returning the smile, Brad focused on business. There were plenty of other customers needing service, and he was ready to move on and not waste his time with meaningless flirting. "What can I get for you ladies?"

The blonde cocked her head. "How about some conversation?"

"I can do that," he replied. "What's the topic?"

"Whatever keeps you right here. I'd like to get to know you better."

No surprise that the veiled offer failed to get a rise out of him. The game had grown stale. Hell, he'd lived like a monk the last six months. With a shake of his head, he slid the bowl of pretzels a little closer to the women. "Sorry. Too many customers to stay rooted to one spot. How about a beer? Something to eat maybe?" A glance to the stage found the first act finishing their setup. "The entertainment should start soon."

The moment he took a step away to check the drink queue on his computer screen, she stopped him. "You're plenty entertaining." She gave him a flirty wink.

He felt not a single tickle of interest. After grabbing a menu, he laid it in front of her. "How about I get you something to eat? We've got great appetizers. Try the fried pickles."

With a pouting bottom lip, she scooped up some pretzels. "Just a vodka stinger." No doubt his abrupt rejection had made her omit any politeness in her request.

Brad arched an eyebrow at the brunette.

"I'll have whatever's on tap." Her attention was directed at the stage, although she spoke to him.

No wonder. The first act of the monthly Indie Night was stepping up to the microphone.

Squelching a sarcastic reply, Brad grabbed a glass and

poured her a foamy Pabst Blue Ribbon. Not his beer of choice, but PBR had seen a resurgence of popularity that he'd never understand.

After serving the women and topping off a couple of nearly empty pretzel bowls, he moved down the bar to slap down drinks for preoccupied customers. By the time the first note of music rang out, Brad was able to take a breather.

The singer launched into a rather ear-splitting rendition of "Take It On Back." Brad got himself a Coke and a handful of pretzels, hoping that the next act wouldn't sound like someone's cat was caught inside a clothes dryer.

After finishing his soda, he leaned back against a wall, closed his eyes, and tried to dismiss the noise as he chewed on the pretzels. Familiar smells filled his nostrils. Beer. Fried food. The mixture of perfumes and hairsprays with a slight hint of cigarette smoke that seemed to be the essence of a large group of people gathered together.

The smell of Words & Music.

God, he was proud of himself—a pride that had been a long time coming. It had taken him so long to accept he'd made more than a few mistakes and was ready to change his life.

Opening his eyes, he let his gaze float around the cavernous bar and restaurant. He took in the tall tables framing the stage and dance floor. They were all full of people who clapped, whooped, or swayed despite the rather dissonant cover of a good song. The large dining area was packed, and there was a decent line in the waiting area, which looked to extend out the door. Every seat surrounding the wooden bar was occupied.

He let a lazy smile cross his face. Words & Music was prospering under his management—and his partnership. The old Brad was gone.

Hopefully forever.

"Man, my joint is jumpin'," he sang softly.

"What d'ya say?" Ethan Walker, one of his two partners, cuffed Brad on the shoulder, near to knocking him over since he hadn't expected it.

"I said we're busy tonight."

Ethan nodded, his eyes following a route similar to the one Brad's had just taken. "Yep, we are."

Brad gave Ethan a quick appraisal, taking in his friend's ragged jeans and well-worn shirt. "Did you come right from the farm?" He chuckled. "I guess chicks like the rugged cowboy bullshit."

"Bullshit? I *am* a rugged cowboy. Besides," Ethan said, "since when do you care if I pick up a woman tonight? The way you've been acting lately, I'm amazed Trojan's stock hasn't plummeted."

That comment didn't deserve any kind of reply. Brad made one anyway. "I'm sure you're more than making up for my slack. Besides, I haven't found a woman worth taking a night off for. Not in a long time."

Unfortunately, the first performer was preparing to launch into his second song. Worse, he'd received enough applause that he'd probably be back to perform again next month—applause loud enough that Brad missed whatever smart-ass remark Ethan made in reply. Probably for the best.

Ethan nodded at the stage. "One to ten?"

One to ten. Their typical way of rating the possibility of any Indie Night act moving to the "big time" and finding a place in the cutthroat world of country music. "Two. Tops."

"You'd know," Ethan retorted.

Brad wasn't so sure. Once upon a time, he wrote songs for the stars, but he'd been on the periphery of that world since he'd vowed to get away from the shit and dishonesty that were such integral parts of being famous. As rapidly as Nashville reinvented itself, a few years might as well be a century.

No, Words & Music was his world now. "Hard to believe," he mused aloud as he looked around the place.

"What's hard to believe?" Ethan asked.

"This used to be two buildings instead of one."

"Yep. The Grand Theatre and Cole's Haberdashery, both of which were toast by the 1970s."

"Glad your parents saw the potential," Brad said.

Ethan let out a chuckle. "What they saw was a tax break—two rundown joints in the middle of town they could turn into a bar? Like they could resist that. No, I'm glad *you* saw the potential."

"We," Brad corrected.

"God, you're a pain in my ass. Fine. *We.*"

Why Brad had so much trouble taking credit was a mystery. Maybe he just wanted Ethan to know he valued the ownership trio they had with Russell Green too much ever to let them think this bar was his own one-man show. But once the three pitched their lots into turning the neglected dive into a showplace, Brad *had* been the one who insisted they renovate the old stage of the theater instead of replacing it. That stage had too much character to destroy. Instead, they'd knocked down walls to open up the buildings and make one enormous bar/restaurant/dance floor/stage. There wasn't another place like it in Nashville, although places like the Black Mustang gave it a shot. Sure, there might be other multipurpose venues, but they didn't have the character of Words & Music.

Instead of commenting, Brad watched a woman preparing for her turn on the stage. Her back was to him as she looped the strap of her acoustic guitar over her head and draped it over her shoulder. She spoke to the two men who were her backup musicians. He'd seen them before, many times. Studio musicians who backed up a lot of different acts, which meant she was probably a solo act and had paid the guys to be her accompaniment.

When she turned to face the crowd, he drank in a deep breath. Damn, she was a pretty thing. Long, blond hair—so sun-bleached it was almost white—which held not a hint of wave or curl. She'd tinted some of the strands framing her face a deep blue, something he found oddly attractive in its quirkiness.

Why did she look so familiar?

Brad moved closer to the stage to get a better look, not

at all surprised when Ethan followed right behind.

The closer Brad got to her, the prettier she got. Her clothes were more "flower child" than Nashville. Flowing, gauzy skirt in a sky blue hue. Ivory peasant blouse, secured around her slim waist with a braided leather belt. She wore several silver bracelets on her left wrist and a necklace of silver and turquoise. There was a small tattoo, the outline of a bird, on the inside of her right wrist.

Once she was settled on her stool and had adjusted the microphone stand, she spoke softly. Shyly. "Hi, everyone. Are you ready for a few songs?" She tucked some long blue strands of hair behind her left ear.

The crowd had grown apathetic during the set change, but she seemed undaunted by their listless applause. It had been years since he'd seen a performer who could exude such innocence and timidity yet still show poise, a stage presence, as though her shyness was part of her act rather than who she really was. Most singers would be shaking in their boots at facing an audience who seemed ready to start complaining at any moment.

With a sweet smile, she said, "Once upon a time when I was all of twelve, I got to meet the best singer that has ever lived. Y'all know her. Reba McEntire."

The audience warmed, applauding her choice of idol and punctuating their clapping with a few approving whistles.

"I doubt she'll forget meeting me," the woman said, adjusting her guitar strap. "After all, I tend to make a perfect first impression."

She gently strummed her guitar—a well-tuned mahogany

Martin. C chord. Then a D4 before she gave the audience another bewitching smile.

The dimple in her right cheek made Brad's heart skip a beat.

Adjusting the mic one last time, she said, "Of course, my family will never let me live it down. How many people spill a Coke in their idol's lap and still get an autograph and a kiss on the cheek?"

The audience chuckled. With her spell now woven around the crowd, she nodded to her backup musicians and started to make music. Her voice, sweet and clear, was perfect for the old Juice Newton song "Queen of Hearts." The up tempo and her infectious enthusiasm had the audience enraptured. The crowd was eating right out of her hands.

So was he.

A hand waved in front of Brad's face. "Earth to Brad."

He ignored Ethan and kept watching the angel on the stage as she sang a second song—a Chelsea Harris tune—and then once again bantered with the audience. A rarity that the rather persnickety stage manager, Randy, was giving her a chance at a third song. He was notoriously stingy with new acts, but he evidently recognized talent when he saw it.

"Um...hello?" Ethan said, all but slapping Brad.

He smacked Ethan's hand away. "What?"

"Where'd you go?"

"Go?"

"Yeah, you zoned out there," Ethan insisted. "Missed a couple of really dirty jokes I was trying to tell you." His gaze followed Brad's to the stage before a knowing grin spread over his face. "Oh. *Now* I get it."

"As dense as you are, you don't get anything."

Ethan let out a snort. "The hell I don't. She's why you trotted up here. You wanted a better look. Damned pretty, isn't she?"

She was a hell of a lot more than pretty, but it wasn't as though Brad was looking for any feminine companionship. Even if he were, he wasn't going to get mixed up with an up-and-coming singer.

Where had he met her before?

"And that voice?" Ethan hooked his thumbs in his belt loops and rocked on his feet. "Do you see how she's seducing the audience?"

"I see." What the woman didn't realize was that she wasn't only affecting the patrons at Words & Music. She was also seducing one of its owners. "What do you know about her?"

"You mean you don't recognize her?"

"I think I do." He rubbed his forehead. "It's driving me crazy 'cause I just can't place where. You know how bad I am with remembering people."

All Ethan did in reply was laugh—too long and loud for a simple question.

"What's so damn funny?"

"Would it surprise you if I said I know quite a bit about her?"

"Where'd you meet?" Brad asked, not able to hide his curiosity.

"I know her birthday."

"Did you date her or something?" Not likely. Ethan wasn't known for being with the same woman long. He surely wasn't with someone long enough to know her age or when her birthday was.

Just the thought of Ethan having slept with the woman made Brad want to hit something. Hard.

"Or something," Ethan replied with a smirk. "I know her address, too. Might be able to get my hands on her phone number and social security number."

"Spit it out already."

"I can also tell you that she works tomorrow from ten 'til five."

"How the hell could you know all that?"

"You seriously don't recognize her, do you? God, what kind of manager are you?" Ethan asked.

"For shit's sake, can you please stop talking in riddles? And what does me being a manager have to do with anything?"

"She works *here*, Brad. Her name's Savannah Wolf. She's been waitressing for us for the last six months."

"What?" Trying hard to picture the woman on the stage in one of the red T-shirts the waitstaff wore, Brad finally made the connection. "Well, I'll be damned." As her song hit the bridge, he realized that he wanted to hear more from her and decided to do something for her he'd never done for an Indie Night performer. "Ethan, I've got a great idea."

"Don't you always?"

"How about we offer this woman a *new* job?"

A broad grin filled Ethan's face. "As a singer, right?"

Brad nodded. "Think Russ will agree?"

"Absolutely."

"Then let's talk to him."

* * *

Savannah Wolf gently set her favorite guitar inside its velvet-lined case. Her satisfied smile couldn't be contained. While she'd hoped for a warm reception for her first time on this stage, having Randy—Words & Music's rather particular stage manager—tell her to sing a third song meant she'd knocked her performance right out of the park. For that third song, she'd chosen "For My Broken Heart" by her idol, Reba McEntire, knowing most of the people she was singing for would recognize the pain behind the words.

Thanks, Juice, Chelsea, and Reba.

Those women represented the kind of country singer she hoped she was—a singer who took risks, who sang songs that meant something rather than churning out silly tunes that jumped on whatever the trend was. Her tactic had worked well the first time she'd stepped into the country music world. She'd started to build a nice fan base.

And then...

Nope. Not going to feel sorry for myself. Never again.

Her mother's mantra echoed in Savannah's mind, a mantra that had helped her through the last five years of hell.

"Everything happens for a reason."

Perhaps her budding career had died because it simply wasn't her turn. After the warm reception from the audience, she now had hope that her time had finally arrived—she could support herself with her singing and bid waitressing good-bye.

She had no illusions of being the next hot ticket, nor was that what she wanted for herself. Just a modest living singing at small venues, doing commercial jingles, or even backing up big names when they were near Nashville would allow her to provide for her family in a way she could never do waiting tables. That's what she wanted. What she'd *needed*.

When she'd finally made the decision to try for her dream again, she'd worked up some guts and dove right into the deep end.

And she'd been able to swim just fine.

Randy held up his hand, waiting for her to give him a high five.

Savannah obliged, even as he grinned and raised his hand a little higher as a tacit tease about her height. Or lack thereof.

"You kicked some ass tonight, pretty lady," he said as the next act launched into their first song.

"Thanks. And thanks so much for letting me have a third song. I sure didn't expect it."

Randy nodded toward the bar. "The bosses want to talk to you."

Shifting her gaze to the bar, she found her bosses standing there—Brad Maxwell pouring drinks, Russ Green and Ethan Walker sitting on stools. "About?"

"You'll hafta ask them."

Setting her guitar case out of the way, she said, "Then I should go talk to them."

"You do that." Randy patted her shoulder. "You really did kick some ass out there, and I'm not just blowin' smoke."

"Thanks, Randy," she said before heading to the bar. Practically floating on air, she made her way through Words & Music.

The place was packed, and despite the fact that a new act was performing, several people stopped her as she wove her way through the high-top tables. She smiled with each kind word about her performance. By the time she reached the bar, she had a broad smile on her face.

"Well, well, well," Ethan said when she took the stool next to his. "Aren't you full of surprises tonight, Ms. Wolf?"

"I suppose I am," she replied. Then she shifted her gaze to Brad. "Randy told me you wanted to talk to me."

After setting the beer he'd just poured on one of the empty trays, Brad nodded. His blue eyes found Savannah's.

The color was so vivid that she could only compare them to the ocean surrounding Saint Bart's that she'd seen so very long ago. The intensity of his stare almost made her glance away.

"You were really great up there," he said.

Her face heated as her smile returned. Here was the

validation she needed from a man who had once upon a time been a successful songwriter. One day she'd find the nerve to ask why he'd stopped composing and now owned a bar.

"Quite a performance," Ethan said with a pat on the back.

She'd met Ethan at her interview. He'd hired her on the spot when he found out she was a single mother. His compassion had amazed her. Most people who came from money couldn't seem to realize exactly how hard it was for other people to earn it. He'd been around the restaurant from time to time to see how things were going for her and the other waitresses, and he always had a kind word for their hard work.

Ethan's hand dropped away. "Funny thing about seeing you onstage..."

She quirked an eyebrow. "Oh? What's that?"

"Brad didn't even recognize you."

Russ barked out a laugh as the scowl Brad leveled at Ethan was hot enough to set the place on fire.

"What?" Ethan's grin could only be described as cheeky. "You didn't, did you?"

Brad held his tongue.

It wasn't as though she was surprised. Ethan had interviewed and hired her. Russ had been in charge of most of her shifts. And the head waitress, Cheyanne, had trained her. The only times she'd seen Brad were on busy weekend nights. There had to be at least a twenty-five servers working on Fridays and Saturdays. She was only one among many who wore the same red T-shirts with the Words & Music logo and black shorts. Since Brad requested that the waitresses keep their hair in neat ponytails, they tended to look like Stepford servers.

Plus, she'd only added the blue highlights to her hair three days ago. From his perspective, Savannah was nothing more than another short, skinny blond waitress. As manager of the place, he'd probably seen hundreds.

She tried to put him at ease. Not because he was her boss but because he looked so awfully uncomfortable at Ethan's teasing. "So you didn't recognize me?"

Brad shook his head.

"No wonder. For pity's sake, you must have to supervise more than a hundred people a day to make this place run as well as it does."

His frown eased then morphed into a crooked smile. "Did you really just say 'for pity's sake'?"

Savannah folded her arms under her breasts, not quite sure of his motives. Sure, it sounded like he was teasing. But he was, after all, the man who signed her paycheck. "I did."

"Who says that?" Since his voice held a bantering lilt, she eased her stance.

"My mom. My grandma. Pretty much *everyone*."

"Not anyone I've ever known," he announced.

If he was open to joking, she could give as good as she got. "At least *I* recognized *you*."

"Touché." With a flourish of his hand, he gave her a corny bow. "I admit it. I didn't recognize you."

"Seriously, though," she continued, "I don't know how you do it, but this restaurant is the best organized one I've ever worked for." Not an idle compliment. She really did enjoy her shifts, although not enough to give up her dream and become a lifelong waitress. But for now, it paid the bills.

"Thanks," he said in an *aw shucks* manner. He pushed a wayward lock of his tawny hair away from his eyes. The man was in desperate need of a proper haircut since his hair was neither short nor long. Just somewhere in between, which gave it an unkempt look.

"You're welcome."

Brad waved to the stage manager, who came to join them. As Randy made his way through the crowd, Brad whispered something to Ethan and then to Russ. Both nodded as smiles broke out on their faces. Then he said something quietly to Randy. His grin was every bit as broad.

Finally turning back to Savannah, Brad put his hand on her shoulder. "Looks like your waitressing here is moot now anyway."

Savannah cocked her head. "It is?"

"Yep, it is."

Since all the men were still smiling, she felt as though she'd missed some joke. There was clearly something they knew that she didn't. "And exactly why is it moot, Brad?" she asked.

"Because you're going to be our new opening act," he replied.

CHAPTER TWO

Brad savored Savannah's surprised expression. Her reactions seemed direct and honest. Having been married to a woman who'd done nothing but play her stupid head games on him, he couldn't help but appreciate a lady who said exactly what she thought and didn't try to disguise what she felt. Her sincerity was a trait he enjoyed.

"What I'd like is for you to be our warm-up act. The Freaky Geeks took an out-of-town gig, and I was going to start auditioning for a new act tomorrow. But I got lucky. The perfect opening act landed right in my lap."

"You want me to sing for you?" She eyed him skeptically. "Just like that?"

His gut knew talent when he heard it. This woman was going places, and Words & Music would be the perfect springboard. It didn't hurt that having someone like her

get her start in his place would add to the partners' reputation for nurturing future stars. Hiring her to sing was a
win-win scenario. "Just like that."

"Would the money be as good as waitressing?" Savannah
asked. "I make pretty decent tips and—"

"We'll make it worth your while," Brad replied.

That dimple of hers was going to be the death of him. It
was so irresistible that he suddenly wanted to tug her into
his arms and kiss her stupid. He wondered how she'd react
if he told her exactly what he was thinking. Then he grew
angry at himself as he wondered what in the hell had gotten into him where Savannah was concerned.

The last thing in the world he needed in his life was a
woman, and he most certainly had no business getting involved with his talent.

He dismissed the weird attraction and focused on business. "We'll start at a higher wage than what you're making now waiting tables—including tips. That I promise
you."

"Should we talk contracts?" she asked.

"We should," he replied. "Who's your agent?"

"Don't have one."

"Manager?"

"Nope."

Of course she didn't have someone handling her and her
career. With a voice like hers, if she had representation,
that manager would already be fielding deals. Brad decided
to offer Savannah a lesson in the music business. "Then I've
got a couple of names and numbers for you. Either would

be a good agent who'll make sure— Why are you shaking your head?"

"I don't want an agent," she insisted.

"You're gonna have to trust me on this, Savannah... Without an agent or a manager, someone's gonna take advantage of you."

She let out a small snort. "Yeah, like that manager."

He tried not to take offense. "I'd only give you the names of people who've earned my trust. Not all managers and agents are crooks and— Okay, why are you shaking your head again?"

"Look," Savannah said, sounding as if she were speaking to someone who clearly didn't understand something, "I appreciate what you're trying to do for me. I really do. But I'm not gonna hire another manager. Is that a deal breaker for you?"

His focus was on the one word she'd emphasized. "Another?"

A wave of her hand indicated the topic was closed. "It's a long story."

"You can tell us," Ethan encouraged.

"Maybe another time..."

Brad shrugged. "Have it your way."

"I always do." Such a saucy reply accompanied by a determined stance.

He still wanted to kiss her for it.

This one could easily get under his skin, but he'd be damned if he let any woman bring him down again.

Then it began, so softly it took him a moment to realize

exactly what was happening. One note. Another. A chord. Until the tune was like a flower bud slowly opening in his mind.

It had been such a long time. So damn long. *Why now?* Why all of a sudden was his head filled with music—his own newborn song?

He didn't fight it. He'd learned a long time ago that trying to ignore a melody that was forming in his mind was useless. The song would always have its way.

"I need to go," Brad announced abruptly, trying to keep the excitement that bordered on panic from his voice. He needed a pencil and some paper to capture the melody that refused to be ignored. He also needed to give Savannah one last piece of information. "Come in tomorrow morning at nine and we'll talk."

Without another word, he turned and hurried away.

* * *

Savannah blinked a couple of times, not entirely sure what had just happened. One moment, Brad Maxwell was talking about giving her a job singing, the next he was practically running away.

Did he think he'd just made a mistake?

"Was it something I said?" she asked.

Russ surprised her with a reply to her rhetorical question. "Not at all. He sometimes thinks of something he should be doing and walks away without a word. If I didn't know better, I'd think he was composing again." He shrugged. "I guess we're all used to it. At least you got a lot of conversation out of him before he ran off."

Since Randy had nodded along with Russ, she supposed he'd seen Brad acting that way as well. "So he wasn't upset?"

"Nah," Ethan replied. "If you knew him as well as I do, you'd realize something important."

"Which is?"

"He thinks you're gonna be a star."

"What?"

"Ethan's right," Randy said. "I ain't never seen Brad jump on an act like that before. When he hired the Freaky Geeks, he made 'em audition three times. They almost told him to take his job and stick it."

"Like I said," Ethan added. "The guy sees something in you, Savannah."

She knew nothing about the terms of the offer, even less about how this job would change her life. She needed backup musicians. Would they be provided, or would she have to pay them? When he said he'd pay her more than she made now, exactly how much did he mean?

Oh, hell. Who was she kidding? Savannah would take the job even if Brad Maxwell wanted her to pay for the privilege.

Trying for a career as a singer again was about taking risks. She'd have to invest in recording more songs, which could be expensive if done right. But she'd vowed to keep control of her own career this time and not let some thief of a manager or some big label recording studio steer her away from her goals. No, she was a proud "indie," and she intended to stay that way.

Taylor Swift could keep her stadiums, and Chelsea Wright could keep her limelight. All Savannah wanted were places like Words & Music. And now, it seemed, Brad was helping her take a huge step toward that goal.

The man used to be called the "Hitman" because of the prolific number of songs he wrote that found their ways to the bestsellers' charts. Even though his last chart tune was over four years ago—a fun song called "She and Me"—Savannah was thrilled he'd taken notice of her.

She smiled at Ethan, Russ, and Randy and asked the only question that really mattered. "So...when do I hit the stage again?"

* * *

The notes were pounding through his brain.

How long had it been since a song came so easily? Hell, how long had it been since a song came at all?

Years. Ever since...

Brad blocked any painful thoughts of the past. If he wanted to dwell on Katie's death—or her betrayal—he'd have to do it some other time when he wasn't in the middle of writing a new song.

A song inspired by Savannah Wolf.

There had only been one woman to serve as his muse.

Katie.

He'd loved her. More than he ever thought possible.

Once she'd come into his life, he'd done everything he could to make her happy. Letting her pretend she was helping with the lyrics to his songs. Taking her to every party so they could be "seen" with all the right people. Introducing her to every star she'd badgered him to meet.

Then, she was gone.

He'd thought the Hitman had died when he'd lost her. But he'd been wrong. The music had still been there, softer and full of hurt, but quietly humming in his head. No, the Hitman hadn't died until the day when he'd learned the whole sordid truth about Katie.

And that truth had devastated him.

God, but he'd tried to bury that part of himself—and the humiliation that came with learning of Katie's betrayal—not long after her funeral. Once the truth had clubbed him over the head, he'd shoved all the bullshit aside and acted as though his marriage hadn't even existed. There'd been no career in music, no long string of hit songs. For a couple of years, there'd been only trysts with nameless women, far too many for him to remember. There'd been nights of drinking and debauchery. He'd been trying to forget in every new face and at the bottom of every glass.

The support of his friends had rescued him. Ethan and Russ had brought Words & Music into his life and given him something else to fill the empty hours.

The restaurant had given Brad a new purpose, a reason to get out of bed every morning—well, *afternoon*.

Mornings simply weren't his thing. But he'd found a motive to get up and go to work and keep putting one foot in front of the other. So he'd left behind anything that tied him to life with Katie and the other fakes in the recording business.

For a few months after he'd started working with his partners, he'd kept his womanizing ways, never seeing a woman more than once and never spending a whole night with any of them. He hated himself for how he treated those women, but they distracted him.

Now, the more time he spent at the bar, the more he began to pity and then loathe people who used other people. So he'd given up drinking and had abandoned the pickup routine altogether. He was content to live in the moment now and pretend the pain of the past hadn't been real.

Sure, he might be compartmentalizing his life, but some days, surviving was the best he could manage. The only thing that mattered was his job, this place. And the only time that mattered was the present.

Until Savannah Wolf turned on the music again.

Why?

Why her?

Why now?

He didn't have time to ponder. Scrawling notes across the hastily drawn staff, crooked lines and all, he struggled to seize the tune. The words were there as well, coming almost too quickly to capture. He sang the phrases just above a whisper, over and over until they were committed to paper. Why hadn't he kept all of his blank pages with their nice straight lines and beautifully printed clefs?

Because Brad had sworn he'd never write another song. After learning that Katie didn't really love him, it was as though all the joy he'd once found in music had vanished. Angry and humiliated, he'd built a bonfire in the backyard and burned her incriminating diaries. Then he'd tossed every blank music page he could find lying around on the pyre. The musical part of his life was over. He'd punctuated his promise by also tossing on his guitar and watching the flames lick at it until it, too, was reduced to ash.

A mahogany Martin.

Morose memories were swept aside as more of the new melody screamed at him. He hastily tried to hold on to each note as he fought a battle with himself. Writing one song wouldn't hurt, wouldn't open a door back into a world he'd left behind.

Would it?

"What in the hell?" a voice called.

As if he needed an interruption. His own thoughts were distraction enough. Brad scowled at Russ. "Shouldn't you be downstairs, tossing some drunk out?"

"Probably," Russ replied. "But it's a helluva lot more fun annoying you." He strode over to the desk, which was now riddled with badly scribbled music. "What gives?"

Brad refused to answer. If he said a word to Russ or Ethan about what he was doing, his friends would have a million questions. Instead, he grunted and pointed at the office door, hoping Russ would take the hint.

Instead of obeying, Russ strode over to the wall of cabinets and jerked one open. "Never mind. I think I know." Then he pulled out the transcribing electronic keyboard that Brad was sure he'd told the guys to pitch.

After plugging it in, Russ flipped the power on, cleared the keyboard's memory, and prepped it to record a new song. Then he put it on top of the small pile of papers. "Try this," he suggested. "'Cause I can't read a single note of that chicken scratch you've got all over the desk."

Brad stared at the keyboard, a bit surprised at being happy to see it. His fingers caressed the keys before he pulled his hand back as if he'd been burned. "Who said I needed that?"

Russ let out a cynical snort as he picked up one of the pages. "You might not have said as much, but you're begging for it." His gaze grew solemn. "Did you suddenly wake up this morning and decide you wanted to be a songwriter again?"

"I think someone else made that decision for him," Ethan said as he strolled into the office. "A very pretty woman who sings like an angel."

Russ scoffed. "No way."

"Yes, way," Ethan said with a nod.

"Don't tell me our Savannah got to him," Russ said.

So Russ knew her, too. Brad wondered when he'd stopped giving any woman notice, especially his own employees. "You heard her sing. You agreed to my hiring her."

"I did," Russ replied. "And she deserves it. I was nice and close for that great performance, too. She asked me to stand close to the stage so she could see a friendly face."

That gave Brad pause. "You're her friend?"

"Well, yeah. She works here."

"I knew that," Brad snapped, but it wasn't the truth. He might've signed her paychecks, but he barely knew her at all.

Ethan shot him a grin. "No, you didn't. But quit beating yourself up about it. She works lunch rush and mostly weekdays."

That explained a lot. Russ or the assistant manager, Ellie, ran the restaurant from opening time until Brad came in to work dinner. He was the one who locked the doors after last call, especially on weekends.

"No wonder he didn't recognize her," Ethan said. "Feel better, Brad?"

"Yeah, I do." Brad glared at them. "Now get out."

With a cluck of his tongue, Russ went to the door. "Such an asshole. I'd forgotten how much fun you are when you're in writing mode."

Writing mode. Russ and Ethan's name for the nearly obsessive state of mind Brad fell into when a new song took control of his mind. He often became so focused on getting that song out of his head before it was lost for all time that he forgot everything else around him. Like eating. Or sleeping. Or running the restaurant. The post-Katie Brad would've grabbed some bourbon and holed up in the office until the song was purged.

This song would have to be born without anesthetic.

"Get out," he repeated, trying to hold on to the bridge that was now drowning out all other sounds.

"Don't worry, old friend," Ethan said. "I'll pick up the slack downstairs until you're done." He joined Russ at the door. "Glad to see you haven't lost your touch."

CHAPTER THREE

Mama!"

Savannah smiled at Caroline's excited call. "Hi, pumpkin." She set her well-worn guitar case next to the stairs as her four-year-old daughter came running across the room, dodging the toys that littered the living room carpet.

"D'ja sing, Mama? D'ja sing pretty?" Caroline reached for Savannah, who picked her up and rested her against her hip.

Savannah kissed her daughter. "Yeah, I sang." She gave Caroline's pert little nose a tweak. "You're supposed to be asleep."

"She was too excited to sleep." Mary Wolf stepped out of the kitchen, drying her hands on a blue dish towel before tossing it back at the sink. Then she started picking up Caroline's toys.

"Good thing tomorrow's Saturday then," Savannah said. "We can sleep in."

As if. Caroline seldom slept past seven. Since Savannah was a night owl, she had no choice but to yawn away her time until her waitressing shift started at ten. She doubted the day would ever come when she got enough sleep—at least not until Caroline hit high school and could drive herself places.

Savannah was more than happy to wait. No way would she wish time to move that quickly. Caroline was everything to her, definitely worth being sleep-deprived.

"Please don't do that, Mom," Savannah scolded as her mother dropped some toys into the nearly empty wooden toy box. "Caroline and I will take care of picking up."

"We could stay," Mary said as she gathered up a few more toys. She glanced at her husband. He'd kicked off his shoes, opened the recliner, and was contentedly snoring. "Daddy's already down for the count."

"No, but thanks, Mom." Savannah set her daughter back on her feet and pushed her toward her grandmother. "You help Grandma pick up." She waited for Caroline to nod her approval. Then she turned to her mother again. "You and Daddy have done enough. Thanks for watching her tonight."

Mary flipped a hand in Caroline's direction as she turned and ran back into her Savannah's arms. "Let's face it, darlin'. We *hate* watching our grandbaby. It's absolute torture."

"Yeah, well . . . I'd don't want to use and abuse."

The last toy now in the toy box, Mary shut the lid. "You still haven't told me how things went." Which meant the discussion was over.

Smiling at the memory of her night on the stage, Savannah rubbed her cheek against her daughter's dark hair. "I got an encore."

"Oh, darlin'!" Mary exclaimed. "That's wonderful!"

Savannah returned the smile with one that had to be as happy as her mother's. "Even better...You're looking at the new warm-up act for Words and Music."

Wrapping her arms around Savannah and Caroline, Mary hugged them tightly as she laughed. "I'm so proud of you."

Paul Wolf jerked to life with a loud snort. He ran his hand over his face, wiping the sleep away. "Did I hear my baby girl's voice?"

"Hi, Daddy."

Caroline kicked her legs hard enough that Savannah had to keep a tight hold on her. "Pop-pop! You're up! Wanna play?"

Savannah set her daughter on her feet. Caroline immediately ran to her grandfather and crawled up onto the recliner, settling herself on his lap.

"Our baby's not gonna wait tables anymore," Mary announced.

Paul knit his brows. "What's this?"

"She gonna sing again."

Savannah rushed to point out, "The boss promised I'd earn more than I am as a waitress."

A smile lit his face. "That's my girl."

The reality of her new job was finally starting to sink in. "I'm gonna sing again," she said in a reverent whisper.

Then worry set in as she realized what her singing meant for Caroline. "I'm gonna have to work evenings now."

As he picked up one of Caroline's books from the end table, Paul said, "So?"

"So," Savannah replied, "I'm gonna need help watching Caroline. There aren't any day care centers that take kids in the evenings—at least none that I know of."

Things were happening so damned fast. There was supposed to be time to prepare, to slowly build a career as a singer. Her head was spinning at all the changes that would happen because of Brad Maxwell's offer.

Mary let out a gasp. "And what exactly is wrong with *us* watching her, young lady?"

After all her parents had done for her, Savannah had a hard time not feeling guilty at needing their help yet again. But how could she let this opportunity pass her by? "You've already done so much for us. I can't possibly ask you to do that."

"Who's askin'?" Her father opened *Chicka Chicka Boom Boom* and started reading to his only grandchild in his rumbling baritone, the one that had comforted Savannah throughout her childhood. God, she was a lucky girl to have grown up with two such caring parents. Maybe one day Caroline would realize she was every bit as lucky to have them as her grandparents.

"You know we wanna help," Mary said. "We can work things out just fine."

Savannah's guilt kept talking. "Yeah, but...several nights a week? That's not fair."

"To whom?" her mother countered. "You don't hear us complaining about spending time with our grandbaby." She laid a gentle hand on Savannah's arm. "You know it'll be fine."

But Savannah didn't know that. Things hadn't been "fine" in a very long time. Only the last year had seen her life approaching something next to normal. And that normalcy was mostly due to the monetary and psychological support of her parents.

The bitterness was still difficult to push aside. Holding on to that anger—mentally counting the money that was stolen from her and the money Caroline's father should be paying in child support—wasn't going to change anything.

At least her heart would heal.

Eventually.

And singing at Words & Music would help her on the road to earning a decent living as a singer instead of a waitress. She'd tucked away a small nest egg, and she hoped to add to that if the new salary was good. The future seemed to have taken on a brighter hue. She just needed a moment to catch her breath and then start making some plans.

"What nights will you be singin'?" her mother asked.

"I'm assuming Thursday through Saturday. That's when the Freaky Geeks opened for the main acts."

"Freaky Geeks?" Paul shook his head. "What happened to normal names for bands? Chicago. The Eagles. Heart."

As if she'd let him get away with one of his "in the good

ole days" comments. "How about Blue Oyster Cult? Credence Clearwater Revival? The Sex Pistols?"

He chuckled. "Point taken."

Mary wouldn't let things drop. "When you're sure about your schedule, we'll make arrangements to come here and take care of Caroline so you won't have to worry."

Although she planned to do some research to see if there were any other arrangements she could make for evening child care, Savannah nodded. The likelihood was that she'd have to lean on her parents. Once she was successful, she had plans to repay them for their endless support. They'd always wanted a boathouse on Old Hickory Lake. Oh, how she wanted to give them that.

Maybe one day...

"Thanks, Mom. I couldn't do this without you and Daddy."

* * *

It's done.

Brad grinned as he punched the Print icon on his computer and then unplugged and set the transcribing keyboard aside. He scanned his basement studio as familiar satisfaction swept through his heart. Rather than grow maudlin over what he'd lost, he let the pleasure of finishing the song lead his thoughts. He believed it was a good, catchy melody. Fun words. But after a couple of years away, he might have lost his touch. One thing was certain—Savannah would do it justice once he convinced her to sing it.

Ready to finally leave the studio, a place he'd all but ignored for close to three years, he went to the door and flipped off the light, knowing he'd be back. He was a composer, and he couldn't hide from that part of his life any longer, even if he wanted to.

In the old days, he'd always raised a bourbon toast to the finished work. Despite the draw to repeat the tradition, he walked past the studio's locked liquor cabinet.

As he climbed the stairs, he was surprised to hear the sounds of someone puttering around his kitchen. A glance at his watch told him he'd worked through the night, an old habit since he had a problem keeping track of time when he wrote. His stomach rumbled in protest to his skipping dinner. Then the smell of something cooking, a scent that made his mouth water, hit him.

Brad stepped into the kitchen to find Ethan standing at the stove, flipping a pancake as if he were a professional chef. Russ sat on one of the kitchen island stools, attacking a stack of pancakes that had been liberally doused with butter and syrup.

"Is it done?" Ethan asked over his shoulder.

"It is," Brad replied with a grin, taking the stool next to Russ.

"How many?"

Ethan's question made no sense. "How many what? Verses? Notes?"

"Flapjacks, moron."

"As many as you can fit on a plate. I'm famished."

"Skip dinner?" Ethan slid the pancake he'd just finished

onto a rather impressive pile that rested on a serving platter. After setting the hot pan aside, he grabbed two empty
plates. Ethan served part the stack to himself, gave a few
more to Russ, then filled the last plate and handed it to
Brad.

"I did. Thanks for cooking." Brad snatched up the syrup
bottle before Ethan could get it. He poured a fair share over
his breakfast before handing the bottle over.

The first bite made him hum in appreciation. If he could
ever convince Ethan to give up his ranch and horses and
become head chef at Words & Music, they'd double their
business.

Ethan nodded as he set about devouring his own breakfast. "You've done the same for me before."

Only one thing could get Brad to leave the food. He
jumped off his stool and went about pouring himself a
large mug of coffee.

Caffeine. A vice that he had no intention of ever giving up.

It wasn't as though he'd planned on giving up sex. That
had just...happened. He'd awakened one morning in a
hotel room, badly hungover yet again with some woman
whose name he couldn't remember. He couldn't have even
described her face had his life depended on it, and he sure
as hell had no idea if they'd both been too drunk to use
protection.

Entirely disgusted with himself, he'd stumbled to
the bathroom—grateful to find a used condom in the
wastebasket. After hastily dressing, he'd muttered some
awkward farewell and gone home to take a long, hot

shower. As he'd let the water beat down on him, he'd had an epiphany.

For the first time in his life, Brad had realized he didn't need to sleep with every woman whose gaze was a sexual invitation. A grown-up man should be able to say, "No."

What had he been trying to prove anyway? That he was a man? That women desired him? That he could fuck any woman in Nashville? In Tennessee?

Ethan was a player, too. And even *he* called Brad a "man-slut" and made a few pointed comments about how often Brad held a glass of bourbon in his hand.

Brad had only been following his father's lead. What a ladies' man Bill Maxwell had been, and most of Brad's memories of his father were of him smelling like booze. As Brad hit puberty, he'd fallen into the same pattern. Drink enough to be numb. Then love 'em and leave 'em. Once he'd met Ethan in high school, they'd become fast friends—brothers, for all intents and purposes.

By the time Brad wrote his first hit song at twenty-two, they were a hell of a partying pair. Brad, the Hitman. Ethan was the son of Dottie and "Crawfish" Walker—the "King and Queen of Country Music," which made their only son pretty much Nashville royalty.

Brad and Ethan made quite a panty-dropping combo.

"When do we get to hear it?" Russ asked. "I'm dying to find out if you've still got the touch—if you can still hit the *Billboard* chart."

Brad shrugged. He might still have the touch, but he hadn't written the song to get himself back on any chart.

He'd written it to get Savannah Wolf on the chart.

The potential was there. The woman was going to be a star. A *super*star. Yet she seemed clueless on how to go about that goal. Since helping singers was something he knew how to do damn well, he figured he'd do what he could to see that she found herself on the way to the top.

Yet a part of him couldn't fight the feeling of regret. For the first time in his life, he had his shit together. No more drunken nights with one-night stands. He had a great job that he was good at. His life finally made sense.

So why in the hell was he writing songs again? That part of his life was supposed to be over. If he opened that door again, even only a crack, would it all come flooding back?

No. Things were different now.

But what if the song wasn't as good as his older works? What if he'd lost his touch? Could a voice like Savannah's overcome bad material?

"C'mon." Ethan jostled Brad hard with his shoulder, nearly knocking him off his stool. "You can't hold out on us. We're your best friends."

"We're your *only* friends," Russ teased. He set his fork down, having polished off the last of his breakfast. "We wanna hear the song." A grin filled his beard-stubbled face. "Why not have our Savannah sing it tonight?"

Brad gathered his brows, not sure why Russ's words bothered him so much. "*Our* Savannah?"

"Well, yeah. She's part of Words and Music, right? She's one of the family."

Brad suddenly remembered that he was supposed to meet her this morning. After checking his watch, he shoveled another bite of pancakes in his mouth. He jumped off his stool, hoping he could make the twenty-minute drive to the restaurant in ten minutes.

Brad snatched up the sheet music and headed to his garage. The confused expressions on his friends' faces could be relished later in the day.

Right now, he had somewhere to be.

CHAPTER FOUR

One of the cooks let Savannah in the back door of the restaurant. As she made her way through the large kitchen, she took note of the prep work being done for the lunch rush, trying to memorize the specials so she could pitch them to her customers. It took a few seconds for her to remember she wouldn't be waiting tables anymore.

With a crooked smile, she realized that she was putting the cart in front of the pony. If she and Brad Maxwell couldn't come to an agreement on a contract, she'd no doubt find herself back in a T-shirt and shorts with a pad in her hand. And she'd probably be taking orders in another restaurant. No way would she grovel to get her old job back. It would be far too humiliating to return to being a waitress among the people who'd seen last night's spectacle. She'd been plucked from utter obscurity to become the opening act for the stars who performed at Words & Music, and she'd be damned if she'd be a server there ever again.

Her imagination was getting the better of her. Last night hadn't been some miracle. No, it had been the product of a lot of really hard work preparing her performance by singing the songs over and over, honing the nuances that elevated a song above a good karaoke cover of a once-popular song.

"Savannah!"

She turned to see Cheyanne skirting around the prep tables to get to her. "Good morning," Savannah said with a hesitant smile. How many of her coworkers knew about her new job?

"Good morning, my ass. Gimme a hug!" Cheyanne gave her a hearty embrace, complete with pats on the back. "I'm so happy for you."

"Thanks," Savannah said, her voice staccato from the enthusiastic thumps on the back Cheyanne delivered.

After turning Savannah loose, Cheyanne grinned. "It's not gonna be easy replacing you. You're my best lunch waitress." Then she frowned. "Why are you back here? Not like you're on today, and I'm already working to get your last few shifts covered."

"You don't have to do that. I'll cover my shifts."

Cheyanne shook her head. "Brad told me you'd be too busy." She linked her arm with Savannah's. "C'mon. He's waitin' for you." She led the way to the stage.

Brad was standing by the bar. He glanced up as she strode to the piano. "Good morning."

Savannah shielded her eyes against the stage lights. "Good morning, Mr. Maxwell."

"Brad. Please."

She watched as he slipped through the side door to the stage. A few moments later, he was heading toward her. He sauntered—the only way to describe the man's confident stride. No wonder. He was, after all, the co-owner of one of the best gathering places in Nashville as well as the man who'd composed hit song after hit song. Not only were tables entirely filled most nights, but artists, both stars and amateurs, scrambled for a slot to perform on this stage—the same stage she'd now be performing on several nights a week.

A shiver of happiness raced over her.

His boot heels clicked in a steady cadence across the polished wooden floor. He was wearing the same clothes he'd worn the night before, which made her wonder exactly what he'd been up to last night. "Ready to get to work?" he asked.

Savannah nodded at the head waitress. "Cheyanne said you told her to take me off the schedule. I don't want to leave her short-staffed." The last thing she wished was to make the other waitstaff resent her for making them work harder.

"Don't you worry," Cheyanne said with a dismissive wave of her hand. "Brad's got Ethan already checking applications. I'll have a new waitress before the day's out."

"We've got it covered," Brad added. "You've got other work to do." He swept his arm in invitation. "Join me at the piano?"

Leading the way, he took a seat on the bench. "Do you

think you can sing this?" He brought the instrument to life with nimble fingers that seemed to fly across the keys.

Savannah listened hard as she leaned in to look at the music, unable to identify the song.

After he played through a verse and a chorus, he stopped and cocked his head. "Helps if you actually sing it."

"I'm sorry... I don't know it."

Brad gave her an enigmatic grin and patted the bench beside him.

After sitting next to him, she focused on the sheet music. The notes triggered no memory of the melody at all, and the words weren't familiar, either. "I'm sorry, but... this one's new to me." When he didn't reply, she glanced over to see that his grin had blossomed into a cheeky smile.

"Then just listen," he suggested before he started the song again, this time singing along.

The man had a passable singing voice. Not that he'd win *The Voice* or anything, but he could hold his own as a cover band singer.

Savannah tried to focus on the song. Other things kept getting in the way. Brad's tousled hair. The heat of his thigh pressing against hers. The timbre of his voice.

What was wrong with her? The last thing she needed was to become attracted to her boss. Even worse, she'd been so preoccupied that only a few lyrics stuck. Should she try to sing the piece, she'd make a mess of it.

"Your turn," he said as he played the intro again.

Normally, she was a quick study, and she could read

music well. Pushing aside as much of the interfering sensations as she could, she tried to sing the song. Although she hit the notes and didn't botch the lyrics too badly, she winced when it mercifully came to an end.

"Hmm," was all Brad said when the ordeal was over.

"Is that a good hmm or a bad hmm?"

"Neither. Just...hmm."

His expression was giving her nothing, which frustrated her to no end. Being a waitress had helped her hone the skill of reading faces. Subtle frowns when the food was too cold or had too much spice. Searching looks when customers suddenly realized there was something they wanted that wasn't on the table. Broad smiles when they left a nice tip for a job well done. But Brad's features were giving her zero to work with.

"Look," Savannah said, fearing the unfamiliar song was the problem, "why don't you pick a different song? I'll sing something else for you. Please don't judge me on a song I've never heard before."

"Why shouldn't I?"

Unsure whether he'd had a teasing lilt to his voice, she replied, "Because I know I can do better. Pick a classic. Pick something on the charts. Pick *anything* else."

"It's okay, Savannah. I don't need to." He gathered up the sheet music and set it aside.

Opportunity had fallen in her path, and she wasn't about to let him jerk it away over one song. "Let me hear it a few more times, then I'll sing it again. I know I can do better," she insisted. She was not only repeating herself, but starting to sound desperate. While singing that song might not have been one of her best performances, she still thought she'd sung it better than most people could probably manage.

Brad turned to face her as an easy smile bowed his lips. "I don't need to hear any more. You did fine."

His words and that smile sent relief flooding through her. "I really can do it better."

"I'm sure you can. And you *will*. I'll help make sure you're ready the next time you're on this stage."

With his declaration, her world was right again. "Does that mean we can talk contract now?"

"Depends," he replied. "Are you negotiating for yourself, or did you give any thought to contacting the guys I recommended?"

"You mean the managers?"

He nodded.

She shook her head.

The smile vanished, and from the hard set of his jaw, she figured he was still irritated with her for not jumping at the notion of having someone handle her career, especially someone he'd recommended.

With a sigh, Savannah decided to be as honest with him as she could in hopes he'd understand. "My last manager all but ruined me."

"Really?" Brad turned to give her his full attention. "Shouldn't you tell me that story now? I mean, I'm bound to hear about it."

She drew her lips into a line, not sure she wanted to trot

her dirty laundry out in front of him. The whole sordid tale still filled her with humiliation, and she preferred to leave the past firmly behind her. "I'm sure there are thousands of people in Nashville who've had crappy managers take advantage of them."

"Thousands? Probably not, and none of them worked for me. I protect my talent."

"I don't doubt that. Which makes me even more sure I don't need a manager."

He let out a sigh. "You're a stubborn lady."

"So I've been told," she replied with her own sigh. "By a lot of people."

But he left her off the hook. "Let's try the song again. Together." The notes of the intro rose from the piano.

The tune was getting more familiar, and she loved the way their voices blended. This time, though, the lyrics came easier. A little practice and she just might have it ready before she gave her first performance at Words & Music.

"Good," Brad said. "Good. You're a quick study."

"Thanks." Savannah turned to offer him a grateful smile.

As though it seemed to be the most natural thing in the world, he took some of the blue strands of her hair between his index finger and thumb, rubbing gently.

Such an intimate gesture; such a devastating effect.

From his wavy dark blond hair to his crystal blue eyes all the way down his lean body, every inch of him appealed to her. Had they been two different people in a different situation, she might have dropped her guard long enough to get to know him better and in a personal way rather than a professional one.

She couldn't think of a worse time to be attracted to someone.

To make it even scarier, he was studying her, his gaze searching hers. Slowly, carefully, he leaned closer as he stared at her mouth.

Heat shimmered through her veins at the mere thought of kissing him. His lips were full and looked exceptionally soft. When he was near enough that his warm breath hit her face, she wanted to close her eyes and let nature take its course, to give in to the chemistry they were generating.

Then the rumors she'd heard came rushing into her thoughts. Brad had a reputation with women. A bad reputation. While the staff wasn't known to gossip notoriously, some of the servers had a few things to say about Brad never being seen with the same woman twice.

Chemistry aside, the man was probably bad news.

Her hands rose between them, and she pressed her palms against his chest as she whispered, "No."

* * *

Brad jerked away from Savannah as though her quiet denial had been a slap across his face.

He dropped her hair and sat back, letting anger flow through him. Not at her, though. She'd done nothing wrong. His anger was self-directed.

Despite his confidence that he'd gotten his libido under

control, he clearly hadn't. Otherwise she wouldn't have gotten to him so quickly.

He couldn't seem to fight this woman's appeal. Everything about her was so utterly feminine. Her hair looked like strands of silk. Her alluring perfume held him captive. Her blue eyes shone when she sang.

Then there was that voice. That incredible voice. When she spoke, he wanted to kiss her. When she sang, he wanted to ravish her.

At least she appeared to be as attracted to him as he was to her, which saved him from utter humiliation. He could see the hint of desire in her beautiful eyes, and before her brain had kicked in, she'd been moving ever so slowly toward him, her pink lips parted.

Thank God one of them was sane.

"Sorry, Savannah." Brad picked up the sheet music, stood, and stepped away from her.

Savannah bowed her head and folded her hands in her lap, looking so damn dejected he wanted to gather her in his arms and hug her tight. Doubting she'd appreciate that intimate a gesture, he struggled to find something to say that wouldn't make an already embarrassing situation worse.

Nothing came to mind.

With a rather loud sigh, she stood. "I'm the one who should apologize."

He shook his head. "I was being . . . inappropriate."

"Instead of arguing over it, how about we just agree to start over?" she offered, holding out her hand.

His anger shifted to agitation. He found it perturbing that she could so easily shake off their near kiss. "Fine," he snapped, shaking her hand a little rougher than necessary.

What in the hell's wrong with me?

This woman had him rattled on so many levels he couldn't even keep track. She'd gotten him writing music again, and there wasn't a more profound way a woman could affect him.

"That didn't sound very convincing." Her voice still bordered on a whisper, which made him feel like a jerk.

"Sorry. You're right. We should start over. How about we talk about your last manager now?" With a swing of his arm, he tried to get her moving. "Let's get a cup of coffee."

Although she was frowning, she started walking.

Brad held both doors open for her and led the way to the kitchen. After grabbing a couple of cups, he began pouring coffee when Savannah stopped him at only half a cup, then proceeded to add three sugar packets and enough cream to turn the drink a light tan.

She shrugged when he cocked an eyebrow. "I need coffee not to taste like...well, coffee."

With a chuckle, he led her to the bar. That time of day, it was the quietest place to talk.

"Tell me what happened," he coaxed.

She set her elbows on the table and put both hands around the cup. "Not much to tell."

"Look, I know you don't want a manager..."

"Or an agent."

"Or an agent. When you're working with me, you won't really need one. I'll give you a fair contract, so don't worry about that. But when you start moving up in this business—"

Her eyes widened. "I'm glad you think I'll keep moving up, but this job is all I've ever wanted."

"You've got talent. You've got stage presence. You're unique. You could take things a lot farther, although I hate the idea of losing you too fast."

"You're not going to lose me. Like I said, this gig is exactly what I wanted. But...what exactly are you offering?" she asked.

"Not talking terms of a contract 'til you tell me at least a little of what happened between you and the guy who ripped you off."

"I never said it was a guy..."

"Didn't have to. You sounded pretty pissed—like you'd lost more than just money. Figured it was a guy you were...involved with."

She twisted the cup in her hands as she lost herself in thought.

He let her have time to decide whether to trust him or not. If she wouldn't open up, he knew more than enough people in the industry to be able to ferret out the story— assuming she hadn't used a stage name. Even then, he'd probably have the truth by the end of the day.

"Fine," Savannah said. "I had a few good breaks six or so years ago. I had an independent album out that was getting some play, and the second single from it was selling well.

There was interest from two labels for a second album. Then I made the mistake of getting a little too...personal with my manager. Because we were a couple, I trusted him when I should've been looking out for myself. I thought he had my best interests at heart."

"Never a good thing to mix business with pleasure," he commented.

"You're telling me?" A sarcastic snort slipped out. "After we'd been together about a year, Michael called me and said the labels both turned me down, that I wasn't seasoned enough." She cast her eyes downward. "Then he said we were through—both personally and professionally. I was so shocked that I had no idea what to do. When I realized I had no clue what he'd arranged as far as future gigs, I went to his office. He'd cleaned the place out—and while he was at it, he'd cleaned out every dollar I'd earned. Guess you could say he cut and run."

"What an asshole."

At least Brad got a hesitant smile from her. "Yeah, he is. I went catatonic, and I couldn't find my voice. I—I couldn't sing. Since I had a mortgage, I worked anyplace I could. Fast food. A laundromat. Found out I was pretty good at waiting tables, so I stuck with that."

"What made you want to sing again?"

"Coming here, working here. It was just...time. Waitressing is fine. It pays the bills. But I wanted to sing. I *needed* to sing."

That sentiment was reflected in his songwriting. Something about hearing Savannah sing had made it the right time—the right voice—to bring the music back. His worry that the new song wasn't up to par had vanished the moment he'd heard her bring it to life.

"But if it weren't for my parents," she added, "and all the help and encouragement they've given me, I wouldn't be here now, singing again."

Although she'd told him about her jerk of a manager, he couldn't help but think there was something she was leaving out. Problem was that he didn't know her well enough to push her. Reliving the hurt and humiliation had to have been hard enough on her. He wasn't about to tell her he thought she hadn't shared everything.

The urge to hug her was nearly overwhelming, but Brad didn't want her to view it as a condescending gesture. Damn, though, the woman deserved a hug. And her ex deserved a punch in the nose. Or the balls. "Tell you what...Let me draw up a standard contract. We'll start with a month and see how things go."

"A month? That's not very long."

"It's usually enough to know if you're ready." He thought she was, but only time could prove him right. "But I'm sure you are."

"And if I'm not?" Her voice quavered.

"Then you'll always have a job working here as a waitress or a hostess. But I honestly don't think you'll be taking orders ever again."

Savannah nodded, pushed her coffee cup away, and stood. Holding out her hand, she said, "Deal."

Brad smiled and shook her hand.

Savannah checked her watch. "I need to be getting home soon."

"Come in Monday morning at nine. We'll work on your first set list."

After seeing her out the back door, he took the stairs two at a time to get to his office. He had some investigating to do.

He had a feeling that there was so much more to the story, and he intended to discover everything she'd left out.

CHAPTER FIVE

Brad took a long pull from his water bottle while he stared at a picture of Savannah performing from six years ago. He'd found the information by dumb luck while searching for any trail of her. A check for her name had turned up a video by a Crystal Bloom. A viewer had commented that he thought the singer's real name might be Savannah Wolf. Not a very catchy stage name, and nowhere as theatrical as Savannah Wolf. She'd made a wise choice coming back with her own name.

Her hair had been the same white-blond, although she'd worn it much shorter. Now, it fell past her shoulders; then, it had framed her oval face. She'd lost some weight over those years, which made her small frame seem even more fragile. There had been nothing then that really gave her an air of originality. The outline of the bird on her wrist hadn't even been inked yet, and there were no brilliant blue strands of hair.

Now, she commanded attention when she took the stage. Something about her, something more than the subtle changes in her appearance, had changed. For the better.

Her eyes, he realized. She'd gotten an air of worldly wisdom in her gaze.

Why he was so utterly fascinated with her remained a mystery. There had always been so many women moving quickly in and out of his life. Only Katie had been able to get him to take vows.

But Savannah wasn't the only one to know what it was like to be betrayed.

He clicked the mouse over the only YouTube video he could find of Savannah singing as Crystal Bloom. She'd been filmed by someone's phone camera at a small club in Louisville. The picture and sound quality were shit, but the touch of magic he'd heard in her voice was there—not nearly as strong as when she'd sung for him, but there nonetheless.

He was watching her singing career as an embryo. Had her ex not pulled the rug out from under her life, she might've enjoyed some success. Surely enough to avoid waiting tables...

The next video he pulled up was from her performance at Words & Music—one of several that people in the crowd had posted. Savannah belonged on a stage, appearing much more comfortable than she had six years ago. Watching her sing again sent chills racing over his skin, and others were noticing her, too. This file had a high number of views for being only a couple of days old.

What exactly had she gone through in those years to change her so profoundly? What had added a mountain of emotion to her voice that had been absent in that first video? Was the experience of being dumped and ripped off enough to put the threads of angst and longing in her voice? When she'd sung on Indie Night, she'd picked three perfect songs to showcase her talent. But the last song—"For My Broken Heart"—had been the one to tug at his emotions. The woman knew love and loss, and every word had been packed full of feeling.

It didn't take too long to discover that the guy who'd ripped her off was named Michael Hart, but learning more about the man was proving difficult—and entirely frustrating. Very few people Brad had reached out to had even heard of him.

"She's really good," Russ said as he strolled into the office. "I could recognize her voice all the way down the hall." He took a seat on the edge of the desk and inclined his head at the monitor. "What'd you find out?"

"She had the start of a career before we hired her." Brad opened the video from Louisville's Riverside Café and started it for Russ. "This was a few years ago."

After about a minute of listening to "Me and Bobby McGee," Russ said, "She was good, but she's gotten better."

Brad switched to the Indie Night video. "There's something...different about her now."

Russ frowned. "Well, yeah. Anyone can see that she grew her hair out."

As Ethan stepped through the door, Brad rolled his eyes. "Why did we make such a dumb jock our partner?" Brad asked.

Ethan chuckled. "He's a helluva bouncer."

"I guess if he can't knock heads on the gridiron anymore," Brad said, "he can knock 'em here when drunks get rowdy."

Giving his knuckles a loud crack, Russ said, "Damn, there are some days I miss being the quarterback."

Ethan flopped on the couch. "So what are you two up to?"

"We're watching our Savannah sing," Russ replied.

"She's not 'our Savannah,'" Brad said with a clenched jaw, unsure as to why Russ's words had bothered him so much.

"Careful," Ethan cautioned. "You're starting to sound jealous."

"And possessive," Russ added. He folded his arms over his chest and glared at Brad. "She's a great person. Can you *please* not do one of your numbers on her?"

A low whistle filled the air. "The ref takes away a point," Ethan said with a smirk. "Brad hasn't done one of his numbers on *any* woman in a good, long while."

"So I've noticed," Russ said. "Then it won't be difficult for him to leave her alone."

Something in Russ's tone made Brad bristle. "Why do you care anyway? Do you like her or something?"

"Not in the way you think," Russ replied with a shrug. "I've talked to her a lot and we're sorta friends. She's a good person, Brad."

"Let's keep her that way," Ethan said, a thread of anger in his voice—the same protective type he'd heard in Russ's.

Not sure what had pissed them off so quickly, Brad drummed his fingers on the desktop. "What?"

Silence settled over the office, and it didn't take Brad long to realize exactly what was wrong. Savannah meant something to his friends. Whatever magic Savannah had begun to weave around him had captured them as well. They were going to act as her champions.

He held up his hands in surrender. "All right. All right. I get it. I promise to keep my interest in *our* Savannah entirely professional. Does that make you two morons happy?"

Ethan nodded.

But Russ was still drilling holes through Brad with his eyes. "You're forgetting something pretty damn important. You *wrote a song* for her. That implies a helluva lot more than professional."

He had a point—not that Brad would concede to it. Shit, but he was already worried about his feelings for her. If only she would've let him kiss her. Maybe then he could have satisfied his curiosity and put aside his fascination.

The problem was that if Brad promised to leave Savannah alone, he was likely to break his word. "How about you two butt out and let me help her get a start in the music business? Or do you think that I'm too much of a heartless, selfish bastard to do that?"

Russ pushed away from the desk and gave him a scorching scowl. "You do what you've gotta do." He marched out of the office.

Brad sighed.

"You didn't even remember her," Ethan reminded him.

"A minute ago, you were her defender. Now you're telling me she shouldn't matter?"

Ethan shook his head. "I never said she didn't matter. I just wanna know this: If you got her, then what? Your record with women isn't stellar."

That was a question Brad couldn't answer. His own thoughts about Savannah were so confusing that he felt like a yo-yo. He couldn't sort out exactly why she was able to crawl so easily under his tough skin. "I'm not looking to date the woman."

He didn't trust his own judgment, though. When Katie had popped into his life, he'd assumed she returned his strong feelings. He'd let things between them flare so quickly, he'd never taken the time to truly get to know her—to learn her true motives for pursuing him. It had been easy to let his ego assume she was falling in love with him the same way he was tumbling head over heels for her.

It was easier to dismiss whatever this was that he was starting to feel for Savannah as lust, which meant the best thing to do was keep his distance. "Like I said, I'll keep it professional."

With a derisive snort, Ethan got to his feet. "Do yourself a favor and try to figure out what you really want before you do anything stupid."

"Like what?"

"Like dropping your monkish ways, sleeping with her, and then dumping her."

Brad kept his mouth shut about how Ethan mimicked a hell of a lot of Brad's old habits where women were concerned. "I already told you I wasn't looking to date the woman."

"I'll believe it when I see it."

"Stop being a dick and close the door on your way out," Brad snapped. "I've got work to do."

The sound of the door closing seemed rather prophetic—as though a part of his life was ending.

Which meant another was beginning?

Hell, now he was waxing philosophic.

Taking a break, he wandered down to the kitchen and poured himself a cup of the strong brew. He sipped it as he leaned back against the walk-in refrigerator's door and watched the kitchen being made ready for the day. The restaurant's famous corn muffins were baking in the oven, the scent making his stomach growl.

"Hey, Brad!" Sous chef Leslie Guinan came hurrying over.

Tall and lanky, the African-American woman been a basketball player in college. A blown ACL ended any potential for going pro, so she'd turned to her first love—cooking. She was number two on Brad's staff, second only to the head chef, Porter Oaks. The restaurant was damn lucky to have them both.

"Can you adjust the meat order for next week?" she asked.

"Depends," Brad replied, loving to tease the woman. "You better have a good reason to make me do paperwork."

"Because," Leslie said, her tone growing insistent, "Porter said we ran out of ribs Saturday night. I promised him I'd make sure you knew. Did you?"

He took another sip of his coffee before he replied. Leslie was a fantastic chef, who ran the kitchen and its staff like a drill sergeant, but she got riled so easily, he wanted to teach her a little bit of patience. "I did."

"And?" Her brows were gathered, and she'd drawn her lips into a stern line.

"Relax, Leslie. I already changed the order."

She took a playful swat at his arm. "I knew it. At least I should've known. You're always on top of things. Did you also ask the produce supplier to—"

"To add arugula to the next order. You told me already. Three times."

With a laugh, she smoothed her hands down the front of her chef's jacket. "You're awesome, Brad." One of the cooks motioned to her, so she hurried to the stove with only a nod in his direction as a farewell.

As the rest of his staff did everything from cutting up mushrooms to stirring the soup *du jour* to rubbing the seasoning on the ribs, he finished his coffee and tried to puzzle his way through his Savannah dilemma.

Although he'd tried to brush his partners' concerns asides, they'd both given him food for thought. His interest in his new singer was going to cause problems.

She'd inspired him; there was no denying it. A second

song was already niggling its way into his thoughts. But if he kept pushing forward with his plans to help her career, he could easily find himself spending more and more time with her—and could easily find himself heading back into the heart of country music.

Katie had wanted nothing more than to be a part of that world, and Brad had been a means to an end for her. He hadn't realized it at the time. No, he'd seen Katie as a woman who knew what she wanted and went for it. His mistake was in thinking that what she wanted was him when what she'd truly desired was to rub elbows with celebrities. Which was exactly what he and Katie had done while she'd been alive.

It wasn't until he'd found her journal shortly after her death that he realized their life together had been one big fucking lie. He'd assumed she'd wanted to share his life. Those entries had shown him otherwise, letting him know exactly how little she cared for him, wanting instead his connections. What she'd shown him was that the country music industry had far too many people exactly like her, people who used other people to get what they wanted.

No matter how much he was drawn to Savannah, she represented a direct path back into a world he'd left behind him.

Or had he learned his lesson where women were concerned? Could he treat Savannah as a woman he might be interested in and then hope she was a better person than Katie?

For right now, he'd treat her like a singer who worked with him.

Brad refilled his coffee and headed back to his office. As he finished off the second cup, he came to an important decision. He would help Savannah get her career up and running, but then he'd step away and convince her to work with a good manager. As he'd promised Russ and Ethan, he'd keep things between them from getting too cozy.

He wasn't about to lose himself to the business again, nor would he let some woman call all the shots and lead him around like some kind of pet. Besides, if Savannah was after him for the people he knew in country music, she'd find herself out of luck. As quickly as things happened in Nashville, most of his contacts had probably moved on.

Satisfied with his plan, Brad grabbed the phone and punched in a number he hadn't called in years. He was going to do everything he could to give Savannah a chance to be more than an opening act, then he'd let his little bird fly free.

"Greg? Hi, it's Brad Maxwell. Yeah, long time, no see. Look . . . I've got someone you need to hear."

CHAPTER SIX

O ne more time," Savannah said, confident she'd finally mastered the lyrics to Brad's new song—"That Smile." She leaned her hip against the piano and waited for him to play the intro again.

Brad shook his head and stood. "You don't need another run. You've got this down pat. Good thing, since I wrote it for you." He winked and picked up the sheet music, set it on the top of the upright piano, and started scribbling a few words.

Blinking a few times, she tried to process what he'd just said. Surely she'd misheard him. "You wrote it for...me?"

"I did," he replied matter-of-factly.

She still didn't believe it. "Really?" Savannah kept staring at Brad.

"You actually wrote 'That Smile' for me?" she asked again. When he shot her a disgruntled frown, she held her hands up in surrender. "Okay, okay. I know I keep asking, but...how often does a girl find out she's the inspiration for a Hitman song?"

He frowned. "Please don't call me 'Hitman.' Not something I like to hear anymore."

"Sorry," she said. That nickname had been used by the press so often, she hadn't realized it might offend him.

Brad quirked a smile to show she was forgiven. "Sit," he ordered as he sat on the bench. "We need to talk about your set list. You go on next Friday so you can open for Southern Pride."

"So soon? Figured I'd need a few weeks to get myself ready."

"You're ready now. All we've got to do is decide which songs work best for you."

"What about the Freaky Geeks?" Savannah couldn't help but ask as she took the place next to him on the piano bench. "I'm not pushing them out, am I?"

Brad shook his head. "They already had one foot out the door. I talked to them yesterday, and they were grateful to have more time to prepare for their next gig."

Although she couldn't help but think the Freaky Geeks were making a huge mistake leaving Words & Music behind, she kept quiet. Their leaving was her opportunity, and she meant to take greedy advantage of it. "All right, then. Next Friday it is."

"Let's hear 'That Smile' once more, from the top." He launched into his song.

Her song. As he played, she sang, knowing the song had new meaning for her. Now, she paid special attention to the lyrics, marveling that those words could describe her—at least they described her through Brad's eyes.

"From the moment I first saw you, all I could think of was that smile."

The tune wove a spell around Savannah. She felt as though he'd reached deep inside her and touched her heart. By the last note, tears were stinging her eyes. Not wanting him to see how deeply he'd affected her, she glanced at the door on the opposite side of the stage and tried to get a hold over her tumbling emotions.

"Amazing," he said, leaning over to give her shoulder a friendly bump with his. "You're absolutely amazing."

She might have nodded in response but honestly couldn't remember. She was too caught up in the revelation that those wonderful words were all about her—words that praised her smile, her eyes, even her voice. Words that spoke of tender emotions that she now realized were already taking root inside her.

I'm an idiot.

"Hey..." His hand moved to her shoulder. "What's wrong?"

With a hard swallow, she blinked back the threatening tears, embarrassed when one escaped her eye and began to trail down her cheek.

"Savannah..." Brad gently gripped her chin to make her face him. Then he brushed the tear away. "Don't you like the song?"

"I *love* the song," she replied in a breathless whisper.

Captured by his gaze, she searched his face, not sure

how to handle the longing his blue eyes sent shimmering through her.

She was playing with fire, which was a stupid thing to do for a woman who'd already been badly burned. Yet as he leaned in, closing the distance between them, she couldn't seem to make herself stop from moving toward him. Her hands moved to his shoulders and then tangled in the hair at the nape of his neck.

* * *

Brad felt as though he'd waited forever to kiss her sweet lips, but the time had finally come. He leaned in closer. Closer. And...

Someone loudly cleared his throat, the sound echoing through the silent restaurant. "Should I come back later?" Randy asked, following his question with a chuckle.

Savannah jerked away from Brad so quickly that it felt as though she'd taken a few hunks of his hair with her.

With an aggravated groan, Brad glanced out onto the dance floor to see Randy grinning like a dimwit.

Savannah's face had flushed a deep red, but Brad had no idea if the change had been caused by their near kiss or the intrusion.

"Well, should I?" Randy asked again as Russ came marching toward the stage.

Russ's boots pounded against the wooden floorboards, clearly showing his agitation, which meant he'd seen the kiss as well.

Combing her fingers through her hair with a trembling hand, Savannah said, "Good morning, guys."

Russ only grunted in reply and headed backstage with Randy close behind.

Since she seemed to be too flustered to do anything except fuss with her hair, Brad tried to push aside the riot of feelings she'd inspired. He struggled for the right words to say when his train of thought was destroyed by notes of music—notes that were rapidly becoming another new song.

Savannah was truly his muse, his inspiration, and he wasn't at all sure how he felt about her having that kind of hold over him.

She knit her brows. "What's wrong?"

The music was coming too quickly for him to form a tactful response. "Nothing," he said before he hurried back to the piano. Snatching up the sheet music, he flipped it over and started scribbling out the tune that now drowned out all his other thoughts. He needed his keyboard or he'd never capture the melody. "Sorry, Savannah. Music's calling. Gotta run," he called over his shoulder as he hurried off the stage. He all but plowed over Russ in his hurry to get to his office.

He had another new song to write.

* * *

Savannah wrapped her arms around her waist, hugging herself. "Sounds like something's wrong to me," she muttered to no one after Brad had fled.

How could she even form a coherent thought? Her mind had been thrown into chaos, and all she wanted to do was run back into his arms and demand that he kiss her and be damned quick about it.

Perhaps his mind was a little chaotic as well. Didn't he say that music was calling to him?

Sweet Lord. Had she inspired another song?

She stood there dumbfounded as she watched him jog away. Suddenly he stopped, whirled back around, and shouted from across the big room, "Draw up a set list and we'll talk later."

Then he was gone.

She had no idea what to say or do.

Russ, who'd passed Brad on his way out, came to stand at her side. "He can be a piece of work."

Savannah shrugged.

"Want me to tell him to back off?"

"Back off?" she asked.

"Yeah . . . *back off*. I saw you two. Has he kissed you yet?"

Embarrassed to the roots of her hair, she shook her head.

"He's my friend, but so are you. I just want you to be careful."

"What are you telling me?"

"Brad can be kind of a . . . jerk. With women, I mean."

Great. The rumors she'd heard were true. Brad was the only man she'd been drawn to in years, and even his friend thought he was on the prowl. Just another reason to keep their dealings entirely professional.

"Look," she said, "can't we just forget about what you think you saw?"

Russ let out a snort.

"I doubt it'll happen again." Trying to put all that had happened this morning behind her, she picked up her purse from where it rested next to the piano. She slid the strap over her shoulder. "You're my friend, Russ, and I appreciate you looking out for me. But I've got to figure this stuff with Brad out for myself."

He thought it over long enough to make her worry she'd endanger their friendship if she didn't take his advice. "Have it your way," he finally replied with a shrug.

With great relief, she went to him. She had to grip his muscular forearm so she could rise on her tiptoes and kiss his cheek. "Thank you for worrying about me."

"Welcome," he mumbled as a blush colored his beard-stubbled face.

CHAPTER SEVEN

Savannah smiled at Caroline, giving her daughter a small wave before her girl directed her attention back to the other kids on the park playground. As she watched Caroline take her turn on the slide, Savannah let her smile fade.

Brad had almost kissed her. Again.

What was wrong with her? This was her second chance at finding a place in country music, and she was going to blow it because of a guy? Especially a guy who'd probably slept with most of the woman in Nashville?

She'd been down that road before and knew it ended in a fiery crash that had all but destroyed her life. Caroline had been the only bright spot. While she wouldn't wish that beautiful little girl away, she could have done without the harsh life lessons that came with her creation.

At least she'd heard from Brad by afternoon. He'd called to tell her he would have another new song for her to learn, and she didn't ask if he'd written this one for her, too. Had she done so, he'd probably think she was a diva with nothing but vanity driving her. She was already embarrassed enough for practically throwing herself at the man. She wasn't about to assume something stupid like she was the reason he'd begun writing music again.

"Hey."

Shielding her eyes against the bright sun, Savannah looked up to find her best friend. "Hey, Jos. What are you doing here?"

Joslynn Wright took a seat next to Savannah on the metal bench. "I was going to go for a run. Saw your car when I parked and figured you'd brought the munchkin to the playground."

Giving Joslynn a quick appraisal, Savannah grinned. Her svelte friend was covered in Lycra—a tight shirt and leggings, both a pleasant shade of lilac. Her long black hair was pulled into a messy bun. "I wish I had your dedication, Jos. Although I wondered if you ran in scrubs."

Joslynn arched a dark eyebrow.

"You're *always* in scrubs," Savannah teased.

"I guess you're right. Such is the life of an ER nurse. I work, I jog, and I try to sleep."

Savannah let out a soft chuckle. "At least scrubs are comfortable. My 'work clothes' are all scratchy or full of sequins and glitter." When Joslynn didn't laugh in response, Savannah turned to see a frown budding on her friend's face.

"Speaking of work... You didn't text me to let me know how things went this morning."

While this morning was the last thing she wanted to

talk about, Savannah needed to share what had happened. Perhaps Joslynn could talk some sense into her and convince her that kissing the new boss would be about as stupid a move as a woman could make. "About that..."

Joslynn folded her arms under her breasts. "Uh-oh. What happened?"

"You know that song I told you about?"

"The one you'd never heard?"

Savannah nodded.

"What about it?"

"Brad Maxwell wrote it for me."

Joslynn's eyes widened as her mouth dropped open.

"I know, right? I told you about his songs, about how he used to write music for every big name in Nashville."

"And he wrote a song for you?"

Savannah nodded.

"Interesting..." Joslynn drawled the word out before she pursed her lips as though lost in thought.

Time for the second dose of crazy. "He almost kissed me." That didn't sound quite right, so Savannah tried again. "I almost kissed him." Since that sounded every bit as wrong, she finally shook her head. "We came close to kissing. Each other."

With a roll of her eyes, Joslynn said, "I think I understand."

"Do you?" Savannah asked. "Because for the life of me, *I* don't."

Joslynn lifted her shoulders in a shrug. "What's to understand?"

Savannah gripped her hands together and glanced at her daughter as guilt filled her. What price had she paid for her impulsivity? "What's to understand? How about how ridiculous I am for blowing this gig?"

"He fired you?"

"No...but..."

"Stop," Joslynn said, her voice hard. "You two almost kissed. No biggie. It sure doesn't mean you're going to lose this job."

"No?" Taking a deep breath, Savannah tried to tamp down her rising panic. "He's my boss, Jos!"

"And you're attracted to him."

"Yeah," Savannah admitted. "I am."

"Then kiss the man, Savannah."

Such a matter-of-fact statement, but not surprising from Joslynn. If she wanted a man, she was straightforward in telling him.

That wasn't Savannah's style. Not only did she lack that kind of courage, but she wasn't sure she was up to another heartache. "I can't. I'd be making the same stupid mistakes I made with Michael."

"I sincerely doubt that, unless one kiss can get you pregnant and make the man suddenly decide to rip off your hard-earned money. It would be a helluva kiss if it could accomplish all that."

How like Joslynn to try to defuse Savannah's worries with a dose of wry humor. And it worked. At least a little. "Okay, okay. I'm overreacting. I know I am. I just..." She kept her gaze on her daughter. "This time, there's a lot more at stake." She let out a sigh. "He's got a reputation."

"Pardon?"

"Never met a woman he didn't screw."

"Oh...that's not good."

"An understatement if I ever heard one. At least I know about his true nature *before* I get involved with him."

Joslynn laid a calm hand on Savannah's arm. "Look, hon...you're a different woman now. You're not the same person you were when you let Michael take advantage of you."

Savannah almost blurted out that Michael hadn't really done that, but she'd be wrong. He *had* taken advantage of her. Not only of her body, but of her trust and her naïveté. He'd used her love for profit.

"I strongly doubt that this Brad is anything like Shithead."

Since Joslynn rarely cursed, Savannah had to smile at the nickname they both used whenever they discussed Michael. "Not from what I've seen." Holding up a hand up to stop whatever Joslynn was going to say, Savannah reminded her, "But Shithead didn't show his true colors until those last few weeks, remember?"

Joslynn let out an inelegant snort that was in direct contrast to her sweet smile. "You mean when he emptied your bank account and left town without so much as a note?"

"I should've listened to you when you said there was something...weird about him. For all I know, Brad could be the same kind of guy."

"Then try to find out," Joslynn suggested.

"Pardon?"

"Put your ear to the ground and start listening. Get on Google. Talk to people in the business. Talk to *him*. Before you get in too deep, see what you can figure out about this guy. Maybe the talk about his women is nothing more than rumors. So find out the truth. If he turns out to be a good guy, then kiss his lips off."

Savannah couldn't help but laugh. "And if he's bad news?"

"Then fulfill your contract and keep your hands to yourself."

Savannah's cheeks heated as her thoughts strayed back to that connection, to the incredible chemistry that had taken her eyes off the prize and made her body so filled with need, she couldn't stop thinking about Brad.

"Ah...so *that's* how it is..." Joslynn grinned. "He got to you, didn't he?"

Savannah's face was hot enough that she might as well spontaneously combust. "I'm an idiot."

"Okay," Joslynn said. "Let's look at this thing from both sides."

"Both sides? I fail to see *sides* in this."

"Look closer. There are two ways this could go." She held up her index finger. "One, you kiss him." She added her middle finger. "Two, you don't kiss him."

"Either way, I'm screwed."

"Pun intended?" Joslynn asked as she let her slender hand drop.

God bless the woman's sense of humor. She always knew how to make Savannah smile. "No, but I'll still take credit for it."

Leaning back against the bench, Joslynn stretched her legs out, crossing them at the ankle as she let her gaze go to the playground, probably looking for her godchild. "Have you told him about Caroline?"

"No. Not yet. No one at the restaurant knows about her—except Ethan, the guy who hired me. I told him I was a single mom."

"You tell anyone else?"

Savannah shook her head. "I wanted to keep my life with her separate from my life at Words and Music—even more so now that I'm gonna be singing there. You know how I feel about keeping her privacy."

Joslynn nodded. "Can't blame you there. I know you don't want Michael anywhere near her. You know, if your career takes off…Might be even more difficult."

"If my career takes off, it'll be even more important to keep her life normal. Besides…you know I hate the idea of being famous," Savannah said. "All I want is to make a decent living."

"And if Michael wants to see her?" Joslynn asked.

"I'll cross that bridge when I come to it. I need to have a career to worry about first."

"Which brings us back to the original problem—your boss."

"My boss." A weary sigh slipped out. "I just don't know what to do about him, Jos."

"What's to know? Even if you kiss him, I think things would stay pretty much status quo. I can't imagine this Brad would hire you as a singer only to dump you over something like a kiss. After all, what does one little kiss matter anyway?" Her gaze came back to Savannah.

Joslynn's penetrating brown eyes wouldn't let Savannah brush aside the truth. "It think it would be more than 'just a kiss,'" Savannah admitted.

Joslynn gave her a quick nod. "Then I suppose the option to not kiss him is out."

"Probably." Admitting it was difficult enough. If she had to try to keep Brad at arm's length, she'd be fighting a challenging battle, even knowing what Russ said about him.

"Ask yourself," Joslynn advised, "what's the worst thing that could happen? You've got a contract, right?"

Not sure she wanted to admit how stupid she'd been, Savannah said, "Not yet. He's drawing it up now. I was going to sign it at the next rehearsal."

"You don't think you should have someone look it over before you sign?"

"Who, Jos? *Who* could I have look at the stupid thing? I can't afford a lawyer, and I sure as hell don't want to talk to another manager."

"Not all of them are crooks," Joslynn reasoned.

"Well, then I guess I've got crappy luck. I found the needle in the haystack of managers. I found Shithead."

* * *

Another one bites the dust... Or at least another song was done.

By the time Brad got Savannah into a studio, he'd probably have a whole damn album for her.

No. No, this was only a one-shot—*two*-shot—deal. She was going to have to take things on her own from here if she wanted original music. He had a restaurant to run. Being back in the music business meant he'd have to constantly be on his guard. He'd learned his lesson well about the fakes who just wanted a taste of fame.

Like Katie. After the way she'd used him, he wasn't going to put himself on the line again. Not for anything or anyone.

If only Savannah hadn't waltzed into his life.

He hadn't even kissed her, yet she haunted him, which pissed him off. He was Brad Maxwell—the man who could have any woman he wanted. He was the one who was always in control, always setting the pace. And he was the one who could and *would* walk away whenever he was ready.

So why couldn't he simply leave Savannah Wolf alone? What about her had captivated him so damned quickly that his head was still spinning?

"You're writing another one?"

Brad glanced up to see Ethan with a shit-eating grin that was sorely begging for a punch in his crooked nose. "No, I'm not."

Ethan's dark brows gathered. "Then what's with all this?" He flipped at the corner of a stack of newly written sheet music.

"I'm not *writing* another one. I already *wrote* it."

"Smart-ass." Ethan flopped on the couch.

"Why are you here? Not enough to do on the ranch?"

"Hardly. I've got two mares ready to foal."

"So why *are* you here? Afraid I'm not doing my job?"

"Again...hardly. I'm here because Russ said you were holed up in the office again and thought you might need a hand with next week's schedule."

"Next week's...Damn. I thought I'd already..." Brad shuffled around the papers littering the desk. "It isn't posted yet?"

"Nope."

"I coulda sworn I'd..." The schedule was on the bottom of the second pile Brad searched. "Shit. I'm sorry. I'll get it up right away."

Ethan held out his hand. "Need me to take a look?"

"No," Brad snapped. Although his anger was self-directed, he couldn't keep it from being shown.

"Alrighty then..." Ethan drawled.

Brad got to his feet and headed to the door. "Sorry."

"You do realize you have two partners in this place, right?" Ethan asked. "That you don't have to do every single thing yourself?"

Instead of replying, Brad stomped to the hallway, pinned the schedule on the bulletin board, and then marched back to the office. "Sorry," he muttered again.

"Look, Brad...I understand. I do. You're writing songs again, and it might be harder to get everything done that needs done. But I can't read your mind. If you need me to pick up the slack..."

Brad settled in his desk chair and glared at Ethan. "I'm fine. And I'm done. That was the last song. Okay? I don't need any help. I can handle the restaurant."

"Easy there, partner. I wasn't saying you couldn't."

"Then what were you saying?"

"What I'm saying is that I think it's great you're writing again, and I think it's great that you seem so taken with Savannah."

Rattled at the thought everyone could see his attraction to the singer, Brad raked his fingers through his hair. "I'm not *taken* with her. I'm—"

I'm what? Falling for her?

That was ridiculous. He wasn't about to let a woman he barely knew disrupt his life.

"I'll handle things here, okay?" Brad let out a sigh. "I wrote a couple of songs, but they're done. I'm back on the job."

Ethan frowned. "I wouldn't mind hanging around here awhile. If you need me, that is."

Even though he was scolding himself for being so interested in Savannah, Brad had come up with what he considered a brilliant plan while writing the second song. If she really wanted to hit the ground running, there was a way to easily jack up the publicity for her first night as their opening act. "Well, since you offered . . . how about you sing one of my new songs with Savannah this weekend?"

The scowl Ethan threw him was hot enough to leave blisters. "You're kidding, right?"

"Nope."

"Admit it. You're pulling my leg."

"Not one bit."

"She doesn't need that kind of publicity," Ethan insisted.

"I know you hate trading in on your name, but the kid needs something...*special* for her first opening set." Although he saw Savannah as anything but a "kid," Brad simply couldn't turn off his desire to help her out.

How old was she anyway? *Twenty-two tops*...Although her Crystal Bloom song was more than six years old, so she'd have to be at least a little older. *Maybe twenty-five?* He felt practically over-the-hill at thirty-five.

He needed to stop obsessing over her when he ought to be working on ordering stock for the restaurant's kitchen. Instead, he was micromanaging Savannah Wolf's return to country music.

Why?

Because she mattered to him.

I'm already in too deep.

Ethan drew Brad back into the conversation. "So you want 'Crawfish' and Dottie Walker's little boy to join the up-and-coming Savannah Wolf in a new song by the Hitman?" He rolled his eyes.

"Something like that."

At least Ethan took some time to think it over. Brad had expected an immediate "Fuck you," and his partner to storm out of the office. Nothing could anger Ethan the way being reminded of his parentage could. The last thing he ever wanted to do was trade in on his parents' legacy.

"Don't do it for me," Brad said. "Do it for Savannah."

Ethan spread his arms against the back of the couch. "I interviewed her, you know."

"I figured as much since I sure didn't remember hiring her."

"Russ thinks she's a great waitress."

"Yeah, well...Russ acts like he has a crush on her."

"And what do *you* think of Savannah?"

"I think she's a great singer." Brad picked up the pages of his new song and then stared at Ethan, hoping he'd see exactly how much singing a song with her could give Savannah a boost. "Just one song, Ethan? Help the girl out. You obviously saw something in her when you hired her, right?"

Ethan nodded. "She hasn't disappointed me. Cheyanne says she's the best waitress we've got. I hate to lose her, even if it's to sing for us."

"Then let's give her the best chance we can. What d'ya say?"

With a drawn-out and rather dramatic sigh, Ethan nodded again. "Fine. One song. But you owe me. Big time. Where's the sheet music?"

CHAPTER EIGHT

Savannah tucked her hair behind her ear. Again. She couldn't seem to control the nervous action. Working for Ethan Walker was one thing; singing with him was beyond anything she'd ever dreamed.

"Just relax. I don't bite. Promise." Ethan sat on one of the stools in the middle of the stage. He took his guitar and settled the instrument against his thigh. As he gently strummed, he gave her a wink. "We're just singing a song. That's all."

A snort slipped out. "That's *all*."

"You weren't this nervous when I interviewed you," he quipped.

"I was. I just didn't show it." She shrugged. "Besides, that was waitressing. Singing is scarier." She almost started babbling on about who he was and why it was so surreal to find herself onstage with him, but she bit her tongue. Ethan probably got sick of people telling him he was special only because his famous mom and dad had procreated.

But it was crazy. Not only was she singing with Ethan Walker, they were going to perform a new Hitman song.

Even though she'd been on the stage at Words & Music only a couple of days ago, she couldn't help but feel intimidated. While she loved performing, she found it nerve-racking to have all three owners watching her. A crowd she could handle; those men were another story.

First, there was Ethan. She'd heard him sing at a charity event a few years back. Whether it came from his parents or was his own God-given talent, he had a voice that touched her soul. A true, rich baritone with a charming Tennessee twang. To sing with him was an honor that she hoped she could live up to.

Then there was Russ. They'd grown close, friendly and comfortable, as he'd kept an eye on the crowds while she waited tables. Even when he'd bounced a drunken customer or two, he'd kept his sense of humor and done his best to keep things low key. When she'd confided that she was going to take a turn on Indie Night, he'd offered to stay close and offer moral support. Just seeing his friendly face in the crowd had calmed her. She loved his rather off-beat sense of humor and dedication to his job, and he was a fantastic person to work with.

Savannah's third "problem" was the biggest. *Brad.* She couldn't help but compare the way he'd captured her attention to him sneaking up from behind and clobbering her over the head. Quite simply, she couldn't get him out of her mind.

There wasn't room for romance in her life, especially with a guy with his reputation. Yet she couldn't stop her thoughts from settling on him. The way his gaze followed her made her both giddy and nervous. At least he seemed as affected by her as she was by him. If either had a lick of common sense, they'd put enough distance between them to douse the fire that flared between them with a hefty dose of cold water.

Since he was here and so was she, it appeared as if they were both idiots.

Ethan nodded to the backup musicians, counted the tempo, and then she joined him in performing "That Smile."

Every single time she sang the song, Savannah found herself near tears by the end. This time was no different and was, in fact, even more moving because of the beauty of Ethan's voice blending with hers. She was able to turn her head and swallow hard before directing her attention back to Brad so she could hear his verdict and hopefully receive some good constructive criticism.

He stood in the middle of the dance floor, facing the stage with his arms folded over his broad chest. "Good, but needs some work," he finally said with a nod.

Ethan shook his head and laughed. Then he leaned closer. "He *always* says that." His voice was a whisper.

"I always say that," Brad said, his voice echoing

through the place, "when a performance needs work." He walked toward the stage. "We'll keep tweaking, and I'm sure it'll be perfect by Friday. You two sound great together."

As Ethan stood, Savannah popped off her stool and placed a hand on his arm. "I can't thank you enough for doing this for me."

"No thanks necessary." He crouched and set his guitar in the case.

"Oh yes, thanks are necessary," she insisted. "You have no idea what you singing this duet means to me."

"You're quite welcome." He flashed her a heart-stopping smile that would've set any woman's heart to pounding—anyone but her.

Seemed her heart had already settled on another man.

Brad appeared on the stage. A frown bowed his mouth when his gaze found hers.

She'd thought the duet sounded great, but he was clearly displeased. "Would you like me to go through the rest of the set?"

He shook his head. "The lunch crew is ready to set things up, and customers will be in here soon. I want to keep you under wraps until Friday."

"But I think the other songs need some work."

"Looks like we're both perfectionists," he said with a grin. "They sound great, Savannah." When she started to protest, he added, "*But* I'd be happy to work more with you on all of them. Just not here." His eyes shifted to Ethan. "Think you can take enough time away from the horses to handle lunch rush today?"

After snapping the guitar case closed, Ethan stood. "Sure. Just for today?"

Brad nodded. "I'd like to take Savannah to my studio. She could use a little help getting ready. We can have some peace and quiet there."

Russ, who'd also joined them on the stage, came striding over to her side. "You're taking her to your place?" His glare was blistering hot.

Brad didn't seem at all intimidated. "Since I only have one studio and it happens to be at my house, then I guess I'm taking her to my place."

"I'll tag along," Russ announced.

Not sure how to defuse the tension between the partners, Savannah focused on another problem—her daughter. "I need to make a call." She shifted her guitar to her side, stepped away, and fished her phone out of her pocket. Then she dialed her mother.

"Hi, darlin'." Her mother's voice buzzed in her ear.

"Mom, do you think you could pick Caroline up? She's playing at Kailey's house."

"You mean her friend on Oak Street?"

"That's the one."

"I'd be happy to. You still working on your song?"

"Actually, I need to work on *all* of them," Savannah confessed.

Her mother scoffed. "You sing like a nightingale. There isn't a single thing wrong with those songs."

"You're sweet, and I thank you for that. But if Brad will

help me work on them, then I'm gonna work on them. I'll pick Caroline up as soon as I can."

"Don't you worry, darlin'," her mother insisted. "You take all the time you need."

Knowing she owed her parents more than she could ever repay, Savannah swallowed back tears. "Thank you. Love you lots."

"Daddy and I love you, too."

* * *

Love you lots.

Brad couldn't tamp down the jealousy that flared at hearing Savannah say those words to whoever was on the other end of that call.

Did she have a boyfriend? Other than the information about her former manager, there wasn't much to learn about her personal life. Hell, he didn't even know if she'd been married to the Hart guy. She'd kept a low profile, including avoiding social media. No Facebook, Twitter, or Instagram. Even her answers on her job application were sparse. Ethan must have been majorly impressed with her people skills in the interview to have hired her when there was so little to go on.

When she came back to stand between him and Ethan, Brad couldn't stop himself. "Talking to the boyfriend?"

"Hardly."

Seconds slowly ticked by until Brad decided she wasn't going to expand on that rather cryptic reply. He'd have to ask her to be specific when he got her away from everyone. Maybe she'd open up a little if they had some privacy.

"Are you ready to work?" Brad eased her guitar strap from her shoulder and took the instrument.

"I'm ready," she replied. As he tucked her guitar into the case, she said, "I can do that."

"Never said you couldn't," he replied, winking at her before he picked up the case. "I'll drive." As he headed toward the stage door, he stopped short and whirled around to face Russ, who'd followed hot on his heels. "You're not invited."

Russ crossed his arms over his chest and narrowed his eyes. "The hell I'm not."

Before Brad could start listing things that Russ needed to do at the restaurant, Savannah stepped between them. She faced Russ. "I really appreciate you wanting to help, but I think it might be better if you stay here."

Russ didn't look convinced. "Are you sure?"

"I'm sure. I want to get these songs just right, and I can do that better without an audience. Okay?"

Russ replied with a curt nod before turning to head to the door leading from the stage to the restaurant.

Brad cocked his head. "I'm not an audience?"

Her laughter was as sweet as a song. "Not really. You're my boss."

"So is Russ."

"He's my restaurant boss; you're my singing boss."

"Well, then. Let's see if we can get you ready for Friday."

He swept his arm toward the back stage door. "After you, m'lady."

She laughed and gave him a small curtsy. "Thank you, m'lord."

* * *

"We're here." Brad pulled his SUV close to the garage door and then punched the opener.

A glance to his right made him worry. Savannah's mouth was agape as she stared at his house. Sure, it was a bit...much. But Katie had fallen in love with it the moment the realtor brought them here. She'd wanted a mansion, and she'd gotten it.

All Brad had cared about was that there was a decent kitchen and plenty of room for him to work. The recording studio had grown out of the need to hear his songs in various stages of completion so he could tweak them until they were right. There were hours of recordings of Ethan singing Hitman songs, often multiple times with slight changes that eventually elevated each piece of music to what Brad considered "ready." Whenever Ethan grew weary of singing the same thing, Brad would do it himself. That was often counterproductive since he hated his own voice when he heard it in playback.

Katie offered to sing, but the poor woman had been tone deaf. Recording wasn't her thing—in fact, she hated it with a passion. To her, the country music world was about partying with celebrities and enjoying everything that he was able to buy her with his royalties.

Including this house.

"This is really your home?" Savannah asked in a breathless whisper.

"For now," Brad replied, leading her from the detached garage to the front door. "I've been thinking of putting it on the market and getting something smaller."

"I figured Ethan lived in something like this."

"Nah. His parents might've been rich, but they were nothing but country folk at heart. Their house is a tourist attraction now. He's got a horse farm not too far from here."

"You live here all by yourself?"

"Yep."

When they stepped into the elaborate foyer, he kept a close eye on her. Even he thought the marble floors and elaborate columned entry leading to the double staircase were a bit intimidating. He honestly didn't even "see" the place anymore. It was just home. But watching Savannah's reactions made him realize exactly how opulent the place was.

He felt like a fool for bringing her there. She had to think he was putting on some kind of show, letting her know exactly how much money he had. That had been Katie's game, not his. He still wore clothes that predated his first hit. There had never been a need to show off, and he made his mind up about one thing as he watched Savannah gaping as she moved through the foyer into the living area. He was putting the damn house up for sale.

The door was open for him to tell Savannah a little more

about himself. She'd asked if he lived alone. Although he'd replied, he hadn't truly answered. If he told her about Katie, maybe she'd open up about whatever it was she hadn't told him.

No. Not now. Not *yet*. They barely knew each other. Sure, they'd almost kissed, and Brad was honest enough with himself to admit that he wanted Savannah. Badly. But telling her about his past would be the first step toward starting a relationship, and he still believed the best thing for now was keeping their connection professional rather than personal. For both their sakes.

Funny, but he was having a horrible time doing that.

Figuring they could break the ice—and that she could get past her stunned silence—by having a bite to eat, he motioned for her to follow him to the kitchen. "I haven't eaten lunch. How about I throw something together for us?"

"Sure." Although she was replying to him, her attention was now fixed on the enormous gourmet kitchen they'd entered.

With the exception of his studio, this was the only room where he felt "at home." Cooking was a hobby, and when they'd bought the house, the kitchen had been why he'd agreed to buy it. While Savannah kept looking around, Brad opened the refrigerator to find out what ingredients he had to work with. Thankfully, his housekeeper also had the job of making sure there were edible things in his kitchen so he could indulge in his passion for cooking.

"Anything in particular you'd like?" he asked over his shoulder.

"You're going to cook?" she asked as she pulled one of the bar stools away from the kitchen island.

"Yes. I actually love cooking."

"You don't have to go to any trouble for me."

"I never want it said that I'm not a good host." Since she didn't say she wanted anything particular, he grabbed some eggs, ricotta, and bruschetta. "How about an omelet?" He set those ingredients on the island, then fetched some sun-dried tomatoes from the pantry.

"That sounds great." She sat on the stool and watched him.

Brad turned on the burner and did his best to put on a performance for her. He cracked the eggs with one hand before tossing the shells into the sink. He added ingredients with the right amount of flair, even throwing in a "Bam" or two like his idol, Emeril Lagasse. The downfall was when he tried to flip the folded omelet.

He tossed it up and then panicked that he wouldn't be able to catch it. In what had to look like a comedy routine, he barely caught the mixture and then shifted this way and that to be sure it didn't fall over the side of the frying pan. Only when he finally had it safely back in the pan did he let his breath out in a rush.

Savannah clapped and laughed. "That was amazing."

"Lunch *and* a show." Brad flashed her a smile. "Would you believe I've never missed before?"

"You didn't miss now."

"Came damn close, though." He slid the enormous omelet onto a serving plate. "Let's eat."

When she started to push back from the island, he stopped her. "We'll eat here. Sit tight."

"Sure I can't help?" she asked as he moved around his kitchen, gathering the plates and silverware.

"Nope. Want a soda?"

"Water's fine."

He filled two tall glasses of water before setting them by their plates. He took the bar stool next to hers and started serving. As he slid her plate in front of her, he said, "Eat up. You're gonna need your strength."

Her blond brows knit. "I am?"

"Absolutely."

"Why do I need my strength?"

"Because you, my dear, are not only going to get ready to sing on Friday. You're also going to record a song for me today."

CHAPTER NINE

Surely she'd heard him wrong. "Record a song?"

"Yep," Brad said with a nod.

Savannah frowned at him. "Here?"

He nodded and picked up their plates then set them in the sink. "C'mon. Follow me." He crooked his finger and inclined his head toward the far side of the kitchen.

Savannah dutifully followed, probably looking like a dork as she tried to discreetly gawk at the hallway's crown molding. She stopped when he opened a door and descended a staircase, a bit apprehensive at what she'd find at the bottom.

It was as though she'd stepped out of a page from *Home and Design* magazine and found herself in the middle of a control room at Blackbird Studio. There was a large desk equipped with consoles that held so many slides and buttons, she'd never be able to learn how to operate them all. Flat-screen monitors were positioned to the left and right of a large window, which allowed whoever was at the controls to watch the singer and musicians in the isolation room while simultaneously keeping an eye on the technology.

"Wow." She let the word slip out before she could call it back.

"I'm glad you like it." Brad pulled one of the leather desk chairs back and took a seat. "Care to give it a spin?" He gestured to the door that led into the recording room. "We can do a few takes now and then see what needs to be tweaked for Friday."

She pointed out the obvious. "There aren't any musicians."

"Don't need 'em." He thumped the back of his hand on the console. "Got all the accompaniment I need right here."

Although she knew it wasn't difficult to synthesize music, she was a purist where her songs were concerned. "I hate canned backup."

"So do I. That's why I played the backup myself."

"You what?"

"It's only a four-piece, but I think it works."

Brad was such a surprise to her. "How do you manage a four-piece backup by yourself?" she asked.

His grin made her heart skip. "It's easy—I played one instrument at a time."

She blinked a few times, processing what he'd just claimed he'd done. "Exactly how many instruments do you play?"

"Depends," he replied with a shrug.

"It depends? On what?"

"How well you expect me to play. I mean, if we're talking about performing or something, well, that's different than if I'm only horsing around." Brad was actually blushing, and she found his humility endearing, especially because he was chock full of arrogance in every other aspect of his life.

Savannah's train of thought ground to a bumpy halt. *Arrogance.* A trait she'd learned to avoid in men. It was one thing to be confident, another altogether to have hubris. Like her ex.

Like Brad?

She sure as hell hoped not.

Since she'd asked a simple question, she expected an answer that wasn't a dodge. "How many do you play, Brad?"

"Six," he replied. "Seven if you count the banjo. I pick it just good enough to not make an ass of myself."

A little in awe of him, she glanced into the recording booth. "So we're going to do this now?"

"That was my plan. You have enough time, don't you?"

Since he hadn't seemed open to telling her any of his personal stories, she felt no real need to explain any details about her personal life. Like the fact she had a child. Caroline was with her grandparents, Brad was obviously hot to get this song done, and Savannah was dying of curiosity to see how well a recording in this little studio would turn out. So she nodded.

"Great." Brad pulled his chair up to the control

console. "Head into the booth, and we'll do a few takes."

As she reached for the doorknob, she was surprised to see her hand shaking. This wasn't her first time recording. She had an indie album under her belt that Michael was supposed to have publicized in hopes of landing a contract. But he never got around to doing anything that helped that album out. Probably because he'd been busy ripping her off.

In retrospect, he'd done her a favor by dropping the ball. Whenever she listened to those songs now, she heard so much room for improvement. Although they were made only six years ago, those recordings were of a voice that hadn't matured, probably because that voice belonged to a young woman who'd never truly been hurt.

She took a seat on the padded stool and lifted the headphones from the music stand, finding herself smiling when she realized there had been one good thing to come from Michaels's betrayal—other than her darling Caroline. He'd forced Savannah to grow up, to endure loss and pain, and her voice had benefited.

After putting on the headphones and adjusting them, she arranged the sheet music for "That Smile," which rested on the music stand. She knew the song well enough that she didn't need to see it printed out, but as nervous as she was rapidly becoming, she found comfort in having it handy. Once she had the pages lined up and ready, she glanced up at the window to the studio, waiting for Brad to start the show.

His voice boomed through the headphones. "Ready?"

Savannah nodded.

"Then let's do this."

* * *

By the fifth take, Brad was losing his patience.

Had he been wrong in thinking Savannah was something special, something new? He sure as hell didn't think so.

Then why couldn't he get her to sing with the passion she'd shown back at Words & Music?

Maybe it was the song. "That Smile" was his first attempt at writing in a long time. Perhaps it wasn't up to snuff?

No. When Brad had heard Savannah and Ethan sing it earlier, he'd known he'd written a strong song with a good melody and a catchy beat.

Something was clearly blocking her talent.

"I'm sorry, Brad." She dropped the headphones from her ears to let them rest around her neck. Then, head bowed, she started shuffling through the sheet music.

He'd never seen her look defeated before, and he didn't like it. This wasn't the Savannah who'd been his muse. This wasn't the woman who brought back his music.

This was...a disaster.

But why?

He watched her closely, trying to find some telltale clue as to what was going on today that had robbed Savannah of the passion and talent he'd counted on. Her hair was braided, the braid an eclectic mixture of blond and blue.

She wore jeans instead of a skirt, and her blouse was made of an airy, gauzy pink material. The white sandals on her feet looked well-worn and comfortable. A blush tinted her cheeks, and he could hear her nervousness through the quaver in her voice, especially in the last notes of her fifth recording.

Something was definitely wrong, and he was going to have to find a way to fix it. But he couldn't do that from another room. Even though he could see her, something told him she needed something more personal. Unsure of whether being closer to her would make a difference, he figured it was worth a shot.

Brad started a new recording so he could capture the song if he was able to help her, pushed himself away from the console, and headed to the recording booth with his remote control in his pocket. He pulled the door open and stepped inside.

Savannah glanced up from the music, offering him a wan smile that made his frustration evaporate. She knew something was wrong, too. Maybe if they put their heads together, they could get back the magic.

After pulling a stool beside hers, he sat. Then he gently took off her headphones, plucked the pages from her hands, and placed them back on the music stand. She let her eyes meet his, and he could see her concern.

"We're going do things a little differently this time," Brad said, keeping his voice low.

"We are?"

He nodded and scooted closer. Then he wrapped his

hand around one of hers. "You're not going to think about recording."

"I'm not?"

"Nope. This time you're just going to sing to me. That's all."

"But you're recording it, right?"

He shook his head, feeling no guilt for lying to her. He'd heard her older songs, so she'd obviously recorded before. But there was something about this session that was blocking her. If a fib helped her put the hurdle behind her, then fib he would.

Her whole body relaxed, and Brad had to fight the desire to smile.

"Sing to me, Savannah. Just to *me*. Okay?"

She nodded, and before she could get a chance to think about what he was doing, he pulled a remote from his pocket and began the music playback so that it echoed through the room.

The notes of the intro flowed around them, and he kept her grounded by not allowing her to glance away. When she opened her mouth to sing, he gave her hand a reassuring squeeze and offered her an encouraging smile.

And sing she did. Each delightful note came from deep inside her, and he found himself caught in some kind of spell, the same type she'd woven around him back at Words & Music. He hung on each rise and fall of that delicious voice until the last note echoed through the booth.

The song might have ended, but not the magic. Brad

found himself leaning closer, his eyes fixed on her soft, pink mouth. Desire ripped through him as she mimicked his action, drawing ever so slowly closer until he could feel the sweet heat of her breath against his face.

With a groan of surrender, he captured her mouth with his own, giving her no warning as his tongue swept deep inside.

Savannah nearly knocked over her stool when she rose to thread her arms around his neck. She was such a little bit of a thing that he could stay seated and draw her between his outstretched legs without interrupting the kiss. As she moved closer, Brad wrapped his arms around her waist and pulled her hard against him.

The kiss turned ravenous, and he realized that he was done fighting this attraction, done fighting whatever these feelings were she'd planted inside him. His tongue rubbed hers as he let his hands slide down to cover her ass. Then he lifted her hard against his erection, hoping she understood exactly how much he wanted her at that moment.

She whimpered against his mouth, rubbing herself against him in response.

It was all the invitation he needed. "I want you," he growled as he embraced her and stood, leaving her feet dangling a few inches above the floor. Backpedaling, he pressed her against the wall. "I want you."

"We can't," she murmured even as her fingers tangled in his hair.

"We can," he insisted before his lips captured hers again. There was no way he was letting her leave him. Not now.

Once he'd made the decision to see where this connection would lead, he needed to show her exactly how desperately he wanted her—and just how much he needed her to feel the same way.

Since when had that kind of link ever mattered to him before? Although he made sure his lovers received pleasure from the exchange, he'd never given a damn about their feelings. Love only complicated things.

Yet he found himself not only wanting to share his body with Savannah. No, he wanted her to want him for so much more than sex.

Brad kissed his way across her cheek before burying his lips against the silky skin of her slender neck. He inhaled, breathing in her irresistible scent and wanting nothing more than to carry her up to his bedroom and make love to her until morning.

* * *

Savannah let out a shuddering breath, trying hard to rein in her tumbling emotions.

Her body demanded Brad, and every ounce of her self-control couldn't seem to help her bring this passionate interlude to a stop.

"Wait," she whispered as a shiver raced the length of her spine. His lips were doing the most marvelous things to her.

"No," he whispered back before the tip of his tongue traced the lines of her ear.

This was reckless. This was stupid. But she wanted him

anyway. The way his gaze had held hers as she sang the song he'd written for her had been every bit as intimate as if they'd already shared their bodies with each other.

"Come upstairs with me." His face came into her sight again. "Let me make love to you." He didn't even wait for an answer as he kissed her again, stoking the overwhelming fire inside her.

One of his hands moved from her back, caressing her waist and then moving higher until his palm covered her breast. It had been so long, and he was making her feel so good . . .

Things were happening too fast. Savannah couldn't think, couldn't seem to find the strength to push him away. She honestly didn't want to, and should she listen to the way her body sang out in need, she'd follow him to his bedroom. She'd give in to his whispered promises and his wicked suggestions.

His hand was under her blouse, and as though he'd honed the skill of seduction to a fine art, he popped the front clasp on her bra. She gasped in surprise when he took her hardened nipple between his fingers and rolled it, making heat rip to her core.

It was that skill, that experience, which finally sobered Savannah. Brad was a pro at getting around a woman's undergarments because he'd had plenty of practice removing them. All the stories of his exploits crowded her brain, and it was a dose of ice water against the desire he inspired inside her.

With that thought, Savannah found the strength to put

her hands against his chest, knock his hand away from her breast, and push. "No."

"Savannah..." He tried to kiss her again, leaning into her hands even as she tried to put some distance between them.

"No. Please, Brad. No." The tremors in her voice made her angry. She didn't want to show him how much he'd affected her.

With a sigh, he pulled back, dropped his hands to his sides, and turned away. "I'm sorry. I didn't mean to...to take advantage." He was out the door and sitting at the control console before she could even gather her wits.

"No need to apologize." A cross between embarrassment and fear filled her as she turned her back and fixed her clothing. By the time she found enough false courage to turn around, she couldn't help but stare at Brad. He was so busy working on something that he might as well have not even been a part of what had just happened between them.

Savannah jumped in surprise when his voice boomed through the small booth. "Want to try one more take?"

"N-no." She smoothed her blouse nervously before deliberately checking her watch, hoping she could find a graceful way out of this horrible situation. Then a laugh bubbled up. "I'd probably sound like a strangled chicken."

At least he chuckled at the comment. "I doubt that... Are you sure? Just one more?"

"I know we don't have the perfect take, but it's getting late." She could barely force her voice to stay even. No, there would be no more singing today. "Do you think you could take me back to the restaurant?" *So I can get my car, drive home, and beat myself up for being an idiot?*

"Sure thing."

Gathering up any ounce of bravado she could muster, Savannah stepped out of the booth to find Brad waiting. He held out his hand to her. All she did was stare at it, unsure as to what her best move would be.

"I won't bite," he said, his voice holding a note of humor.

She put her hand in his.

"Look, I really am sorry." He squeezed her fingers.

"No, I'm the one who should be sorry," she insisted.

"For what?"

"For...for..." She jerked her hand away and wrapped her arms around her waist, hugging herself. "You know, I have absolutely no idea."

His grin was charming. "Good, 'cause neither do I."

The stilted silence lasted for a few moments until he let out an exaggerated sigh. "Can we talk for a minute?"

Now she'd done it. He was going to fire her. She nodded at his question because she wanted to know exactly why he was going to can her. Was he angrier that she'd overstepped their boundaries by kissing him, or was he more upset that she'd turned him down when he'd responded to her kisses with an invitation to have sex?

"C'mon." He flipped his hand. "Let's go upstairs and have a cup of coffee."

CHAPTER TEN

Cradling a warm cup between her hands, Savannah waited to see if Brad was going to say something or if she'd have to broach the subject. He'd been the one who wanted them to talk about what almost happened in the recording booth. She would've been much happier pretending none of it ever occurred.

But instead of fleeing, she'd straightened her spine, followed him upstairs, and waited while he made them coffee.

Her patience was now at an end.

Brad sat down next to her, sipping from his cup. He finally put it aside and turned to her. "So..."

"So..."

"We need to talk."

"Yep. We need to talk." Savannah almost rolled her eyes at herself for sounding like a parrot.

His face was hard to read, downright stoic. "First of all,

I want you to know that I didn't bring you here to try to get you into bed."

"And I didn't come here to get *you* into bed." She let out an amused snort. The whole situation certainly was absurd. "It wasn't like I was thinking about anything other than singing, either. It just...happened."

"That's the problem, though. It didn't just *happen*. Judging from the way things were between us in that isolation booth—the way things have been between us almost from the beginning—we were both thinking about *it*, probably far too much."

"I suppose..." She took another sip and debated over what to say. Did he want her to admit how attracted she was to him? Did his ego need her affirmation? Or was he enjoying her embarrassment?

He raked his fingers through his hair. "I also want you to know that this is virgin territory for me."

Another laugh bubbled out before she could stop it.

His response was a confused frown.

"I'm sorry," she said, trying to sound contrite. "It's just...I've heard a few stories. You know, about you." *Virgin territory, my ass.*

"About me?" Brad let out a weighty exhale. "I can only imagine. Russ, right?"

Hoping to keep any friction from developing among the partners, Savannah shook her head. The last thing she needed was to be the wedge being driven between them.

"You don't need to lie, Savannah. I know he probably had a mouthful to say about my...um...dating habits."

"He really didn't say all that much..."

He scoffed. "I know I was a jerk, but that's why what's happening between us is virgin territory."

Confused, she put her mug down and slid it away. "I don't follow. I thought you'd been married."

"I might've been married, but I don't know shit about"—he pointed to her and then to him—"this. This starting a healthy relationship stuff. Making things work between two people."

Surely she'd heard him wrong. "Relationship? You think we're in a relationship?"

"Well, not yet, but I was kinda hoping we were heading in that direction."

"I honestly don't know what to say." Her thoughts whirled as she tried to think of all the time they'd shared. Were there hints that he wanted something more than her singing in his restaurant? That he wanted something more personal?

There were the times they'd almost kissed. But incidents like that weren't enough to make a relationship. She'd clearly been so concerned about her budding career that she'd missed any signals he'd sent that he thought of her as something more than an employee or a great warm-up act.

Brad combed his fingers through his hair again, something she'd realized was his version of a nervous tick. "I'm doing this all wrong. Let me try again..." He took her hands in his, turning her so she was fully facing him. "I'll admit it. I tried to ignore you, I mean as anything other than a singer. I really tried. But you were there anyway. Hell, I wrote two songs for you already, and I'll be damned if there isn't another one in my head trying to work its way out."

"For me?" she squeaked, taken aback by the forcefulness of his tone. One song was merely a fluke. She'd somehow done something inspiring. But two songs? Or three? There had to be more to this than dumb luck.

He nodded. "I figured I'd just get you singing for Words and Music and treat you like any other act, but I can't keep my distance. And I honestly don't want to."

In all the times she'd had dealings with men, Savannah had never had one come out and lay his cards on the table the way Brad was doing.

If that was what he was doing. Or was this simply another attempt to finish what they'd started in the basement? Was he only trying to get laid?

"I'm so confused," she admitted, sounding far too forlorn for her taste.

"Would it help if I tell you I am, too?" he asked with a chuckle. "I've never been this...open before. I'm just sick of playing games with women. I'm tired of saying what I think a woman wants to hear. I want to do things differently with you."

"I'm honored. I think."

He shrugged. "It is what it is—whether that's good or bad, I don't know yet."

* * *

Brad was shocked by his own admissions. After the way Savannah had not only returned his kiss but passionately responded to him, he'd decided he would try something he had never done before.

He had been honest with a woman about everything he was thinking and feeling.

It wasn't easy, especially when she looked so damned confused. No wonder. He hadn't been lying when he admitted he was in virgin territory. He'd never taken the time to get to know a woman before.

Except Katie, and that hadn't turned out at all well because he obviously knew nothing about the *real* Katie. He'd never been able to see through her façade, the mask she'd worn to win him over simply so she could use him.

But Savannah was...different. He could feel it. She deserved something more than his usual modus operandi, and he couldn't help but think this change in his approach was for the better. Once he'd made up his mind to stop fighting whatever was flaring between them, he also decided that he would try to make a positive change in himself. He would stop using women. While he wanted to make love to Savannah, wanted to be inside her so badly that he hadn't lost his erection yet, he also wanted something more. To get to know her. To learn what she liked and what she didn't.

Why couldn't he finally be the "good guy" he'd always wanted to be?

That tactic had worked for Brad where the restaurant was concerned. He'd made positive changes and had taken great strides to become the man he wanted to be. So why not approach his feelings for Savannah the same way?

He'd decided to go for broke. Although he was still concerned about being dragged back into the music scene, he would simply have to be more careful in whom he trusted. He'd steer clear of the parties that were always full of opportunists of every shape and size. That was all there was to it. He'd stay the hell away from anything that could hurt him again.

"Brad, I should probably go." Savannah tried to pull her hands away.

"Not yet. Please. We need to talk."

"We've been talking, and I don't think it changed much."

"You're right," he admitted. "So here's the truth of it—there's something about you that makes it impossible for me to leave you alone. And I'm not talking about your voice. You already know how I feel about that." He squeezed her hands. "I want to see if we can try to be together. You know, date or something."

"Date?"

He nodded.

"Like go out and see movies and stuff?"

"Whatever you'd like to do, we'll do it."

"You want to make plans now?" she asked.

"How about we just take things as they come?"

Her laughter made him smile. "No pun intended?"

"No pun intended. I'm not that clever."

She shook her head. "You're very clever."

"Thank you."

"You're welcome."

"Are we now reduced to nothing but polite conversation? Have I scared you away?"

The longer she thought the question over, the more nervous he became. About the moment Brad was going to break the stilted silence, Savannah beat him to it.

"Fine," she announced with a terse nod.

"Fine?"

"Fine, we can go on a date and see how things go."

Since he hadn't been at all sure how she'd respond to his honesty, he was a bit shocked that she'd agreed. "Great."

Now he only needed to figure out the perfect thing to do on a date. God knew he hadn't been on a real date since high school. Even then, he'd approached the girl of his choice with the idea of getting laid upmost in his mind.

Katie had been a different story. She'd approached him at a party thrown by a mutual friend. They'd left together at her insistence. The more he thought about it, the more he realized she'd targeted him. They hadn't truly dated, but instead had sort of fallen into a relationship because he fell for her so damn hard. She'd moved in with him after only two weeks.

Savannah glanced at her watch. "I really should be getting home."

"Tell me about home. All I know about you is that you were a waitress and that you tried to start a singing career that was sabotaged by a jerk."

"That's plenty to know." Standing, she picked up her cup and inclined her head toward his. "Want me to put these in the dishwasher?"

Brad shook his head, took her cup from her hand, and grabbed his own. "You're the guest." After finishing the quick chore, he led her back to the front door, a bit worried that she hadn't taken his hint that he wanted to know more about her. Then he realized he'd been every bit as guarded.

So he took the first step. "You were asking about why I bought this place. My wife wanted this house. I really didn't. But I figured she deserved it for putting up with me."

"What happened to her?"

"Katie died a few years back."

Sympathy filled Savannah's face. "I'm so sorry."

"It was another lifetime." He opened the door for her and set the alarm before shutting the door behind himself. "At least it seems that way. Just wanted to be honest with you. I think honesty should be our battle plan." He cast a glance back at the house when they reached his car. "I think it might be time to give this place up and look for something smaller."

"If I had a place this wonderful, I'd never give it up."

Then perhaps his call to his realtor would be postponed. For now.

Once they were in his car, buckling their seat belts, Brad tried again. "Let me drive you home. I'll need directions."

"My car is at Words and Music. We can just go back there."

The woman couldn't take a hint, so he abandoned subtlety. "You've seen my place, so tell me about yours. What kind of house do you live in?"

"It's not much. Only a small fixer-upper town house."

Despite his best efforts, he could pull very little personal information from her. Before he knew it, they were pulling into the restaurant's parking lot. After he turned off the engine, she tried to open the door.

"Wait a second." Brad jumped out and raced around to open the passenger door, mad at himself that he hadn't opened the door for her when they'd arrived at his house. He grinned at Savannah when she was out of the car. "I might have a bad reputation, but I promise you that I always treat a lady like a lady. Now, let me walk you to your car."

Her brows had gathered and a frown bowed her mouth.

"Savannah...what's wrong?"

"You really want to know more about me?"

Such a strange question since he'd just spent the last hour trying to convince her he was serious about dating her. "Yes, ma'am. I really want to know more about you."

Her sigh was acquiescent. "Fine." She took his hand and dragged him down the line of parked cars until she stood by an ancient Honda sedan that had more than its share of dings and scratches in the silver paint. "This is my car. It has almost two hundred thousand miles on it."

And what exactly was he supposed to say about that? "Sounds dependable."

"Hardly, but it's all I could afford after...Well, after Michael. At least when he left, I didn't have to divorce him. We never got around to getting married."

Brad waited, hoping the door was now open for him to find out more about the misery Michael Hart had inflicted on her. His wait was in vain as Savannah fell silent again. Yet she stared at him, cocking her head slightly as if deciding something important. If that decision involved him, he hoped the verdict was in his favor.

Instead of saying anything, she took a step that closed the slight distance between them. Then she put her arms around his neck and pressed her lips to his.

All his thoughts fled as he wrapped his arms around her waist and pulled her hard against him. Before he could heighten the kiss, her tongue was in his mouth, rubbing against his. He growled deep in his throat, letting her know how much he appreciated her being the aggressor this time.

She ended the kiss as abruptly as she'd begun it, stepping back and out of his arms. His ego loved the fact that she was panting for breath until he realized she'd had the same effect on him. He was nearly shaking with desire.

"If we're going to do this," Savannah announced, her voice no longer hesitant, "if we're really going to be honest, then there's something you need to know about me."

"Fire away."

CHAPTER ELEVEN

I have a daughter," Savannah said, watching Brad closely for any reaction.

"You're a mom?" he asked.

"I'm a mom."

He stared hard at her. "You must've been pretty young when you had her."

"Not so young. Twenty-three."

"That's what I figured you were now," he said with a grin.

"I'm twenty-eight." She shot him a smile. "But thanks."

"What's her name?"

"Caroline. If you're coming to my place, you're going to meet her. But I'll only introduce you as my boss right now, okay?"

"If it means I get to meet her, that works for me." His gaze went to her car. "Should I follow you?"

With a nod, she chirped off the alarm, which surprisingly still worked, and allowed him to open the door for her. "I drive kinda fast, so try to keep up."

* * *

The moment she pulled up next to her town house, Savannah feared she'd made a huge mistake. Bringing Brad to her home went against every promise she'd made to herself about keeping business and personal matters as separate as humanly possible. Not only that, she hadn't had a chance to warn Caroline or her parents since her phone battery had died. They were in for a shock.

She was being foolish. They hadn't even gone on a single date, and she was dragging him home to introduce him to her family. Her daughter shouldn't have to worry about what Brad's role in her life might be—if he even developed a role at all. The poor kid had enough problems trying to understand why her father had never so much as sent a birthday card.

And her parents... What would they think, especially after helping her through hell when Michael had abandoned her and left her penniless? They didn't need to meet Brad. They'd only start speculating—and probably encouraging, considering how often they'd told her she needed to "get back out there" again.

Of course, they had no clue about Brad. If they knew his reputation, they'd probably pitch a fit.

Before she could think of a good reason to tell him she'd changed her mind, he'd pulled up behind her and parked his car. She lightly banged her head against the steering wheel, wishing an enormous sinkhole would open up and swallow her whole.

A knock on her window forced her to face her rash choice. Popping off her seat belt, she pushed the door slowly open before Brad took over the chore. Once on her feet, she opened the back door. He gently moved her aside to get her guitar. Then he stood there, waiting.

She swallowed hard. "This was a bad idea."

He shook his head. "Honesty. Remember?"

She glanced at the town house, worried that he'd think the place was a dump. His home reeked of opulence. She lived in a row house that had probably been last renovated before she was born. The place was comfortable and cheap, but he was sure to see her as bordering on poverty.

"Savannah, what's wrong?"

Gaze still fixed on her home, she frowned.

"It's a cute place, if that's what you're worried about."

"Cute, my ass."

He took her hand in his and gave a reassuring squeeze. "It really *is* cute. Lots of character."

Her eyes found his. "I thought you said we were going to be honest with each other."

"I did."

"Then stop lying to me." With a resigned sigh, she headed toward the stoop stairs, tugging him along with her. "We're here now. You might as well come in."

The door was unlocked, something she'd have to scold her parents about again. They'd always lived in the boonies and knew all their neighbors, so they'd never developed the habit of locking their doors. Once they were inside, she took her guitar case from Brad. "Are you ready?"

"Mama!" Caroline's excited squeal echoed down the staircase.

Savannah set the case down next to the coat tree and crouched down to open her arms to her daughter, who was practically flying down the stairs.

Caroline threw herself into Savannah's embrace, and Savannah lifted her into her arms to stand next to Brad. After they hugged, Caroline eased back to look at him.

"Hi," he said as he slid his hands into his pockets.

"Hi," Caroline said before looking back at Savannah. "Who's that man, Mama?"

"Is that my baby girl?" her father called from the kitchen.

Brad quirked a brow.

"My father. He and my mother are my babysitters," she replied to his tacit question.

Her father came strolling down the hall before stopping short as his eyes widened. "Well, hello, young man."

"Hello, sir," Brad replied. He thrust out his hand. "Brad Maxwell."

"Paul Wolf." He shook Brad's hand before breaking the connection to adjust his thick glasses. "You didn't tell us you'd have company, little miss."

Little miss. The only time her father called her that was when he intended to scold her.

"I didn't know he'd be visiting when I asked you to babysit." Savannah shifted a squirming Caroline in her arms since her daughter was intent upon staring at Brad, even if it meant crawling over her mother's shoulder to do so. "Brad, this wiggle worm is my Caroline."

He made a point of giving her hand a shake, which set the girl to giggling. "How old are you, Caroline?"

"This many!" She held up five fingers.

After gently tucking Caroline's thumb against her palm, Savannah smiled at her daughter. "You're this many."

Caroline put her thumb back. "Gramma said I'd be this many soon."

"How soon?" Brad asked as he kept grinning at Caroline.

Caroline returned the smile as she shrugged hard enough that Savannah almost dropped her.

"Six weeks, Miss Caroline," Mary said as she joined them in the foyer. As though she knew exactly how much trouble Savannah was having holding on to her daughter, Mary took Caroline and set her against her hip. "Hello. I'm Mary Wolf."

Brad inclined his head in greeting. "Now I see where Savannah gets her good looks."

Paul chuckled. "Don't try to make brownie points with either of 'em. The women in this family are immune to compliments." Flipping his hand in invitation, he led everyone into the living room. After he sat in his favorite place—the worn recliner—he waited until everyone else found a place to park themselves. "Might I ask how you know my daughter, Mr. Maxwell? Where'd you meet? How'd you come to be her date tonight?"

Resisting the urge to let out a groan, Savannah fired a frown at her father. "Daddy, we weren't on a date."

"If you weren't on a date, what exactly were you doing?" He narrowed his eyes at Brad. "Just what are your intensions toward my daughter?"

"Dad..."

"It's my right to know," he insisted. "What with all the trouble you had with Michael—"

"Dad! Stop!" She narrowed her eyes. "Brad is my boss, okay? He owns Words and Music and he hired me to sing. Those are his intensions."

Mary, who'd sat on the arm of the recliner, cocked her head. "Your boss, eh? Can't say I ever went to the trouble to drag any of my bosses home to meet my family. So tell me, Brad...are you wanting to date our Savannah?"

"Mom! Stop!" Hands fisted against her thighs, Savannah took a deep breath, trying to calm herself. This was exactly what she'd feared, but it wasn't as if she could—or would—tell her parents to go home. All she could do was hope Brad would find some reason to leave. Quickly.

Caroline had plopped herself on the sofa, right between Savannah and Brad. She kept staring at him as if he were the strangest thing she'd ever seen. No wonder. The only male adult in her life was her grandfather. Over the years since Michael had abandoned her, Savannah had gone on a date or two, but never once had she let any of those dates near her daughter.

What had she been thinking? Just because Brad had opened up a little about his life didn't mean she had to drag him home and share everything she'd always tried to protect. No wonder her parents were grilling him.

You know why you brought him home. He's... special.

Shut up, stupid heart. You get me in too much trouble.

As though he knew Caroline was staring at him, Brad turned his head and smiled down at her. "Are those your books?" he asked as he nodded toward the stack of books Caroline kept on her play table.

Her whole face lit with a grin in response. "Yeah."

"You like *Where the Wild Things Are?*"

Caroline began to bounce with excitement. "It's my favorite!"

"Mine, too," he said. "Do you wish Max had stayed with the wild things?"

She picked up his hand and held it fast, still smiling at him as she nodded. "Wanna read it?"

"Not now, Caroline. Brad isn't staying long," Savannah explained, hoping to spare Brad an ordeal. One book was never enough for her daughter, and although she was pleased that Caroline loved reading, Brad sure didn't need to lock himself into an extended session of children's books.

The poor man had to wish he could leave tire marks getting away from them all. Her father was drilling him on his "intentions." Her mother eyed him as though she was ready to measure him for his wedding tux. And her daughter was clearly enamored with him.

"I'm sure he needs to be going soon. Right, Brad?" Savannah was sorely tempted to take his hand away from

Caroline and drag him to the door. "It was nice of you to make sure I got home safely."

"So *that's* what this is all about." Her father slapped his hands against the armrests. "You having engine problems again? I wish you'd let me buy you something nicer. You're just as stubborn as your mother."

Her mother patted his shoulder. "Thank you, dear."

"It wasn't a compliment, woman."

"Sure, it was." She patted him again.

Cheeks burning, Savannah bowed her head and started rubbing her forehead, hoping to relieve the headache that had suddenly appeared. "Dad, no. I told you, the car's fine."

Caroline crooked her finger at Brad until he leaned closer. "I wanna tell you somethin'," she whispered.

"Go ahead," he whispered back.

"I got a ghost under my bed."

"Really?"

She nodded. "Can you come scare it away, Brad? Please?"

"Mr. Maxwell," Savannah corrected.

"She can call me Brad," he countered as he let go of Caroline's hand and stood. "I don't mind." Then he held his hand out to her in invitation. "I'd be quite happy to chase away your ghost. I'm great at ghost removal."

"You are?" Caroline, eyes as big as saucers, took his hand and hopped off the sofa.

"Yes, ma'am, I am." He extended his free hand toward Savannah. "Would you care to help us with some ghost-busting?"

6666666666

Anything to get away from the Wolf Inquisition. "Absolutely."

"Hang on there a minute, little miss," her father said. "I'd like to have a word with you first."

Since she had no intention of being grilled about Brad, she shook her head.

Her father got to his feet and hitched up his pants. "I insist."

Caroline dragged Brad to the stairs, then thankfully the two of them were gone.

"Dad..."

"I like this one," her father announced. "Respectful. Good financial prospects."

Her mother was more subtle. "Has he asked for a date?"

Savannah nodded.

"Well, good!" her mother said. "Just let us know when you need a babysitter."

She frowned at them. "You're both making too much outta this."

"We are, are we?" her father asked.

Her mother matched her frown for frown. "Tell me this, darlin'...Why? Why bring him here?"

"Honestly? I don't have a clue." And now she wished she had thought a bit more about introducing Brad to her family. All it had done was complicate things, and that was exactly what she didn't need. Complications. "Look, I don't know where it's going. Okay? We did some recording and... well...I..." She threw up her hands. "Like I said, I haven't a clue. Just don't make more out of it than it is, okay?"

Her father nodded and strode to the coat tree. He held her mother's jacket so she could slip into it before donning his own.

Relieved they were going, Savannah was anxious to see exactly what Caroline had shown Brad. No doubt her daughter's room was in its typical state of chaos. Considering where he lived, he probably thought this place was pathetic.

"Thanks for watching Caroline," she said as she gave each parent a quick hug.

Her mother's face lit with a sly smile. "Like I said, just let us know when you're going on a date with Brad. We'll be glad to babysit."

Instead of giving her mother the satisfaction of knowing she was right, Savannah said nothing. Once her parents were out the door, she hurried up the stairs.

* * *

Brad flipped on the light when they got to what he assumed was Caroline's room.

Pretty typical for a girl. Lots of pink and plenty of toys, which were scattered around as though she'd tried to play with them all at the same time.

Caroline tugged on his hand and pointed. "It's under my bed."

"How do you know?"

"He makes sounds. He's gonna get me."

He squeezed her small hand. "I won't let him get you."

After turning her loose, he knelt on the floor next to her twin bed. Then he lifted the dust ruffle and tried to see what exactly was scaring her. He came face to face with two feral eyes. "You don't have a ghost under here, pumpkin. But you do have a guest."

"A guest?" The floor creaked as she took a few steps closer.

Unsure whether the cat was friendly, he resisted the urge to scoop it up and show Caroline what was making the noise under her bed. The animal was staring at Brad as though sizing him up, which was exactly what he was doing to the cat. "Do you have any pets?"

"Pets?"

The question had come from Savannah. "Yeah," he replied. "Like a cat?"

Braving the possibility of being clawed, he slid his hand under the cat and dragged it closer. When the animal didn't fight him, he pulled it out from under the bed. He held the cat to his chest and stroked it, hoping he'd won its trust. A purr assured him he had.

"Mr. Whiskers!" Caroline ran to Brad's side and scratched the yellow tabby's head.

Savannah took the cat from Brad and set him on the floor. The tabby trotted out the door, tail twitching. "He's never hidden under there before. He tends to hide out in my room. Thanks for fishing him out."

"My pleasure. Just glad he wasn't a ghost."

"Caroline," Savannah said, a note of censure in her voice, "you need to thank Brad for getting Mr. Whiskers for you."

"Thanks." After her muttered appreciation, the little

girl went skipping out of her room. "Mr. Whiskers?" she sang from the hallway. "Come play with me!"

"And *that*," Savannah said, "is why he hides in my bedroom."

Brad waited a few moments to be sure Caroline was out of earshot. "I'll bet she's a handful."

With a chuckle, Savannah began to gather up the toys strewn across the wooden floor. "And then some."

While there were so many questions he wanted to ask, he figured a date would give them a better chance to get to know each other. After her agony over her parents asking him questions, he didn't think she was in the mood to tell him much about herself.

Since she seemed intent on picking up toys—and all but ignoring him—he started to help. He hadn't so much as grabbed a teddy bear when she tossed the toys she was holding into a wooden toy box and snatched the bear from his hand.

"You don't need to be doing that." She set the toy on the small bed and then folded her arms under her breasts. "You should probably be going."

"Are you anxious to get rid of me?"

She'd been staring at her shoes. His question made her head pop up. "No! I mean . . . you've got to have much better things to do than hang around here."

"There isn't anything I wanna do as much as spend time with you."

Her gaze left his. "I never should've brought you here. I'm sorry about my parents."

"They're only looking out for you," he said.

"I know, but...they come on a little too strong."

"I didn't mind," he insisted. In fact, he found their asking about his intentions not only quaint but wise.

Two steps put him right in front of her, and he laid his hands on her shoulders. "I really didn't mind, Savannah."

She glanced up, giving him her full attention. "Thanks for being so great with Caroline and my parents."

He wasn't sure he'd ever get used to the way her blue eyes affected him. The worry he saw there now made him want to gather her into his arms. "Thank *you*."

"For what?"

"For sharing your life with me." He brushed a quick kiss over her lips, wanting more but willing to wait.

Long moments passed before Savannah cocked her head. "So we're really going to do this?"

Brad quirked a tawny brow. "This?"

"This...relationship stuff."

"Yes, Savannah, we're really going to do this. How about we start with that date—except it'll be you, me, *and* Caroline?"

CHAPTER TWELVE

"Chaos," Brad muttered to himself. "Absolute chaos."

When he'd suggested that they bring Caroline on their first date, Brad had figured they'd do something like go to a movie—some kid flick—and then take the munchkin to a babysitter. Then he and Savannah could hit a nice restaurant. After all, why would Caroline want to spend so much time with him? She barely knew him.

He'd been dead wrong.

As he surveyed the crowd of kids at Planet Pizza, he couldn't help but shake his head. There were so many children that he could hardly keep track of Caroline's frenzied flight around the play area. He glanced at the bracelet on his wrist. The costumed employee had snapped one on each of them when they'd entered the restaurant. That gave him "claim" to Caroline should she get separated from them. All she had to do was find an employee, who would immediately page her first name and tell her "parent" to come retrieve her.

Yes, it was *that* crowded. But he was actually okay with it, and he enjoyed seeing how thrilled Caroline had been when they arrived.

His gaze finally found her as she surfaced from beneath the colorful balls in the huge pit. Brad had never seen the likes of it before. Kids swam through the sea of red, blue, yellow, and green plastic balls as though they were in a pool. When her head popped up in the middle, she let out a loud laugh as though she were having the time of her life.

Savannah came to stand at his side. "Finally found her, huh?"

He nodded.

"Thanks for bringing us here." She looked around the restaurant. "I know you probably had something else in mind when you asked where she wanted to go."

"I didn't even know this place existed," he admitted. "Does she come here often?"

"God, no. I can't handle the noise. We haven't been here since she went to a birthday party a few months ago, although she's begging to come again for her birthday."

"When she'll be this many." Brad held up five fingers, and was happy to hear her chuckle in response.

Caroline had crawled out of the ball pit and was sliding her feet back into her shoes. Flushed and grinning from ear to ear, she sprinted back over to them. "I want pizza now!"

Savannah held out one of the small pagers many

restaurants used to alert a customer. "Already ordered it. As soon as this lights up, it's ready."

"Where do we sit?" Brad had no idea where they'd find a place to have a meal. He couldn't see anything but video games, skeeball alleys, and far too many other things for kids to do he didn't even recognize. Places like this probably didn't exist when he'd been a kid. If they had, he'd never heard of them.

Grabbing his hand, Caroline started dragging him away. "Tables are back here."

He let her lead him, although he kept glancing back to be sure Savannah was following. It wasn't as if he hung around a lot of kids, but Caroline seemed not to know or care about his lack of experience. From the moment he'd picked them up, she'd been stayed close to his side. She'd even asked her mother if she could ride "shotgun," and he'd laughed.

Since when did four-year-olds know what shotgun was?

Savannah had insisted kids her age belonged in their booster seat and in the back, not the front.

Caroline sure didn't talk how he thought a little kid would. Hell, the girl could string words into sentences that went on just about forever. When did she even have a chance to take a breath? So far, she'd told him about her school, her teacher, her favorite books, what happened on the last episode of something called *Word Girl*, and the fact that her cat liked to lick her fingers after she ate because she always forgot to wash her hands.

"Which table, Mama?" she asked Savannah.

"Number twelve." Savannah pointed toward the left side of the room.

That's when Brad saw the numbers posted on each table. "What kind of pizza?"

"Popperoni!" Caroline replied over her shoulder as she skipped toward their table. "Mushrooms are too gross."

"Popperoni?" he said softly to Savannah. "Cute."

"Good stuff," she replied. "Because mushrooms *are* gross."

"Sit by me, Brad." Caroline patted the seat on the bench she'd taken.

He obliged her, finding it interesting that she wanted so badly to spend time with him. When he got Savannah alone, he was going to find out more about her daughter. The assumption was that Michael Hart was the father and that he'd run out on Caroline the same way he'd run out on her mother.

Had Caroline even met the man?

His guess was that Savannah protected her, which meant the child had never known a father. Was her grandfather the only man in her life? An older guy...That would explain her utter fascination with Brad right now.

After the waitress, who was dressed like an astronaut in a silver suit, dropped off their pizza, Brad spent most of his time listening as Caroline filled the time with happy chatter between her wolfing down bites of her food and big swallows of her drink. Only when she asked her mother if she could go back to the ball pit and skipped away did he finally feel as if he was no longer caught in a hurricane.

"Do all kids talk that much?" he asked.

Savannah frowned. "Sorry. She can be a chatterbox."

"Please don't take that wrong. I love listening to her. She's got so much to say. I just don't have much experience with kids." He let his eyes wander the big room. "Judging from the noise level in here, I'm guessing they like to talk a lot."

"Mine sure does," she said with a lopsided smile. "She has two speeds: all out or asleep. As much as she's run around here tonight, my guess is she'll conk out in the car on the way home."

So many questions crowded his mind, but he bit them back. Even coaxing Savannah into going on a date had been difficult, and she'd been so hesitant to accept that he wanted to see how well they worked together. If he started tossing her queries about her daughter and her ex, she'd balk.

Brad would bide his time and wait to see when her guard dropped.

* * *

Savannah found herself brushed aside when she tried to retrieve her slumbering daughter from the backseat of Brad's SUV.

He gently unbuckled her booster seat strap and lifted Caroline into his arms. "You want her put in her bed?"

"Please." Quickly hurrying up the porch steps, she got the door open and held it as he carried Caroline inside. Then she rushed ahead to pull back the comforter and remove Caroline's shoes so Brad could set her down.

"Should you put her in her pajamas or something?" he asked as he laid Caroline down.

"I'll do that if she gets up to go to the bathroom later," Savannah replied, a bit surprised that he so tenderly covered the little girl up before she could do so. "C'mon, let's go downstairs. I'll make us some coffee or something."

Brad followed her to the kitchen, and she was grateful she'd found the time to get the dirty dishes done before he'd arrived. She wasn't much of a housekeeper, but she didn't want him to think she was a slob. The town house was usually in a state of orderly disorder, the type she was sure most parents understood. When a person had a four-year-old to chase around, priorities had to be set, and dirty dishes weren't at the top of the list.

"Coffee?" She held up the empty pot. "It'll only take a few minutes."

"No, thanks."

"Tea? Soda?"

He shook his head.

From the perplexed look on his face, he had to have a million things he wanted to say—or perhaps ask.

So why was he holding back?

Savannah broached the topic she was most sure bothered him. "Michael is her dad."

"No, he's not," Brad announced.

"He is. He's—"

"He's her sperm donor, but he's sure not a dad, 'cause Caroline didn't mention him once tonight."

He had her there. "Point taken. He's never even met her."

"Have you seen him at all since he...um..."

While she appreciated his tact, it wasn't necessary. "Ran out on me and stole all my money?"

Brad nodded.

"Nope. But I let him know about her when I found out I was expecting, and I even tried calling when I went into labor."

"Why? The guy deserted you."

Savannah shrugged. "I guess I thought knowing about her might change things? That he might come back?"

"And return the money?"

"I don't know. I was pregnant and emotional. Once I saw Caroline, I realized the best thing for her was to keep Michael out of her life."

"Did you ever hear from him about Caroline...or the money?"

She shook her head. "And I'm glad for that. Caroline is happy. My dad is sorta like a father figure to her." Then she remembered exactly how clingy Caroline had been and worried that Brad had gotten the wrong impression. "I'm not looking to find her a stepdad or anything..."

He cocked his head. "Where'd that come from?"

"She was sorta glued to your side tonight. I was afraid you might think..."

"I thought she was having a good time with a new friend, Savannah. That's all I thought."

A sigh of relief slipped out.

"Seriously, don't overthink this," Brad suggested. "She's a great kid, and I like her."

"I think she's great, too. Thanks for tonight."

"Want to do something on your day off? Take her to the zoo or something? I've never even been there," he said.

"You mean tonight didn't scare you off?"

He was in front of her before she could blink. Arm around her waist, he tugged her against him. "Not one bit."

Then Brad was kissing her, and Savannah smiled against his mouth. All her fears vanished in the wake of his passion—passion that she met and matched as he deepened the kiss.

The most terrifying step was past. He'd accepted her role as a mother and had forged a tentative bond with Caroline.

Maybe this relationship stuff wouldn't be so damn tough this time around.

CHAPTER THIRTEEN

Another burger?" Brad asked Savannah's friend, Joslynn.

"God, no," she replied. "But thanks. I'm absolutely stuffed." She set her now empty plate on the stack that had piled up next to the sink.

He'd never used the outdoor kitchen much. Katie had thrown a few pool parties, but she'd always insisted they be catered, always wanting the best. Such a shame considering how great the grill was and that there was a refrigerator and a sink, all under an enormous thatched roof that protected guests from the midday sun.

A glance around showed Savannah sitting next to the pool with Caroline, smearing sunscreen on her daughter's arms before applying a liberal amount to her own. Since the summer day was warm and sunny, they'd both need some protection—especially as fair as their skin was. The last thing Savannah needed was to get a nasty sunburn when she was going on a date with him that evening.

She looked amazing in her red bikini, and he caught her taking a few long looks at him in his blue trunks. Those heated glances were almost enough to make him want to steal her away from the group.

Joslynn grabbed a soda from the fridge, popped the tab, and then leaned a hip against the counter. "It was nice of you to invite us out for lunch and a swim."

"No problem." He inclined his head at Caroline, who was pulling blown-up floaties up her arms. "I want to get to know Caroline better."

"And her best friend," Joslynn said with a wry smile.

"Yeah, you, too."

"Ethan's a lot different than I expected."

"Most people say that when they meet him."

A loud whoop drew Brad's gaze to the pool. Ethan was running toward the small diving board. He launched himself at it, sprang in the air, and cannonballed into the water. The splash was big enough to hit Savannah and Caroline. First they squealed; then they laughed.

Turning his attention back to Joslynn, Brad couldn't help but ask, "Have I passed whatever test you had for me?"

"You're blunt," she retorted, wiping some of the condensation off the side of her bottle.

"Let's just say I hate playing games. You're her best friend. Your opinion means a lot to her—and to me."

At least she didn't lose her smile. "So far, so good. This was a nice gesture. Shows you care about more than... Well, that you care."

"About more than getting in her pants. That's what you were going to say, right?"

"As I said, you're blunt. I appreciate that. So, yes. You care for her more than a fling."

He killed the gas on the grill and then flipped the last couple of hamburgers onto the serving platter. "I'm going to be eating leftovers for a month."

"You cooked enough to feed an army." Joslynn glanced around. "Didn't you invite your other partner? What's his name... Ross?"

"Russ—Russell Green. He's got the late shift tonight, so he's probably sound asleep right now. I'm sure you'll meet him sometime."

"I'm sure." She started to walk toward the pool but stopped after a few steps. "I like you, Brad. Try to keep it that way."

The woman was the epitome of honesty, and he couldn't help but admire the trait. Trust was something he was reticent to give, especially to someone new. But Joslynn seemed to have only one true motive—Savannah's happiness. The women's bond was evidently as tight as his was with Ethan and Russ.

Caroline came skipping toward him. "Wanna swim?"

After sliding the platter onto a shelf in the refrigerator, he smiled down at her. She was the spitting image of her mother, minus the blond hair. Caroline's was dark, but everything else was pure Savannah. The pert nose. The blue eyes. Even the high cheekbones. No doubt the little girl would be a heartbreaker when she grew up. "Sure thing, kiddo."

As though she'd known him forever, she took his hand and led him to the pool. He whipped his polo shirt over his head and tossed it on one of the deck chairs. Then he picked Caroline up in his arms and said, "Hold your breath." A moment later, he jumped in the pool.

* * *

Savannah laughed when Caroline surfaced, giggling and splashing. She'd let Brad know that Caroline was a strong swimmer and that her daughter loved to play in the water. He'd obviously taken that advice to heart.

Tonight was their first "official couple" date, as Brad had called it. But he'd insisted on the lunch cookout as a way to let Caroline know she was important to him. He'd also suggested that inviting their friends would be a nice gesture and would make the atmosphere more relaxed. Perhaps he was worried that Savannah would think he was trying too hard to win over Caroline, or perhaps he really wanted Joslynn to see he was genuine in his feelings.

Whatever the reason, things were going swimmingly.

She chuckled at herself. The puns were getting to be a bad habit.

Brad swam over to the edge of the pool, Caroline at his side. They rested their crossed arms on the tile and stared at her.

"You coming in?" Brad asked.

"Yeah, Mama! Come swim with us!" Caroline insisted.

Before she could reply, Joslynn took the seat next to

Savannah. The intent look on Jos's face meant there was something she wanted to say. So Savannah waved Brad and Caroline away. "In a little bit. You two go have fun."

Without a backward glance, Caroline swam off, joining Ethan in a game of Marco Polo.

Brad's eyes searched hers.

"Go. Swim. Have fun," Savannah insisted.

"Caroline made me promise we'd take her to the zoo next week," he said.

"I'm not surprised."

A splash from behind him made him whirl around to a giggling Caroline. "Come play, Brad!"

Ethan, eyes closed, yelled, "Marco!"

Brad growled and lunged after Caroline, making her let out a squeal and try to swim away.

"They're cute together," Joslynn said.

"I know, right?" Savannah tried not to read too much into the easy way Brad and Caroline seemed to accept each other.

"Aren't you worried about Caroline getting too attached?"

"Of course I am," Savannah replied. "But what am I supposed to do? I like the man. I can't keep my daughter at a distance. She's too important to me to ever act like my time with him is separate from my life with her."

"Things just seem to be moving awfully fast," Joslynn pointed out.

As if Savannah wasn't aware of that fact. She simply didn't know how to slow things down. Brad hadn't drawn close to her life, he'd plowed right into it—almost like he'd always been a part of it.

"I know, I know," she said. "I can't...Things are going well. Okay?"

"I can see that," Joslynn said. Caroline's happy shouts brought a smile to her face. "It's going very well. For both of you. But you know me...I just worry about you. You'd do the same for me."

"I would." Savannah let out a sigh. "I wish I knew how to keep my distance. He seems to know how to break through any wall I try to build."

"Do you love him?"

"It's too soon, Jos."

"I know that. But do you love him?"

Savannah didn't bother to reply to the absurd question.

Probably because she didn't know how to define the whirlwind of feelings she was having.

* * *

"This place is lovely," Savannah said as Brad helped her take a seat at the table. "I didn't realize you liked Vietnamese food."

"I enjoy all kinds of food," Brad replied as he sat opposite her. "Not many people know about this place."

A waitress came over to the table, and before she could say anything, Brad ordered something called *nem cuon* and a couple of sweet teas.

"You've been here before," she said.

He nodded. "Russ and I like to try new foods. Once we found this place, we had a new favorite restaurant. The spices are so different than anything you can get anywhere else. I hope you like things hot."

"And if I don't?" she asked.

"Then I chose the wrong restaurant," he said with a crooked smile.

"Don't worry. I do. The spicier the better."

Nem cuon turned out to be a version of vegetable egg rolls. Since Brad knew his way around the menu, Savannah let him order for her and was treated to a soup full of spaghetti that brought enough heat to her mouth to make her nibble on the flat bread he'd insisted upon.

"Don't worry," he said. "The entrée is less intense."

"That's a relief. That soup has turned me into a fire-breather," she quipped.

His eyes showed his concern. "I shouldn't have—"

"Stop it. I told you. I love heat," she insisted.

"You don't have to lie to me."

The sentence gave her pause, making her wonder why he'd think such a thing. "I'm not lying."

He shrugged, and she could almost feel him withdrawing.

Reaching across the small table, she put her hand on his. "I'm not lying, Brad. Why would I?"

All he did was shrug again.

The waitress broke the tension, setting the entrée on the table and refilling their drinks. Little was said as they ate, although Savannah had lost her appetite. Brad barely touched his food as well.

As they walked back to his SUV, she stopped him when he was opening the door for her. "You need to talk to me," she insisted. "Why are you so distant?"

His hands slid into the back pockets of his jeans. "Why'd you lie to me, Savannah?"

"I didn't lie. Why would you assume I did?" When he didn't reply, she pressed the point. "This isn't about me at all, is it?"

"What?"

"Was it your wife? Or some other woman?"

"What are you talking about?" he asked.

"Someone lied to you. Someone you cared about. So now you're assuming that's what I was doing—lying to spare your feelings."

Brad took a few moments to think things through. Then he gave her a curt nod.

"We agreed on honesty, right?" she asked. "I wouldn't tell you something I didn't mean. Look, I know about people being dishonest. Trust me, I do."

"I imagine you do."

"You've got to learn to trust me."

He nodded, and then silence settled over them. They simply stood in the dim parking lot lights and stared at each other.

Then he spoke. "It was Katie."

"Do you want to talk about it?"

"No." A few seconds passed. "Not . . . not yet. Sometime."

"I'd like to hear about it," Savannah insisted. "And I think it might do you good to talk about it."

* * *

She was right, but Brad wasn't ready to let Savannah know exactly how foolish he'd been.

He'd been every bit as stupid jumping to the conclusion she'd been lying when she said she enjoyed the soup. Such a petty thing to be angry about, and he realized exactly how sensitive he was to the prospect of her being less than truthful.

Which meant his feelings for her were growing—at a rapid pace. What other reason could account for his overreaction?

The woman was owed an explanation, but other ideas crowded his thoughts.

She looked so damned beautiful tonight that he couldn't fight the urge to kiss her a moment longer. Taking her hand, he pulled her into his arms. A smile blossomed on her lips before his mouth settled on hers.

Brad loved how she was the first to heighten the kiss, her tongue tickling his lips until he opened to her. She put her arms around his waist and then pressed her palms against his ass. Had they been somewhere more private, the kiss would have easily gotten out of hand quickly, which was why he'd chosen to take her out to eat instead of cook for her at his home. After the way the recording session ended, he knew he wouldn't be satisfied with only kissing her. He'd take her to his bed.

If he was going to convince Savannah that she truly meant something to him, that she wasn't only another notch on his bedpost, then he needed to take things slow. That didn't mean he was going to end their kiss.

Her tongue glided over his. He grasped it between his teeth and tugged gently, loving how she pressed herself harder against him in response.

Reluctantly, Brad eased back. At least she appeared as rattled as he felt.

"I should take you home now." There was no way she'd miss the hesitancy in his voice.

"You should. My parents are probably exhausted."

"It was nice of them to babysit."

"Yeah. They're great with Caroline." She tilted her head and smiled at him. "So are you. Thanks for the cookout today."

"You're welcome. I want her to know that since she matters to you, she matters to me, too."

Savannah rose on tiptoes to give him a quick kiss. "Take me home, Brad, before I demand we go to your place."

So her hunger was as deep as his... "One day soon, I'll give in to that demand," he promised.

"I sure as hell hope so."

CHAPTER FOURTEEN

I'm what?" Savannah shifted her cell phone to her other ear, hardly believing what Joslynn was telling her. "On where?"

"YouTube!" Joslynn said. The sounds of her fingertips clacking on a keyboard were easy to hear. "I'm sending you the link now."

"How did I end up on YouTube?" Opening the laptop that she seldom had time to use, Savannah waited as it booted up.

"Did'ya get it yet?" Joslynn asked.

"Hang on." Savannah had to bite back a comment about the lack of speed on the laptop. Joslynn had given it to her when she'd bought a new one for herself, and Savannah considered herself lucky to have such a generous friend.

"Did you know he was going to post the song?" Joslynn asked.

"Who's he?"

"I'm assuming it's Brad since the poster is a guy called The Hitman."

"He wouldn't." *Or would he?* He'd never told her what he intended to do with the recordings she'd made. He'd been too busy coaxing her to sing.

One thing was for sure. This strategy had his name written all over it.

"Did'ya get it yet?" Joslynn, normally patient, sounded agitated. "Check again."

When Savannah opened her e-mail, there were only three items in her in-box, and two of them were spam. "Yep, I got it." She opened Joslynn's message and then clicked the link. "Oh my..." YouTube appeared with the title of the video.

Who's Nashville's Newest Star?

"He doesn't use your name," Joslynn pointed out. "He's obviously trying to create buzz about who you are."

"Then how did you know about it if it doesn't have my name?" Savannah asked.

"I caught it on the news. I was sitting there, drinking my coffee, and the anchor started talking about the top five videos of the week. Before they showed yours—which, by the way was number one on their list—they talked about how it had gone viral. Everyone's trying to figure out who you are."

Savannah watched herself inside Brad's basement isolation room, singing to him as though the words were meant only for him. Simply watching how she slowly moved toward him, how she'd been drawn to him in such a dynamic way, made heat shimmer through her. The memory of her desire for him, of how she'd felt each time he'd kissed her, had haunted her sleep and intruded upon her thoughts thousands of times.

Why hadn't he bothered to tell her he had a camera aimed at her while she recorded his new song? Still dumbfounded by his temerity, she couldn't even focus on whether she'd done a good job covering the song. Then her jaw dropped as the video continued after the last note rang in the air, capturing their kiss. Thankfully, he ended the clip with her melting into his arms, so she didn't have to live with the embarrassment of knowing how intimate they'd become after.

"Look how many hits!" Judging from the chair's squeak and her excited tone, Joslynn had to be bouncing in her chair. "And the comments! So many great comments!"

All Savannah could do was blink. The video had been posted three days ago and already had close to five hundred thousand hits. Scrolling down the long list of comments, she fought back tears.

Best voice ever!

Who is this woman? She's amazing!

I have GOT to see her in concert!

Then there were Brad's fans.

Is this a new Hitman song?

Rock on, Hitman! U have a fucking awesome new song & u get the grl!

"Oh my..." Feeling the fool that she couldn't seem to

decide how to react, she just kept repeating herself.

Brad had been busy since the last time they'd been together.

She'd seen neither hide nor hair of him since their last date three days ago. Rehearsals had been run by Ethan, who was now spending more time at Words & Music. Brad was evidently still working as manager, judging from his hand-written comments on the work schedule and the rehearsal notes he'd given to Ethan. Unsure as to why he hadn't called or texted, she could only assume he finally realized he'd made a mistake in pursuing her.

Although Joslynn, true to her assertive nature, had encouraged her to reach out to Brad and find out why he'd been silent for so long, Savannah wasn't about to put her pride on the line to contact him, only to be rejected.

If he didn't want to be a part of their lives, maybe his silence was for the best. Caroline was already asking why he hadn't come for another visit. The last thing Savannah needed was her daughter getting too attached to him.

Damn it. All her worry about Caroline caring for Brad was nothing compared to how much he already meant to Savannah. Each day that passed without a call made her heart hurt.

"This is a good thing," Joslynn insisted.

"I suppose. I just...it's so much like something Michael would've done."

"I hadn't thought about that."

Savannah tried to keep a grip on her temper, which was quickly heating up. "Seriously, this reeks of Michael. Doing something that affects my career without even asking how I feel about it."

"Calm down, Savannah. Sure, Brad should've asked first, but it's not like anything bad could come of this."

"Probably not. But why wouldn't he at least tell me?"

"Maybe he likes surprises?" Joslynn asked.

Maybe he likes to run the show. After Savannah had told him she didn't need a manager, perhaps he'd taken it upon himself to try to jump-start her career.

Without asking permission.

Although she had to admit the idea bordered on brilliant, and realizing she hadn't truly come up with a plan of her own, she couldn't seem to get past the irritation over him acting on her behalf without so much as a peep explaining his plans.

But a look at the number of views on YouTube showed his strategy was working remarkably well.

"You okay?" Joslynn asked. "I hate to leave you, but I've got to get to the hospital."

"I'm fine," Savannah replied, even though she really wasn't.

"Are you sure? You sound—"

"I'm fine, Jos. Go to work. Thanks for telling me about it. I'm going to head to the restaurant and talk to Brad."

"When you talk to him, Savannah, remember one thing."

"What's that?"

"Everyone who watches the video absolutely loves you."

* * *

Brad leaned back in his desk chair, letting a smile bloom.

Things were working out better than he had a right to expect. Although he wasn't particularly concerned with social media, he'd taken Russ's advice and bombarded the Internet with the video of Savannah singing "That Smile."

Russ had softened his anger over Brad being personally involved with Savannah. The change in attitude came right after he'd showed Russ the video. The connection between them was so obvious that there seemed to be invisible wires pulling them together. Russ evidently figured out that Savannah wasn't being coerced, which meant the friction between him and his friend could end.

Brad's first inclination had been to stop the video right after the last note of the song, but Russ had insisted the kiss—at least the beginning of it—would make more people talk about her. And "talk" was what he'd aimed for.

The Hitman was back, and his new songbird clearly belonged to him. How funny that he didn't even mind the nickname any longer. If it helped her, so be it.

Once the video was ready, he'd followed Russ's advice and bombarded different sites, posting it for everyone to see. There was no trying to hide that this was a Hitman song, which ramped up speculation. Especially since one big thing was missing.

Her name.

She was going to be so pleased. What singer didn't want to be the newest rising star? Katie had based her whole existence on it, but had none of the talent. Savannah was the genuine article.

After watching the flurry of activity that had exceeded his expectations and Russ's predictions, Brad was ready for the next step. Today, he'd solve the mystery of her identity and let everyone know exactly who she was and where she'd be performing tomorrow night—and from then on until she was popular enough for larger venues. Probably far too soon for his taste.

An insistent knock on the office door drew him back from his smug satisfaction of a job well done. "Come in!"

Savannah walked into the office. "Stormed" was probably more descriptive, especially since she slammed the door shut behind her. Her cheeks were flushed, and her slender fingers were clenched into fists that rested against her hips.

"Why?" she demanded.

"Why what?" Her anger took him by surprise because he had no clue as to what had set her off.

"Why would you post that video?"

He blinked a few times when her mood suddenly registered. "You're *mad* about it?"

"Hell, yes, I'm mad."

Confused, Brad dragged his fingers through his hair. "About..."

"You know what about," she replied. "You didn't even tell me that you'd filmed the song. You told me you weren't even recording it!"

"I film everything in my studio. It's set up for video and audio. You never know when there'll be magic in a performance." Considering how hard she was glaring at him, his explanation hadn't helped. His own temper began to rise in response. "I posted that video to build an audience. For you. I did it for *you*."

"Without asking! You didn't even tell me you'd recorded that take!"

"I *wrote* the song."

"I *sang* it."

He narrowed his eyes. "It's working, isn't it? Have you seen how many hits it has on YouTube? How many shares on Facebook? On a ton of other sites?"

"Yeah, I did. But..."

"When I release your name today—"

"Today?" At least she no longer sounded pissed.

Brad nodded. "Just in time to get Words and Music packed to the rafters for your first performance tomorrow night."

The fight drained out of her in the blink of an eye. "Look, I know you posted that video to help me. I just..." She let out a weary sigh, reminding him of a balloon deflating. "Michael used to do stuff and not tell me."

Like a flash of lightning, Brad understood. And he felt like an asshole. Sure, his intentions had been good. He'd been trying to get her career up and running. But he'd taken total control. Not once had it occurred to him to talk to her. He'd figured she was busy enough simply getting herself and the music ready for opening night. He'd stayed away from rehearsals because Ethan had told Brad he would be too much of a distraction. Since he couldn't be there to help, he'd busied himself with building an audience for her. After all, wasn't being a star what every singer wanted?

"I'm sorry," he said.

Her head shot up. "You are?"

Brad stood and came round the desk. He placed his hands on her shoulders. "I should've talked to you first."

"It's just...I have a hard time trusting people," she whispered.

He smiled at her. "I've got the same problem, as you're well aware."

"I told you that I don't want someone ruining my career."

"How about we do it together?" he asked.

"Ruin my career?" At least she was teasing now. Her eyes were full of laughter.

He grinned. "*Build* your career. I can still act as a sort of manager, but from now on, I'll run all my ideas by you."

She eyed him skeptically. "For how much? Fifteen percent? Twenty?"

Although he was a bit insulted, he understood why she was asking. "How about zero?"

Her eyes flew wide. "Zero?"

"I don't want money, Savannah. Especially from you. I only want to help you the way you helped me."

"How did I help you?" Savannah looked genuinely surprised.

"I hadn't written a note in just about forever. All I had to do was listen to you and..." He shrugged even though he felt anything but casual. This was an important time for them in a relationship that was an embryo. He would have to earn her trust, and to do that, he had to assure her she wasn't a meal ticket. Sure, he might be paying penance for another man's sins, but God only knew Brad had been quite a sinner himself.

Perhaps a little penance would make him a better man.

"Besides," he added, "you're singing my song. I'll be making plenty of money once you're a star. Which reminds me...I'd really like to get the second song on tape. We can release it soon, while the buzz is still strong."

* * *

Savannah wanted to believe him. Wanted to believe *in* him. History had taught her how foolish it was to blindly trust.

On the other hand, Brad was right. His concern for her career was also concern for his own. Those songs represented his comeback, although he hadn't truly been absent from the music scene for too long. Why not hitch her wagon to his star? At least they were both heading in the same—correct—direction.

But there was one thing she really needed to know, and she had to ask him about it before she lost her nerve. "You haven't been at rehearsal. And you didn't call. Why?"

He looked surprised by the question. "Ethan didn't tell you?"

"Ethan?"

Brad nodded. "He told me I...distracted you. Said I should let him run rehearsals and to give you some space until the first show. I can't believe he didn't explain that to you."

"Not a word," Savannah said, pleased to know he hadn't been avoiding her.

"You could come over tonight," he said, his voice growing husky. "We could do a few takes and *you* pick the one you think is best." Still holding her shoulders, he caressed her arms, sending chills racing across her skin. Then he drew her closer and wrapped his arms around her. Staring down into her eyes, he smiled—a lopsided and entirely too seductive grin. "I could make us dinner afterward."

As if she didn't understand exactly what he was inviting her to do, especially after their frankness on their last date. No, if they were alone in his home again, she'd end up sleeping with him. She'd probably be the one to suggest it.

Am I ready?

They were just starting to learn about each other, and yet she felt as though she'd known him forever. Her whole life she'd wished for the kind of passion she felt whenever they kissed. Michael had never shown her any. Sex with him had been clinical and cold. What Brad made her feel was warm and intoxicating, and even though they'd spent only a short time together, in some ways she felt closer to him than any other man she'd known.

"Will you come tonight, Savannah? To my house? I've got a surprise planned for you."

"Another surprise? I'm not sure I can handle that."

"It's a good surprise."

Since she figured he was planning seduction, she nodded. "I'll come."

Then Brad's lips were on hers, and all she could do

was melt into him. Her hands smoothed over the broad planes of his chest and she twined her arms around his neck. Whatever it was inside her that he touched, she both welcomed and feared it. Whenever he kissed her, all she wanted was to get closer and closer. To let him reach parts of her she'd never shown to any other man.

As his tongue slipped between her lips, she had her answer. For now, she would go wherever this man led. It would be easier to live with regrets over having been too daring and for having reached too high than to always wonder what might have been.

CHAPTER FIFTEEN

"Welcome back," Brad said as he held open the door to his home.

Savannah took a backward glance at the vehicles in the driveway, including a souped-up muddy pickup. Since she'd assumed they'd be alone, she had no idea what was going on. "Um...thanks. But"—she nodded at the vehicles—"are those yours?"

He let out a chuckle. "Hardly. That's Ethan's truck. He's waiting for us inside."

Her heart sank. All the fantasies she'd nurtured that afternoon about making love with Brad were going to have to be postponed. "What about the cars?"

"That's the surprise." Another chuckle. "Actually *two* surprises." With a gentle hand against the small of her back, he guided her through the door.

The last thing in the world she wanted to do was scold him, but she'd never been so disappointed. "You gave me your word that you'd run everything by me first."

He held up his hands in surrender. "I told you there was a surprise." Shutting the door behind them, he nodded toward the kitchen. "Everyone's waiting for us."

Ethan smiled when they entered the kitchen. Dressed in an apron that looked like a curvy woman's body wearing pasties and pink panties, he was flipping steaks on the indoor grill. "You're just in time. These rib eyes are a perfect medium rare, and all the sides are ready."

Two women sat on the same bar stools Savannah and Brad had used only days ago. One was a blonde who had an incredible smile. The other was a brunette who had to be a good foot taller than Savannah. Even sitting down, her lofty stature was plain. Both had more curves than Savannah's thin body would ever boast. They were putting serving spoons into several types of covered dishes.

Motioning to the blonde first, Brad said, "Savannah Wolf, meet Leah Brooks." Next, he gestured to the brunette. "And this is Maggie Sims."

"Hi." Savannah gave them a goofy half-wave. Then she fixed her attention on Brad. "Should I know them?"

"They're your new backup singers," he announced as though he'd done something wonderful for her. What he'd done was make plans for her career without asking. Again.

"Backup singers. So now you think I need backup singers?"

Ethan was the one to answer as he slid the steaks on plates that had been set out on the counter. " 'Need' isn't the right word. Brad and I talked it through, and we think they'd be a great complement to your voice. His songs always sound great with harmonies."

"We listened to your older stuff, too," Brad added. "Your voice is phenomenal, but a couple of backups would really add some power to your performances."

Ethan untied the apron and tossed it aside. "With your wit, you could bounce things off the girls when you're chatting. Trust me, the crowd will eat it up."

Leah and Maggie must have picked up on Savannah's anger because both of their smiles had faded. Feeling like an ogre, she tried to put them at ease even though she was still skeptical. "I'm sure it'll be fine."

"And no worries to commit to anything permanent," Brad said, pulling out a stool for her. "We'll do a couple of takes and just see how it goes first. You get to make the call."

One by one, Ethan was putting plates in front of everyone. The food smelled so good that her stomach let out a loud rumble in anticipation. Her own fault for having skipped lunch. She'd been fretting—and fantasizing— about being alone with Brad too much to eat. All that worry had been a waste.

With a theatrical flourish, Ethan swept his hand over the food. "Let's get our feedbags on!"

* * *

Settling himself at the console's chair, Brad kept a close eye on the people in the recording booth. Savannah was trying to get comfortable with her new backup singers. She'd moved her seat back to be closer to theirs, and the three of them chatted amiably as their headphones rested around their necks.

He'd hired the singers before he'd made her the promise that he wouldn't act on her behalf without discussing it with her, and for a moment, he'd wished he had called them off for tonight. But his experience had told him that they would add so much depth to the recording of his new song and to Savannah's sound. He was also going to have them do a new cover of "That Smile," then he could get it into release tomorrow so people could start downloading it right after her debut at Words & Music.

He wasn't at all used to running ideas by anyone, especially singers who were recording his songs. He was the Hitman. He knew exactly what worked and, more important, what didn't. With very few exceptions, Brad just did what needed to be done. End of story.

But a man could change, and Savannah Wolf—his beautiful muse with her blue tresses and delicate bird tattoo—was a woman worth changing for. Signaling Ethan to put on his headphones, Brad spoke into his mic. "Tell the girls to get ready. We're just gonna do an easy rehearsal of 'All She Is.'"

"You mean 'All *He* Is.'" Ethan winked.

"Smart-ass." Since Ethan already had the ladies putting on their headphones, Brad went on with business. "Like I said, an easy rehearsal is all we're doing."

A lie, and judging from Ethan's scoff, he knew it. There

was never a song done in Brad's studio that wasn't recorded. The first time singers performed a piece was sometimes the best because they were trying so damned hard to get it right. Although he'd be spending most of the wee hours of the night going through all of tonight's recordings to make adjustments and finally choosing which one to release the following morning, he had a sneaking suspicion he was about to witness something amazing.

Once the girls were ready, Brad smiled at them through the window. His eyes fixed on Savannah. She'd changed the moment she'd put on the headphones. Her gaze was now determined as she stared at the music stand and nudged the mic a little closer. He knew that look well. He'd seen it on Indie Night when she'd blown his life out of the water.

"Nice and easy, everyone," he said. "Let's have some fun with it."

Their nods were his cue to start playback. The opening notes of the song filled the air.

* * *

Savannah forgot the backup singers. She forgot Ethan, too. The moment she began to sing Brad's song, her world was reduced to him.

Holding his eyes, she let his music flow through her, from her soul to his. The connection was there, exactly as it had been the last time she'd been in this studio, but this time there wasn't an ounce of nervousness. Only confidence and a feeling of rightness. This performance had nothing to do with her wanting to please an audience or gain new fans. She sang now to open her heart to the man who was rapidly capturing it.

When I see you, everything's right.
Let your future start with me tonight.

There was no way she'd ever find the words to tell him how much he was coming to mean to her, how much he'd already become such an important part of her life. And in such an embarrassingly short time, especially considering how he could make her angrier than anyone ever had.

You're the one I thought I'd never find.
What do I have to do to make you mine?

But she could reveal that affection—even a bit of her vexation—as she sang. The old adage about a thin line between love and hate crossed her mind, then she pushed it aside so she wouldn't stumble over the lyrics.

Vaguely aware of how much Maggie and Leah's accompaniment made her voice ring clear and strong, she answered each of Ethan's words with Brad's snappy lyrics.

When the song ended, she held her breath, waiting for Brad's verdict. Her heart told her there was no way she could ever sing it better, but he was a perfectionist. No matter how emotionally draining it would be, she'd probably have to sing it twenty more times, especially since this version was nothing but a rehearsal. She'd do as he asked, knowing appeasing his exacting standards would be good for her, and he'd be sure the song they released would be the very best take.

A grin bloomed slowly on his face, and her hopes rose. Then the grin became a full-blown smile. His voice buzzed in her ear. "You were *amazing*."

Ethan let out a chuckle. "Damn shame it was only a rehearsal."

"That's okay," Savannah said, returning Brad's smile. "Now we know we're ready."

"Oh, sweetheart," Brad said. "You should know me better than that."

When Maggie and Leah started laughing, Savannah chuckled, too. "I forgot. You record everything,"

"And I think he just recorded a hit song," Ethan said.

* * *

The crowd was loud and rowdy, which made Savannah very happy. These people would engage, and that made her job a hell of a lot easier. Thank God they weren't a dead audience. Zombies were the worst because they turned entertaining into conquering. And some crowds couldn't be conquered.

A hand settled on her shoulder. She turned, smiling because Brad had come to give her some last-minute advice.

Only it wasn't Brad. "Hey, Ethan."

Towering over her from his exaggerated height, he gazed down at her. "Nervous?"

"Yes...and no." She peeked out at the crowd again. "I think we hit the jackpot with these folks. They're ready."

He grinned. "Yep. And judging from how fast the wait-staff is moving between the tables and the bar, they're likely to get nice and juiced."

"I hope they don't get too drunk and turn hostile."

"No way," Ethan said, his tone sincere. "That crowd came for one reason tonight, honey—to hear you. I'd wager every single person has watched at least one of your videos."

Brad had been true to his word, releasing the two new performances to social media early this morning. The new cover of "That Smile" had a staggering number of hits. "All He Is" was only slightly less watched.

Maggie and Leah slipped up beside her, both bubbly with anticipation. Leah couldn't seem to stand still, popping back and forth between her feet while Maggie compulsively stroked her long ponytail. Dressed alike in black sequined tops and faded skinny jeans, they made a nice complement to Savannah's white sequined blouse and tight denim miniskirt.

Ethan appeared to eschew any costume, choosing instead a flannel shirt with the sleeves rolled up to the elbows and snug, well-worn jeans with ripped knees. His long hair was tied back neatly, and he would probably be the recipient of a large number of leers from the females in the audience. There was already a high-top table of women close to the stage having a bachelorette party, complete with tiaras and white sashes labeling bride and bridesmaids.

They were talking loudly and pointing to where he stood in the wings.

If Ethan decided he didn't want to go home alone tonight, he'd have plenty of company to choose from.

No wonder male singers and musicians ended up being such horndogs. What man could resist that sort of temptation all the time?

Which explained Ethan's reputation.

And Brad's.

Songwriters who were as visible as the Hitman enjoyed a large number of groupies as well. The video on which she and Brad kissed had more than its share of lewd comments from women who claimed they wanted to be in her place.

Two women claimed they *had* been.

Savannah took in a deep breath and let her jealousy go. In a few minutes, she'd be onstage. She didn't have time to worry about what Brad had or hadn't done. There were people waiting to watch her, and she intended to give them the best show of her life.

Where's Brad?

Stop it. Focus on the music.

Then she saw a grinning Joslynn sitting at a table to the left of the stage with Savannah's parents. Savannah's neighbor, Brianna, had graciously offered to babysit Caroline. Since Caroline often played with Bri's daughters, she'd begged to spend the night. Bri had told her that was a great idea, which would allow Savannah to stay out as late as she wanted.

Just seeing the smiles shining from her parents' faces was enough to give Savannah the boost she needed. They had always been her biggest fans, and tonight she'd sing her ass off for them.

The band played the intro, an up-tempo piece that was meant to get the crowd going. And going they were. By the end of the three-minute piece, the crowd was clapping and stomping.

Closing her eyes, Savannah cleared her head. On her next inhale, the delicious smells of the food being passed around the patrons wafted toward her. The sounds floating her way, from the people in the restaurant to the soft sounds of Ethan, Leah, and Maggie warming up, filled her. Her heart sped, pounding in her chest, and heat raced through her limbs and sent a flush across her face. Yet in the melee of sensations, she found the calm that always came before a performance and made her ready.

She hummed her favorite song to keep her vocal chords warm. She'd used the ditty for her first public performance—at the Jacob County Fair Talent Show—when she'd been all of thirteen.

God, had she ever been that young?

When she'd won the blue ribbon, she'd convinced herself that her warm-up routine had brought her good luck.

"'Blue Moon of Kentucky'?"

Whirling fast enough she had to catch her guitar before it swung wide, she laughed at the man who'd correctly named the song she'd been humming. Then she smiled. "I wondered if you were coming."

Brad moved close, cradled her face in his hands, and gave her a kiss so gentle she sighed when it ended. "I wouldn't miss it for anything."

"'Bout time," Ethan said, clapping Brad on the shoulder just as soon as he'd turned her loose. He fixed his gaze on Savannah. "Ready to go, little lady?"

She returned his smile, feeling ready to conquer the world. "Darn tootin'!"

Taking her hand in his, Ethan tugged her along with him as he approached the stage. "Then it's show time!"

CHAPTER SIXTEEN

Although Savannah was only supposed to be the opening act for Southern Pride, Brad quickly realized that this crowd was hers. Sure, the band had been climbing the charts with "America, I Love Her," and Words & Music would normally be filled with their rabid fans.

But not tonight.

The crowd belonged to Savannah Wolf. From the moment Randy introduced her, they were chanting her name.

As she and Ethan took center stage, her face was radiant. She brushed her loose hair over her shoulder before settling on one of the bar stools and getting her guitar ready. While her backups got into position, she turned those hypnotic eyes to the crowd and gave them one of her beguiling smiles, and the chanting morphed into applause.

"Glad to see y'all come out tonight," she said with that endearing touch of a Southern drawl to her voice. "I'm so pleased to see you! We've got a great show, including one of my favorite trios, Southern Pride." A glance to her right. "I'm also tickled to death to sing my first two songs as duets with the son of Nashville Royalty, Ethan Walker." She waited a few beats to let the women quit whistling and calling out a few bawdy things to Ethan. "So to start out your night, how about Ethan and I introduce you to the latest song by the Hitman?" Without waiting for the applause to die down, she launched into "That Smile" with Ethan following her lead.

Pride washed over Brad, but not at the success of his music. That ship had sailed. Sure, he loved writing songs and hearing them recorded. And the money was nice, although he was good and set for a long time. His pride tonight was for Savannah. The woman wove magic not only with her voice but with each grin and glance. She engaged the crowd as if each individual were the most important person in the world, handling them in a way that couldn't truly be taught. Her talent and her ease in performing were God-given gifts.

He tried to stay in the background, not wanting to distract her or Ethan. Savannah's gaze found him anyway, her grin broadening, lighting her eyes with a spark that seemed to race through him like electricity. Had there been a fire erupting at his feet, he'd have been unable to look away.

Her star was rising. Rapidly. Because he wanted to be with her meant that Brad would find himself back in the world he'd left behind. There'd be parties to attend. There'd also be stress for her to crank out new releases, and he'd be damned if he'd let her sing anyone else's songs. So he'd have to put his nose back on the grindstone and start writing as a business rather than through strikes of inspiration.

Yes, Savannah's career was taking off, and she would now be an integral part of the world of country music. Although he'd sworn he would never go back into the music business, he realized he wanted to be by Savannah's side when she became a star.

Damn it all if that didn't give him an idea for a new song.

While he wanted to watch Savannah sing, words began flying through his mind like shooting stars. If he didn't catch them quickly, they might be lost, so he hurried to the bar, snatched up a napkin, plucked a pen from a waitress as she passed by, and started scribbling down the lyrics.

* * *

Savannah came close to stumbling over the lyrics when Brad hurried away from the stage. It took all her concentration to keep going, and damn, if that didn't make her angry. She shouldn't be so affected by the man, especially by something as simple as a smile changing to a scowl. When he focused on writing something on a bunch of napkins, she needed every ounce of her concentration not to stop singing right then and there to ask what his problem was.

Never in her life had she allowed someone to distract her

when she was singing for a crowd, and she'd be damned if she'd let whatever Brad was doing cause her to botch the most important performance of her life!

A glance to Ethan told her that the change in her hadn't gone unnoticed. With a wink to him, she pushed aside all thoughts except making beautiful music.

God, she loved to sing.

The music whirled around her, filling her mind and her heart. The lyrics drove her on, and she and Ethan finished "That Smile" on a lingering note that seemed to go on forever.

Applause erupted, fueling the fire growing inside her. If Brad couldn't be bothered with paying attention to her performing his songs, she'd sing for this crowd. For Ethan, Leah, Maggie, and the fantastic musicians performing with them tonight.

And for herself.

Her whole life, Savannah had been a singer. She'd been able to carry a tune from the time she was three. Her parents loved to show videos of her taken when she was little and crooning whatever song caught her fancy. As she'd aged, her voice had matured to a rich alto that a judge at a talent competition had compared to Karen Carpenter in her prime. Since Savannah had spent most of her childhood listening to her parents' records on an ancient turntable, she'd been well aware of who Karen Carpenter was and exactly how beautiful her voice had been. That comparison had been the push she'd needed as a young woman to keep looking for opportunities to sing.

Amateur nights. Open mics. County fairs. And then Michael had found her and promised to make her a star.

Problem was that she didn't want to be a *star*. No, she had no desire to find herself in Taylor Swift's snazzy little shoes. Savannah wanted only to earn a living singing, enough to give her and Caroline a comfortable life.

Savannah refocused herself for her second duet with Ethan. They launched into "All He Is"—with Ethan modifying to "she" on his verse—and all she thought about from that point on was the music and the faces of the people she loved and the people she didn't even know who'd come to hear her sing. Ethan's smile told her she was back in her groove, so she dismissed whatever bee Brad had up his butt and allowed herself to simply enjoy making beautiful music.

* * *

"So this is where you went to hide after we sang."

Brad glanced up to find Ethan leaning a shoulder against the door frame. "I wasn't *hiding*. I was *writing*. I stayed for all six songs." He hated how defensive he sounded. "You two sounded great. You heading home?"

"Yep." A contented smile crossed Ethan's face. "She was holding those people in the palm of her hand from the first note. She didn't even need me."

"Probably not," Brad replied. "But I appreciate you being willing to put yourself out there for her."

"She's with her parents and Joslynn right now."

"I figured." Brad would have to keep an eye out for when she was done talking to her family. She didn't know it, but he had a reception planned for her and her guests in one of the private rooms at Chez Jacques just down the street. Then he hoped to whisk her away for an even more private reception. His house. Her place. He didn't care. All he wanted was to be alone with Savannah, and her enthusiastic response to his kisses and caresses showed she wanted him—maybe even as badly as he wanted her.

"So what's the new song about?" Ethan rubbed his chin and hummed as if in thought. "Oh wait... what else? Your new muse."

"Smart-ass. I can't help it. The woman inspires me."

"Exactly what do you intend to do about that?"

"Do?"

Ethan pushed away from the door frame and folded his arms over his chest. "She's not like your other women, Brad. And she's not like Katie."

"What's that supposed to mean?"

"You know exactly what I mean. Katie pursued you. You didn't have to lift a finger."

Ethan got that right. Katie had practically stalked Brad, wanting to be a part of the country music scene desperately when she had no true talent. She'd thrived on the parties and the soirees. The concerts. The appearances. She'd enjoyed them a lot more than Brad ever had.

All those had done for him was make his life miserable. He'd have been content writing songs and staying home. And not the home Katie chose. What he wanted was a cabin in the mountains, someplace private and a bit rustic where he could hike and be alone.

At least that was what he used to want. Now, he thought being alone would hurt. He wanted Savannah with him.

"Savannah deserves better," Ethan added.

"Are you insulting me?"

"Easy, pal. What I meant was that she deserves to be treated well. You know, courted."

"You think I don't get that?" Brad snapped. "Stop hounding me, okay? I've only got her best interests at heart."

Ethan cocked an eyebrow. "And what do you think are her best interests?"

"She's going to be a star, buddy. You know that. I know that. Everyone in the crowd out there knows that."

"So because people love to hear her sing, you think her becoming a celebrity is in her best interests?"

"She'll be rich, and she'll be able to make a great life for her kid."

"It's just...I think you've got Savannah all wrong. I don't think she really wants to be the latest country singer popping up on every talk show and touring arenas from here to Timbuktu."

"How would you know that?" Brad asked.

"Just picked it up from a few things I've heard her say in rehearsals." Ethan's brows gathered. "Have you ever had a conversation with the woman? Or are you too busy trying to give her what you think she needs?" He scoffed. "Or trying to get into her pants."

Fed up, Brad pushed aside the song he'd been working

on and directed a hard glare at his friend. "It's not like that with her, and you damn well know it."

The last thing he needed was another person playing Savannah's champion, but in walked Russ anyway. "Sounds like I'm missing all the fun. Any punches thrown yet?"

"Not yet," Ethan replied.

"But getting close," Brad added. "Look, let me lay it on the line for both of you so hopefully you'll get off my case."

"Since I walked into this conversation late," Russ said, "how about you tell me why Ethan's on your case?"

"Savannah," Ethan replied. He inclined his head at Brad. "He's ready to turn her life upside down to make her the next great country music star. By the end of the week, he'll have a thirty-week cross-country tour with at least two stops every week."

"No wonder you're mad at him," Russ replied. Then he frowned at Brad. "Have you sat down and asked Savannah what she wants for her career?"

Everything he'd done since she'd made that first damned song pop into his head had been for her. To give her what she deserved. Her talent shouldn't be destined to linger in bars and clubs, even one as classy and popular as Words & Music.

"Look," Russ said, sitting on the couch and spreading his arms over the back. "Would you take a piece of advice from a friend?"

"Two friends?" Ethan added.

Brad swallowed his pride and nodded.

"Talk to the woman," Russ said. "Just sit down and talk to her. Find out what she wants."

"Find out," Ethan said, "if you're trying to turn her into something she may not want to be."

Much as he hated to admit it, they were right. Things had happened so quickly. Too quickly.

Everything went fast now. Friendships. Relationships. Careers. Thanks to the Internet, one minute a person was a nobody...the next, she was Savannah Wolf.

"Fine," Brad said. "I'll talk to her." He tossed a frown to his friends. "Will that get you two off my back?"

Neither appeared fazed by his pique, and Ethan replied, "For now."

CHAPTER SEVENTEEN

So you forgive me?" Brad asked. "I just couldn't turn the words off. I had to write them down. But I listened. Honest I did. You blew everyone away. Including me."

Savannah nodded, no longer angry that he had seemed so distracted while she'd been onstage. "I finally figured it was something like that. It was just a...surprise that you were so busy writing on napkins. Then my parents acted like they were in such a hurry. I can't believe they didn't stay to talk to me for more than a few minutes after the set. Joslynn left, too. It's like they all ran out the door."

"I'm sure they had a *damn* good reason for not sticking around," he said with humor she didn't understand in his voice. He led her through the restaurant and stopped at the door to a private dining room. "How about I give you a *real* surprise?" He flung open the doors.

"Surprise!"

Tears pooled in her eyes when the people waiting in the big room greeted her with their shouts. He'd told her he was starving and wanted to get away from the crowd. The restaurant was a close walk. Her stomach was making enough whale calls to reveal her hunger to anyone nearby, so when he'd suggested Chez Jacques, she'd taken his hand and walked with him to the trendy new eatery.

She hadn't expected to be led to a private room, nor had she anticipated a party to celebrate her opening night.

A large banner was draped above the table. Written on the white surface in forest green letters was "Congratulations, Savannah!" Scrumptious-smelling foods waited for the guests.

There were a lot of people, but not a crowd. Just enough to make her feel as though she'd accomplished something important. Her parents were beaming at her, and to see their pride in her on their faces was almost her undoing.

Hurrying forward, her mother embraced her. "Oh, darlin'. Like I told you before, you were wonderful!" She took a look around. "Isn't this nice of Brad?"

Savannah nodded as she was quickly turned to her father.

"Couldn't be prouder of you," he said before he kissed her cheek.

After greeting a few more people, including Joslynn, Russ, and Ethan, Savannah turned to Brad. "You arranged all this?"

"Yes, ma'am." He draped an arm over her shoulders and leaned closer to whisper in her ear, "Hope it makes you happy."

"It does, Brad. It really does."

Then he brushed his lips over hers, right in front of everyone, which made her smile even more.

Motioning to a lady Savannah didn't recognize, Brad said, "There's someone who asked to meet you."

The woman, looking a bit out of place in a navy blue pencil skirt and starched gray blouse, strode over on her high heels and offered her hand to Brad. "Thanks for the invite."

"My pleasure," he replied before turning to Savannah. "Savannah, I'd like you to meet Marie Allen." A glance at Marie. "Marie, this is the woman you've been asking me about—Savannah Wolf."

Marie held out her hand, and Savannah shook it, a little surprised at the intensity of Marie's grip.

"I'm happy to finally meet you," Marie said. "As Brad could attest, I've been anxious to talk to you."

Unsure why Marie was at the party since she wasn't family or friend, Savannah couldn't help but ask, "Brad's been talking to you about me?"

"Actually, *I've* been talking to *him*," she said, her voice enthusiastic as she grinned at him as though they shared some inside joke. "Talked and talked and talked."

Feeling a bit off center, Savannah frowned.

"She demanded to meet you, Savannah," Brad said, at least sounding a bit apologetic, "Since she wouldn't take no for an answer, I figured this might be a good place for you two to connect."

Marie had a rather practiced smile. "I'm here representing Allied Sound. We'd like to discuss the possibility of a recording contract with you. Brad assured me you hadn't signed with anyone yet, so I asked him to arrange a meeting as soon as possible."

Savannah couldn't decide whether to be thrilled by a company like Allied being interested in her or to be pissed that business was going to interrupt this evening. Only Caroline's birth could eclipse the way Savannah felt after her most successful opening night, and she didn't want to come down from that high.

"I complained until he gave me an invitation to meet you since I was going to be at your performance." Marie shifted a worried gaze to Brad. "Is now a bad time?"

"It's fine," Savannah assured her. "Thank you for coming."

* * *

Brad almost let out a sigh of relief. He'd been afraid Savannah would be angry that he'd invited Marie Allen to the reception.

Marie had contacted him, which was an unusual thing. Allied had no reason to search out clients, and that spoke volumes about Savannah's talent. He and Marie were peripheral friends through some of Allied's artists who'd recorded his songs, but he hadn't heard from anyone in the company in a long time. They'd been good to him, and the organization was kinder to singers than any other recording company in Nashville. If Marie Allen wanted to meet

Savannah Wolf to talk shop, then by God, he'd make sure she got exactly what she wished for.

Hopefully Savannah would understand that he'd been acting in her best interests by not telling her that Marie was in the audience. News like that would've surely thrown her off her game, and tonight was too important for her to be flustered at the possibility of recording with Allied.

No longer lost in thought, Brad tried to play catch-up with the conversation.

"You really need to consider hiring a good manager," Marie suggested. "Once we start talking brass tacks, you might want someone who's been down that road to look out for your best interests."

An odd suggestion from a recording executive, which only went to show that Allied was an honest company that actually cared about its talent.

Savannah was shaking her head before Brad could add his two cents. "A manager is out of the question."

His girlfriend had a stubborn streak.

My girlfriend.

That sounded...right. So he jumped in the debate. "I tried to tell her that, too, but..." He shrugged. "For now, I'll be there to help look over anything you offer."

Marie's smooth smile told him he was correct. Allied wanted to offer Savannah a recording contract. "So you think I'm going to make this incredibly talented woman an offer?"

"Of course. I know you, Marie. You'd have never reached

out to me if you hadn't already made up your mind you wanted her."

Switching her attention back and forth as Brad and Marie bantered, Savannah looked a little shocked. "You want me to record for Allied?"

With a nod, Marie said, "Why else would I be out this late? I've got three kids." She thrust out her hand again, this time holding a business card she seemed to pluck from midair. "Give me a call next week. We'll have a meeting." She smiled at Brad. "Drag yourself along so we can chat about your new songs, too." Turning on her sharp heel, she strode away.

Savannah rubbed her fingertips against her forehead. "I feel like I just got caught in a storm."

Brad barked out a laugh. "That describes Marie perfectly." After Savannah slid the business card in her skirt pocket, he took her hand.

"You should've told me she was coming."

"That would've spoiled the surprise of the party," he teased, hoping to defuse any anger she had over him not telling her he'd talked to Marie.

Her frown was stern enough to show he'd taken the wrong tack. "Don't try to charm me, Brad. You promised me you'd tell me if you were planning anything to do with my singing."

"You're right." He kissed the back of her hand. "I should've told you. Anyone else would've been a bundle of nerves at knowing Marie was watching them. You're obviously stronger than other singers. Am I forgiven?"

"You are...if you promise to keep your promise from now on. Seriously."

"I really am sorry, Savannah."

"You're forgiven." She lost herself in thought for a moment, a frown forming on her mouth. "I still can't believe Allied wants to talk contracts with me."

"May I make a suggestion?" Brad asked, hoping that she'd be a little less reticent to protect her interests now.

She slid a skeptical gaze his direction. "Go ahead."

"Why don't you talk it over with someone who knows contracts?"

"A manager?"

"No commitment. Just pick his brain so you go into the Allied meeting properly armed."

Her frown eased. "You already have someone in mind, don't you?"

Brad let out a chuckle. "I do. Greg Jorgensen. He's a talent manager. Things are getting serious now, sweetheart. You need someone to watch out for you."

Savannah let out a snort.

"I know what you've been through," he said. "But you can't let that jerk ruin this chance for you. Would you consider meeting with Greg?"

"Fine. But I'm not promising anything."

Brad brushed another quick kiss over her mouth. "That's all I could ask." Then he leaned in closer and whispered, "How about we go talk to your guests and get back to celebrating? Then we can get out of here and be alone."

Her features softened as a sly grin bowed her lips.

"Alone? What makes you think I want to be alone with you?"

Moving in even closer, he brushed his lips against the hollow under her ear. He loved how she shivered in response. "I sure want to be alone with you."

She tilted her head just enough so he could press a kiss to her slender neck. "I guess there's only one question I'd want to ask."

"And what is that?" He blew in her ear and then eased back to find an incredible and hopefully seductive smile on her face.

"My place or yours?"

* * *

The ride to Brad's house seemed to take forever. The satellite radio was tuned to a seventies channel, which made her happy. The last thing she wanted to listen to at that moment was country music. No, her restlessness and need required something more sensual, and the tunes of Led Zeppelin and Peter Frampton suited her just fine.

She had no idea what he liked, and her experience with men was rather limited. Orgasms had been few and far between, but she loved the closeness and the intensity of sex, even if she was often left wanting more.

Now she wanted Brad with a passion that was new and rather frightening. Never one to run from a challenge, she embraced that fear and let it feed her desire. His experience was vast, and while that might have been a turnoff, it wasn't. She counted on that past to make him the man to show her everything she'd been missing.

If only she could show him how badly she wanted him.

She gathered her courage. Popping her seat belt, Savannah shifted to face Brad and reached over to run her hand from his knee to his thigh, dragging her nails along the fabric. His sharp intake of breath made her bolder, so she let her fingers walk over to the obvious bulge in his jeans. The way his breathing sped made her tug on her bottom lip with her teeth to keep from laughing in relief.

She might not be a skilled lover, but she was getting to him.

"You keep that up," he said with a growl in his voice, "I'm gonna drive us right off the road."

Savannah rubbed the length of his erection. "It seems as if you're a bit...*anxious* to get home."

"I'm so far past anxious, I doubt we'll make it to the bedroom."

"Fine with me."

Driving with his left hand, he slipped his right from her shoulder to her breast, giving it a light squeeze that made her tingle.

Her bravado fled, and she wasn't sure what approach to take next.

Did he want dirty talk? That was a skill she couldn't fake.

Did he need her to be more aggressive? She was already pushing herself.

Oh Lord. What if he was into really kinky stuff?

Joslynn had mentioned BDSM, and Savannah had needed to Google it to know exactly what it was. When Bri loaned her a copy of *Fifty Shades of Grey* a few years back, Savannah had closed the book at the first sex scene.

Kink was evidently not her *thing*.

On the other hand, she wasn't sure exactly what her thing truly was. At that moment, she felt inadequate and downright virginal.

He pulled into the garage, killed the engine on the Escalade, and lowered the door behind them.

Savannah rose to her knees and cupped his face in her hands, turning him to look at her. "You know we really need to talk."

"Talk? You expect us to talk? *Now?*"

She nodded, knowing he was every bit as wound up as she was. Any conversation between them at that moment would be nothing but gibberish. "We'll talk about a lot of things. About Allied Sounds and Marie Allen." Then she pressed her lips to his. A quick but very sweet kiss. "But we'll talk *after*."

"*After* sounds great." But Brad didn't seem in a hurry to get out of the car. Instead, he dragged her from her seat across the console and onto his lap. A little awkward at first, he shimmied her around until she straddled his hips on the big leather seat.

His kiss was full of hunger that fueled her own. He made her body frantic for more of his touch. Welcoming his tongue when he thrust it into her mouth, she moaned deep in her throat. The heat he created inside her, from her breasts to her core, was incredible, and she was ready to be rid of any barrier between her skin and his touch.

Savannah broke away from the kiss, breathing hard. "Inside now?"

Before answering, Brad captured her lips for another fierce, tongue-dueling kiss. "Inside. Now."

He shoved the door open and then somehow carried her out of the car without either of them banging head or limb. Using his butt to push the door shut, he leaned back against the SUV and let her slide down his body until she was on tiptoes, still kissing him.

If one of them didn't find some strength to pull away, they'd never make it out of the garage. And she was pretty sure there weren't any condoms on one of the pegboards full of tools.

Dropping to her flat feet, she easily broke the kiss. His height wasn't normally intimidating, but she felt so petite at that moment. Too petite. And with her lack of curves, a bit inadequate.

She frowned, wondering if he'd be disappointed when they were finally skin to skin.

He gripped her chin and tilted her head up. "Hey. What's wrong?"

"Nothing important. Just a little...insecurity," she admitted.

"Insecurity? Over what?" When she shrugged, he set his hands on her shoulders, traced them down her arms, and took her hands. "Savannah, you had me make you a big promise, remember?"

"Of course."

"Then I want a promise from you, too."

She arched an eyebrow. "You haven't *exactly* kept that promise."

"I'll do better. And I want you to try to always be honest with me."

"I *am* always honest with you!" she insisted.

He shook his head. "Not right now you're not. Tell me what's making you insecure."

The tenderness shining in his eyes stripped her of her defenses. "You've been with all sorts of women..."

"My reputation is making you insecure?"

"I'm sure most of them were really...pretty." She hurried to add, "And curvy and..." She shrugged again, uncomfortable with being so vulnerable.

Brad smiled, but not a grin of condescension. One full of what appeared to be understanding. Taking her hand, he pushed away from the Escalade and dragged her through the door and into the house. Once the door was closed behind them, he swept her into his arms and headed toward the stairs without saying a word.

And yet she didn't feel as if he'd ignored her worries. The forceful way he was bringing her to his bed actually made her feel desirable. Wanted.

Setting her on her feet, he pulled her into his embrace and stared down into her face. "You, Savannah, are beautiful."

Part of her wanted to argue back that she had no boobs and was too skinny. But the heat in his gaze as he leaned down to kiss her made the disparaging words fly right out of her thoughts.

Savannah welcomed his kiss, looping her arms around his neck and opening her mouth to his probing tongue. By the time he eased back, her legs were trembling. "Oh..."

"Come to bed with me," he coaxed. "Let me show you exactly how beautiful you are to me."

CHAPTER EIGHTEEN

Brad had a hard time walking up the steps as Savannah tugged at his clothes. Since he was doing the same to hers, their progress toward the bedroom came in fits and starts as they left behind them a trail of crumpled clothing.

By the time they hit the master bedroom, he was down to his briefs, and she stood before him in her white bra and lacy panties.

Her body was sleek, her legs incredibly long considering her petite height. The moon shone down on her through the skylight, painting her pale skin an ethereal blue.

She was exquisite.

And he had to have her.

Sweeping her into his arms, Brad carried her to his bed. After setting her on her feet, he jerked back the comforter and plucked the remote from the nightstand. He clicked on his sound system, and a playlist of classic hits filled the air. Then he reached for Savannah again. With a shake of her head, she took a small step back and reached behind her to pop open her bra. As she gave him a shy smile, she shrugged it forward and then dropped it on the rug.

Having never preferred busty women, he found her high, firm breasts exquisite. Her nipples had hardened, and he couldn't stop himself from wrapping his arms around her waist and lifting her until he could take one of those tips into his mouth.

The sound Savannah let out as he suckled her was one of pure pleasure. She raked her fingers through his hair, tugging enough to sting. As he shifted to the other breast, he said, "Easy there, love. I'd like to keep some of that hair on my head." Her responding chuckle turned into a hiss when he pulled the nipple between his teeth.

He turned to set her on the bed, then knelt in front of her and began to drag down her panties. The hesitation that crossed her gaze made him stop. "What's wrong?"

"I...um..."

"Honesty."

"I'm not very good at...this." She stumbled over her words. "I mean, I can make sure you enjoy it. I just sometimes have trouble with my...you know. With me."

"You?"

"Me...enjoying it."

"Ah..." So Savannah's ex had been not only a heartless bastard about her money, but a selfish prick in bed. Brad intended to show her that was definitely not the case now. Her pleasure would always take precedence over his own. "Trust me?"

"Of course."

Her quick answer pleased him so much that he knew she wasn't walking away from this room until she realized there wasn't a single thing wrong with her. "Then relax and lie back."

Although she knit her brows as though she had no idea why he'd given her that command, she slowly obeyed.

He eased her panties down her legs, letting them fall to the floor. Damn, but she was even more beautiful with her clothes off than with them on. Hands on her knees, he eased her legs apart as he kissed each slender thigh.

"Brad?"

"Shh." Then he moved closer to press his lips against each hipbone. "Let me," he coaxed when she tried to squeeze her legs shut. "You'll like it." With no warning, he ran his tongue between her slick folds.

Whatever Savannah had been about to say came out as a squeak that quickly turned into a moan.

She tasted so sweet, and Brad indulged himself in something he'd only done with Katie. It was something he never felt quite right doing with someone he barely knew. In a lot of ways, oral sex made a person more vulnerable than intercourse, so he'd made a rule that it was off limits—to both give and receive.

At that moment, he was glad he'd made that rule. Now he could give Savannah something he'd offered to only one other woman.

* * *

Savannah let the throbbing beat of "Lovin', Touchin', Squeezin'" seize her. Brad seemed to be in rhythm with the music as he pushed away all her control.

She'd never felt more alive.

Tunneling her fingers through his hair, she let a throaty moan loose as heat from her core raced through her limbs. She raised her knees, not at all ashamed of how she'd opened herself up to him. His tongue, his teeth, made her wild with want.

And then the pleasure crashed over her, making her twist and squirm until the storm passed. As she tried to catch her breath, she waited for Brad to rise above her and sink himself into her body. Instead, he went right back to business, sending her rising again to the precipice before she came a second time.

Then he let out a growl full of masculine need. With a speed that was astonishing, he snatched a condom from his nightstand and donned it. He grabbed her under the arms to move her up the mattress, spread her legs, and settled between her thighs. Entering her in a thrust that startled her rather than hurt her, Savannah let out a little yelp.

Brad held himself up on his elbows and looked down at her with concern in his gaze. "Did I hurt you?"

She wrapped her legs around his slim hips. "Not at all." To get him moving, she cupped his neck and pulled him down into a heated kiss.

Accustomed to Michael pounding into her in a quick frenzy before he came, Savannah had to adjust all her thinking where sex was concerned. Brad was in no hurry. In slow strokes, he'd pushed inside her before easing back until he was almost free. Then his lips would find hers again as he thrust forward. Again and again until she thought she'd go mad. The heat was unbearable and she suddenly wanted it faster. Harder.

With a little nip on his shoulder, she tried to let him know what she desired. Or did he need the words?

Hovering above her, he smiled. "Tell me what you like, Savannah. I want to please you."

Since she could find no other words, she simply said what her body demanded. "Then let's go!"

A small chuckle escaped before he gave her exactly what she needed, moving within her at a pace that stole her breath and made her reach yet again for the joy he seemed to easily give her. When she climaxed, she called his name in a voice full of wonder and a bit of awe.

Brad gripped her hips almost too tightly, sinking into her until his body shuddered. Burying his face against her neck, he whispered her name in a way that was so sensual, it sent shivers over her skin.

Only after he'd rolled away and made a quick trip to the bathroom did Savannah begin to come back to her senses. Never had she felt so relaxed. So lethargic. And so damned fulfilled.

"Scooch," he said, waving her toward the far side of the bed. Then he settled beside her, pulled her into his arms, and covered them both with the sheet.

She pillowed her head against his shoulder and let out a contented sigh, waiting for him to begin some kind of conversation so that things didn't get awkward. But the only sound in the room was the voice of Stephen Perry, and Brad had turned the thrumming volume down until the music was merely background white noise.

Pushing up on her elbow, she let any annoyance ebb away when she caught the satisfied smile on his face. His eyes were closed, and had he not been grinning, she might have thought he'd fallen asleep.

Not wanting to shatter the peaceful interlude, she laid her head against his shoulder again. Why bother fighting the first time she'd felt relaxed in just about forever?

Her last thought before sleep claimed her was that she could easily get used to ending each night in his arms.

* * *

Brad awoke at three in the morning, the same way he did almost every night—a weird type of insomnia that had plagued him as long as he could remember. Before he'd cleaned his life up, he'd kept a bottle of bourbon on his nightstand. A good, strong drink or two while he surfed the Net on his phone and he'd always been able to get back to sleep.

Not anymore. Now he still played around on his phone, but it took him a good hour to relax enough even think about sleeping again.

Tonight felt...different. His body, while humming in satisfaction, was already responding to the feel of Savannah curled up against his side. It had been a long time since he'd spent the night with a woman. Not since—

Nope. He was done comparing Savannah to his dead wife. Katie was his past, and it wasn't fair to Savannah to constantly equate them. In all honesty, they weren't equal. Not at all.

The time had come to let Katie go. For good. Her death had been tragic. A young woman gone far too soon. But she represented his past, a past he wanted to leave behind.

Savannah represented his future.

Brad hugged her a little closer, wondering if he could wake her up and make love to her again. To have her still there was comfortable. Right.

Damn. He was in over his head, but he didn't care. Savannah was like no other woman he'd known. The sweetness in her smile was bone-deep, and he suddenly worried he was making a huge mistake getting tangled up in her life.

This wasn't a woman a man walked away from. She wasn't a woman to take as a lover for a while and then part to go their separate ways. This was a woman a man grabbed on to and then held tight.

"Brad?"

Smiling, he pulled her closer and leaned in to give her a gentle kiss. But then a gentle kiss wasn't enough. He wanted more.

He wanted it all.

There was a welcome in her lips, her tongue heightening the exchange before his could. Before things got too hot and heavy, he grabbed a condom and donned it.

As he tried to take control of their lovemaking again, Brad was surprised to find Savannah shaking her head as she gripped his upper arms and urged him to his back. Thrilled that she was taking the reins, he obeyed, sprawling on his back. She rose on her knees and then worked her way over to straddle his hips before leaning in to kiss him again.

* * *

The way Brad had made love to Savannah had freed something inside her. She wasn't truly cold like Michael had always said. Her body was clearly very capable of enjoying sex, and now she wanted to indulge in her newfound sensual side, the part of her that Brad had touched so expertly.

Since rolling on a condom wasn't a skill she'd learned, she was happy he'd taken care of the task. If she worked up more bravado, maybe she'd ask him to let her practice. That could be fun. As it was, she felt brave enough simply wrapping her fingers around his erection. Michael had never liked to be touched too much, always saying that he was too sensitive or that she didn't know what she was doing. In reality, the man had no self-control and would come in ten seconds flat. If she'd stroked him intimately, he'd have been done in five.

No wonder sex had been such a disappointment. There was nothing wrong with her. Instead, her ex had been a selfish jerk, caring about his own pleasure rather than what they could share.

Brad didn't have that problem. The man was a revelation. She'd never known someone as unselfish, who cared as much—if not more—about her pleasure as he did his own. She wanted to show him exactly how much she not only wanted him but also appreciated him.

His cock was hard as granite, and the heat was incredible, even with the thin sheath between her fingers and his skin. She loved his shape, tracing the crown with her fingertips and wondering if she'd eventually be able to go down on him. It was something she really wanted to try, and Brad was probably the right man to help her learn.

But right now, she wanted to return the pleasure he'd given her rather than dwell on her naïveté. She'd had only two dates since Michael left, and neither of them got anywhere near her bedroom.

Savannah rose over him, moving her hips until Brad slid home, making her feel delightfully full. Complete. He grasped her waist and pushed his hips up until he was buried deeper inside her. Closing her eyes, she let out a ragged moan.

Warm hands covered her breasts. "God, you're beautiful," he said, his tone husky.

Staring down at him, she smiled as she lifted herself up and down, trying to find a rhythm that would satisfy her. When she leaned forward to kiss him again, Brad took over, holding tight to her as he thrust inside her in a way that rubbed against her sensitive nub with almost the same intensity as he'd used with his tongue. It wasn't long before the pleasurable pressure built inside her, and before she could marvel at how easily he could make her respond, her climax raced over her.

* * *

The moment Savannah threw her head back and called out his name with a bit of surprise and wonder, Brad gave up his own self-control. He drove into her again and again until he came, an overwhelming experience that left him panting for breath and full of his own surprise.

What was it about this woman that had turned sex into something that felt so new? So damned satisfying? Never had he known this type of contentment.

She collapsed against his chest, and he wrapped his arms around her shoulders. A laugh bubbled from her. "That was...amazing."

Brad combed her hair with his fingers. "I sure as hell thought so. Glad you did, too."

Since he was softening and about to slip free from her body, he eased her to his side and took care of cleanup. The chore bought him a little time to think.

Amazing?

Oh yeah.

In fact, it was a lot more than that. He just didn't know how to explain exactly how important this night had been to him.

He went back to the bed, still unable to find the right words.

Savannah sat with the sheet pulled up to her collarbone. Her expression was wary.

Brad slid between the sheets, getting in a short tug-of-war with her as she tried to keep herself covered.

"We never talked," she said, her voice soft as though she was trying not to wake someone up.

He flopped back against his pillow and stacked his hands behind his head. "No, we didn't."

"I can't believe that Allied sent someone to the reception tonight."

"Should we be discussing this at four in the morning?" he asked.

"I'm wide awake now," she insisted even as she lay down beside him, stretching out on her side to face him and covering them both with the sheet. "Are you sure you don't have any more surprises for me?"

"Not a single one. I promised, remember?"

"Did your wife like it when you made all the plans? Seems like a habit with you."

Savannah had just opened the door to discussing Katie. He warred with himself over whether to share his past with her. He hated rehashing things, especially a mistake like his life with Katie. But the way he felt after making love to Savannah told him that what they shared was so much more than what he'd shared with any other woman.

Savannah deserved to know everything.

"My marriage wasn't...good," he said.

* * *

Hearing nothing forlorn in Brad's voice, Savannah hoped that he would open up to her now. "How did she die?"

"Katie had lupus. Her kidneys slowly stopped working until she ran out of options and time."

Quiet settled over them until she lifted his hand and kissed his fingers. "I'm sorry. That must've been rough."

All he did was give her a squeeze.

"You loved her."

"At the time."

"'At the time'? What's that supposed to mean, Brad?" she asked.

He breathed a loud sigh. "Do you want to know the truth?"

Why did that question frighten her so much?

Didn't matter. Not only did she want to know about his first wife, she suddenly realized that she *needed* to know. "Yes. I do. If you want to tell me..."

"I loved Katie," Brad said. "I loved her so damn much, and I thought she loved me."

"She didn't?"

"No, she didn't. After she was gone, I was packing away her things. I couldn't bear the idea of throwing them out, so I was going to put them in boxes and store them for God knows what reason. But I found some fabric-covered books buried deep in her bureau. Turns out she kept diaries for quite a few years—even before she met me."

Savannah didn't like the way this story was unfolding, and her heart ached from the pain in Brad's voice. "You don't have to—"

He gave her another quick squeeze. "I do. And you deserve to know."

"The diaries. They were…bad?"

"Really bad. She wrote about who she liked, who she hated, what she thought she deserved, which was pretty much everything. She actually had her sights set on Ethan. When she didn't get anywhere with him, she targeted me."

"Targeted?"

"She wanted to be famous, even if it was through other people. I was a door for her to get into the world of country music."

"But she married you," Savannah said. "That's an awfully big step just to meet a few people in the business."

"She wanted a lot more than that," he explained. "She thought she could be a famous singer. I guess she figured I'd write her some hit songs and introduce her to the right people. Like it's that simple."

"So did you?" She'd never heard of a Katie Maxwell, but she might've used a stage name.

His chuckle was hollow. "The woman couldn't carry a tune in a bucket. I could've written the best song in the world for her and it wouldn't have mattered."

"What did her diaries say about that?"

"She thought I was wrong, that she was full of talent, but I was too dense to appreciate her. Besides, she didn't love me and didn't really give a shit what I thought. That was pretty damn clear from what she wrote. In fact, she said several times she wished Ethan was with her instead of me."

Having heard more than enough, Savannah hugged Brad tightly. "I'm so sorry." What else was she supposed to say after hearing about such abject cruelty? She found it a bit amazing that he didn't bear some ill will toward Ethan just because of Katie's obsession.

"Over and done with," Brad insisted.

As though it could be that simple...

Savannah rolled to face him and wrapped her arms around his waist. "Thank you."

"For?"

"For telling me. It helps me understand you better."

He pressed a kiss to her forehead. "You told me about your ex. The least I could do was tell you about Katie."

Feeling as if they'd cleared some important hurdle, she fell asleep with a smile on her face and wrapped safely in his arms.

CHAPTER NINETEEN

Savannah walked through Brad's office door as he held it open. She had an hour until her performance, and she'd rather have been warming up her vocal chords than talking to a manager she didn't want or need.

Or did she need him after all?

Much as she still felt burned by Michael, she had to admit Brad was right. The circumstances of her career were changing rapidly—probably too quickly for her to handle alone, especially when she was a single mom who already felt guilty for not spending enough time with her daughter.

Perhaps a man with Greg Jorgensen's stellar reputation— something Joslynn had discovered while researching to help Savannah out—could benefit her. At the very least, she'd try and keep an open mind.

"Savannah Wolf, meet Greg Jorgensen," Brad said, nodding at the impeccably dressed older man sitting at his desk. "Greg, this is the singer I've been raving about."

Greg stood and held out his hand. "As you should have. I caught your opening night, Savannah. You were amazing."

Face flushing hot, Savannah smiled. "Thank you." Then she turned to Brad. "Why didn't you have him come to the party if he was already at the show?"

"If Marie hadn't insisted on being there," Brad replied, "I wouldn't have even let her come. Last night was for family and friends."

"Marie Allen was there?" Greg asked. "Interesting..." He stroked his salt-and-pepper Van Dyke beard.

"I'd say so, considering *she* called *me*," Brad added.

Savannah listened to the two discussing Marie Allen's penchant for always getting what she wanted while she tried to take in other tidbits about the woman. Greg seemed to know quite a bit about her, which was a point in his favor. Not that Savannah was ready to sign a contract. Far from it.

She was, however, a bit off balance after meeting Greg. She'd expected someone younger. Someone more like Michael. Judging from his gray hair and the laugh lines around his dark eyes, she'd have a hard time believing he wasn't well past sixty. His age put her more at ease than if Brad had planned for her to meet some hungry up-and-coming twenty- or thirty-something. A manager needed to have experience. Greg seemed to fit that bill.

"So, Savannah," Greg said, gesturing to one of the two seats on the opposite side of the desk, "tell me how you came to be at Words and Music."

She and Brad sat down before she launched into the story of her being a waitress who was lucky enough to appear on Indie Night. The tale was fun to tell, but she worried he'd think she was painting herself as some sort of overnight sensation. Her past was littered with failures, including her one real relationship. Brad wasn't helping her stay humble by tossing in exaggerated compliments about her voice and stage presence.

"I have to admit," she said, wrapping up the story, "that I was really, really fortunate."

Brad took her hand. "No. You were really, really *good*."

Leaning back, Greg tented his index fingers and tapped them against his lips. "Interesting..."

His comment threw her off balance. "What's interesting?"

The glance he gave Brad was enigmatic. "Just nice to know the Hitman is back in business."

Although he hadn't truly answered her question, Savannah let it go. Besides, she was more comfortable talking about Brad's career than her own. "His new songs are wonderful."

"I heard them," Greg replied. "You sang them beautifully, which is why I'm here. I saw you on YouTube, and I knew I had to hear you sing live. So I stopped by to watch your opening. I liked what I saw."

"I knew you would," Brad said. "So are you willing to take her on as a client?"

"Whoa there..." Greg's eyes found Savannah's. "You might have gotten us together for this meeting, but I think now's the time for Savannah and I to talk business. Alone."

Brad leveled a frown at Greg. "You're kicking me out of my own office?"

"It would appear I am," Greg replied with a cocky grin. "If you'll please excuse us for a bit..."

Although he appeared annoyed, Brad left the office, closing the door behind him.

Savannah took hold of the situation by raising her hand palm-out when Greg began to speak. "I'm not sure exactly what Brad told you, but I'm not sure I'm looking for a manager."

"Ah, yes. I have to say that after he explained about your last representation, I can't blame you for that attitude." Greg pulled a legal pad from a leather portfolio and laid it on the desk. Then he opened an expensive-looking fountain pen and settled it and his folded hands on the pad. "Quite frankly, I'm different than that failure. In fact, I'm the polar opposite. If I didn't think I could be an effective manager who has impeccable ethics in his fiduciary responsibilities to his clients, I wouldn't waste your valuable time."

Having nothing to lose from hearing him out, she nodded. "All right then. Why don't you tell me what you think you can do for me?"

"I believe, my dear, that as far as a music career, I can give you whatever your heart desires."

* * *

Brad couldn't stop pacing as if he were an old-fashioned father-to-be, anticipating his first child's birth. In a way, Savannah's career *was* his baby. If only she'd put aside her stubbornness and appreciate the opportunity sitting across the desk from her.

To sign with Greg Jorgenson would be a coup any rising star would envy, but after what her ex had put her through, she might not want to hear about all the things Greg could do for her career. She sought to be the next Carrie Underwood? He could and *would* do that for her because Savannah had the talent and Greg had the skill as a manager.

Ethan's voice echoed through Brad's thoughts.

"Find out if she wants you to turn her into something she doesn't want to be."

Brad had promised to do exactly that.

A check of his watch irritated him. They'd been talking for almost thirty minutes. She needed to get ready to perform. The door mercifully opened, so he hurried back down the hall to find a rather grim Savannah. Greg was still sitting at the desk, jotting something down on a legal pad.

"So?" Brad gripped her shoulders to get her to look at him.

"So..." was all she said.

"Did you two work something out?"

When she nodded, he sighed in relief. "Fantastic," he said before brushing a quick kiss over her lips. "You should go get warmed up."

"Thank you for introducing me to Greg. See you after my set." She headed toward the stage.

Brad frowned, unable to understand why she wasn't excited. Hell, she'd just signed with a man who'd made more stars than any other manager/agent in Nashville.

Greg was packing his pad into his briefcase when Brad returned to his office. The man's face was almost as grim as Savannah's had been. "What's wrong?" Brad asked.

After latching the case, Greg set it on the desk. "Wrong? Nothing is *wrong*. I do have a question to ask you, however."

"Fire away."

"Have you ever sat down and had a conversation with that sweet woman about what she wants for her future?"

He sounded exactly like Ethan and Russ. Perhaps it was time to listen to all of them, but getting a hint of what they saw that he obviously didn't would help. "What do you mean?"

Greg stepped around the desk to stand directly in front of Brad. "I distinctly remember you telling me that Savannah not only had the talent to succeed but that she was—using your word here—hungry."

"She is."

"Not for what you think. She doesn't want to be a celebrity, Brad."

"Of course she does."

With a shake of his head, Greg walked to the door. "You two are involved, aren't you?"

"Why does that matter?"

"It doesn't matter to me in the least. But I believe it should make you pay a little closer attention to what I'm about to tell you."

"You sound like my father," Brad grumbled.

Greg put his hand on Brad's shoulder. "What she wishes to do is earn enough to make a comfortable living for her family. She'd like to buy a nice home for herself and her daughter and to buy a bigger house for her parents."

"What are you talking about? She'll be famous enough to do both of those things...and then some."

"Her dreams for herself aren't the same as your dreams for her. If you're dating, then you should be considering what she wants more than what you think she deserves." Holding out his hand for Brad to shake, which he did, Greg gave a parting shot. "Savannah and I came to a tentative agreement for me to represent her."

Every word Brad had heard, but understood none of it. "If she didn't want a career, why would you take her on?"

With a chuckle, Greg shook his head. "You're not listening to me, my friend. I never said she didn't want a *career*, and I have every intention of giving her exactly that. On *her* terms." A quick check of his watch. "If you'll excuse me, I promised my wife I'd be home early tonight." Another chuckle escaped. "If one can call home by seven 'early.'" On that, he left.

Brad sprawled on his desk chair before leaning back and dragging his fingers through his hair. Hard as it was to admit, his friends had been right. He'd been so focused on giving Savannah what he wanted for her—what every other singer he'd known had wanted—instead of finding out what she wanted for herself. No wonder she'd been so upset over all he'd done for her.

Or was it done *to* her?

Unfortunately, he was accustomed to Katie's overwhelming desire to be a star, which made it difficult to recognize that he didn't know what was best for Savannah. The decisions should have been up to her.

The sound of Randy introducing her reached the office. It was time to watch her perform—something he knew he'd never tire of doing. Brad left the office and headed toward the restaurant.

When the show was over, he'd make sure that the two of them had a nice, long talk.

This time, he'd listen.

CHAPTER TWENTY

Savannah left the stage feeling as though she were walking on clouds. The audience had been supportive and enthusiastic, and she'd sung her heart out to please them. Adrenaline still raced through her after she took her last bow and left the stage.

No, not just adrenaline. There was something else, something deeper than a mere performance "high." What she felt was more passionate. Primitive.

Downright sexual.

Every song had been about Brad. For Brad. And since the singing was done, she needed him, and she needed him right *now*.

As her eyes adjusted to the dimmer backstage lighting, she found him waiting for her. Leaning one shoulder against the wall, arms crossed over his broad chest, he grinned. "You had them eating outta the palm of your hand tonight."

Without a word, Savannah set her guitar down and went to him. She wrapped her arms around his waist and rose on tiptoes to kiss his lips. He didn't miss a beat as he enfolded her in his embrace, kissing her back with the same sort of desperation that was ripping through her.

There might have been people staring—Randy, Leah, Maggie—she didn't give a damn. Whether it was the thrill of performing or the knowledge of how Brad could make her burn that drove her on, she kissed her way across his cheek to whisper in his ear, "I want you."

His arrogant smile didn't dampen her ardor. Instead, his confidence made heat pool between her thighs. "Where?"

"My place." She needed to head home to thank her parents for helping with Caroline, who would be sound asleep. If he followed her home at a discreet distance, then her parents would be long gone before he got there. "Give me a twenty-minute head start."

"Hell with that." He kissed her again before she could explain, his tongue driving her wild.

She was about to ask why he wouldn't let her leave first when he took her hand and led her away from the stage. Using the back hallway, he headed to his office. He shut and locked the door behind them.

Could she do this? Make love to Brad right there in the place she worked—that he owned? What if someone started knocking? What if—

He tugged at her shirt, whipping it over her head before she could ask him any of her questions. Only one word spilled out. "Condom?"

"Got one." He left her long enough to pluck one from his desk drawer. After tossing it at the couch, he gathered her into his arms. Any will to resist him fled, and she snatched at his shirt, needing to be skin to skin.

The rest of their clothes were thrown about the office. She thought she saw her bra fly into the trash can, which made a giggle bubble up. Brad kicked his pants and briefs aside, rolled on the condom, and then smothered her laughter with another kiss. He tumbled her onto the couch, where they lay side by side.

"Are you ready?" he asked as his hand smoothed down her stomach, moving lower. When he reached the junction of her thighs, his fingers moved between her folds, finding the sensitive nub. "Close, but not quite. Let me help."

She let out a little moan as the heat inside her grew with each stroke. "That feels so good." Her words seemed to drive him on, and the speed of his caresses increased. One finger, then two, slipped inside her, and she raised her hips with each thrust.

"Now you're ready," he pronounced. He settled himself between her thighs and entered her slowly, maddeningly, until she palmed his tight ass and pulled him inside her.

The longer he moved within her, the closer Savannah came to the release she craved. She wrapped her legs around his hips as the tension rose. Higher and higher until the climax raced through her, making her close her eyes and surrender to the wonderful sensations only Brad could inspire.

As she basked in the afterglow, he finished, holding

tight to her hips as he let out a loud moan. Then he rested his face against her neck, his breath choppy and hot.

Sanity returned, making her face flush warm. "I can't believe we just did...*that* in here."

He let out a little chuckle as he moved to look into her eyes. "We can do...*that* anywhere you'd like. Even on the stage after hours if that would turn you on." A wiggle of his eyebrows. "It would turn me on." After a kiss on the check, he withdrew, hurrying to reach for the tissue on his desk.

Savannah rounded up their clothes. She dumped his on the desk and tried to don her own as quickly as possible. "I'm afraid I'm not quite that daring."

Once they were dressed, he grabbed her around the waist, turned her to face him, and then kissed her until she sagged against him. "Then I'll have to make it my mission to make you that daring."

Feeling awkward, she tried to ease away from him. The moment they stepped out of the office, everyone would be staring, no doubt knowing exactly how they'd spent their time.

He grabbed her shoulders. "Hey...what's wrong?"

"People will know what we were doing in here."

"People won't care."

She rolled her eyes at his nonchalance.

"Trust me on this. They really won't give a shit. And even if they do know, all they'll think is how lucky I am."

"Lucky?"

"To have you. Want to come back to my place?"

Although she would love waking up in his arms, she had to shake her head. "I need to go home."

"Then I'll follow you there. Up to you if I spend the night."

Caroline would have a million questions if he did, but at her house, she and Brad could finally have a much-needed talk about her career.

* * *

"Thanks again, Mom." Savannah leaned against the open door, waiting as her parents walked through on their way to their car.

Mary patted her cheek as she passed her. "You're welcome, darlin'. See you tomorrow."

A sigh of relief almost slipped out until Savannah realized how ungrateful it sounded, even if her parents were out of earshot. One day she'd find a way to pay them back for everything they'd done for her. She'd see to it.

Checking on a slumbering Caroline, Savannah took a few long minutes to simply watch her precious daughter. Then she changed into yoga pants and a comfortable shirt and waited for Brad to arrive. He wasn't long in coming. Despite all the time she'd spent with him already, she was anxious enough to meet him at the door.

She took his jacket and hung it on the coat tree. Then she took his hand and led him to the couch. Folding her legs under her, she settled in and hoped to heaven he'd understand what she was about to tell him.

"So...now we talk?" she asked.

He nodded, then leaned back to drape his arm across her shoulders. "I assume we're talking about Greg."

"Yes...and no." The words should've been easy. This was a man she cared about. Why couldn't she open up about what she wanted for herself, for her life?

Because, she suddenly realized, she'd lost the battle to protect her heart.

It belonged to Brad, and damn if that didn't terrify her. How was she supposed to share a plan for her career with him since his actions had made it crystal clear his goals for her were different than those she set for herself? She was sure about what she wanted, had been from the time Michael walked out on her. He'd dreamed big, and she'd latched on to those dreams as though they were her own.

But they weren't. Not then.

Just like Brad's dreams weren't hers now.

Would he still want her if she refused to follow the path he wanted her to walk?

Savannah was ready to follow her own dreams, yet she feared it might cost her this new and wonderful relationship.

She firmed her resolve. Life's harsh lessons had changed her in so many ways, and she was ready to stand up for herself and what she wanted. Even though acknowledging that she was in love with Brad had been enlightening—and rather liberating—she refused to change her plans simply to be the woman he wanted rather than the woman she was.

He'd either learn to accept her and her hopes for the future, or he'd turn away from her. It would hurt like hell, but she needed to know. Even if telling Brad forced him to walk away. Better now than after they became even more tangled up in each other's lives. Or worse, before Caroline grew even more attached to him.

"Savannah?" Brad coaxed.

"One of the reasons—actually the main reason—I agreed to work with Greg was because he understands what I want. For my singing career, I mean."

"He'll be good for you, love. He's also good for us."

"Pardon?"

Brad pulled his arm away from her shoulders and leaned forward. "I set some goals for you. I thought you wanted what Katie wanted—to be the best thing that ever happened to country music."

"But I'm not," Savannah insisted.

He tossed her a lopsided smile. "That's debatable. But Greg—and Ethan and Russ, for that matter—opened my eyes. My goals aren't your goals."

"No, Brad. They're not."

Picking up her hand, he cradled it in his. "Then tell me what you want."

"First, I want to make enough money to stop waiting tables."

Turning his head to look at her, he furrowed his brow. "You already accomplished that."

She nodded. "Then I want to be able to buy a house."

His gaze swept the room. "But you have a—"

She put her fingers against his lips. "This place might be a house, but it's a dump. You know it. I know it. I want a place where Caroline can play in her own yard and not have to walk to the park to see grass. I want her to be able to swim in her own pool. I want her to go to a good school. It's not like I need a home as grand as yours or anything. Just a nice place on a big lot in a great neighborhood. Picture a Cape Cod on a half acre. *That's* what I want. And I think it'd also be great to buy a bigger house for my parents—a place close to mine. I'd get them a housekeeper. A gardener. I owe them so much for all they've done for me."

Brad squeezed her hand. "Do you have any idea how high you could climb in Nashville if you wanted to? You could be the next Taylor Swift and—"

"That's the last thing in the world I'd ever want. I'm thrilled just singing someplace like Words and Music. It's a dream come true."

"Then we're on the same page, and we'll work together for the same goals from now on."

She kissed him, a quick kiss. He pulled her back for more, leaving her humming in happiness when he ended their connection.

"You understand now?" she asked.

"I do." An enigmatic smile filled his features. "I also think I can help with one of your wishes."

"You can?"

"I can. How about you and the squirt move in with me? I'll get some great playground equipment, and I've already got a pool."

"I can't move in with you."

He quirked an eyebrow. "Why not?"

"For pity's sake. We barely know each other. We haven't even been dating two months. It's too soon."

He shook his head. "I'm a guy who knows what he wants when he sees it, then he goes for it."

Exactly like he'd done when he'd tried to dictate her career. "I can't. Not yet, at least. You're gonna have to give me a little time before I can jump into that kind of commitment. I have to think of my daughter, too. What message would I be sending her if I moved in with you so quickly?"

"She loves the house."

Savannah chuckled. "She loves the pool. That and you've been indulging her every whim every time you see her."

"So you won't even consider having the two of you move in?"

"Not yet. Not now."

Silence descended for long enough to make her worry. Then he sighed. "Fine. I get it."

"Do you?"

"What's that supposed to mean?"

Savannah had promised honesty, so she gave it to him full force. "I'm falling in love with you."

Eyes wide, he just stared at her. Was he angry or... afraid?

"But like we just discussed, you need to let me make my own choices. I know you've only got my best interests in mind, and your heart is in the right place. But you need to let me decide what's best for me."

His body began to relax, which boded well.

"I love that you invited us to move in, especially that you're welcoming Caroline without hesitation. But you can't try to solve all my problems."

"I do that?"

She nodded. "Let me be the one to tell you what I need."

He cocked his head. "What do you need, Savannah?"

"Right now, all I need and want is to be able to sing for a living—a comfortable living—without trading away my private life in the process."

"That might not be in your control," Brad pointed out.

Savannah nodded, understanding that the snowball was already rolling down a very steep hill. Despite her reticence to hire a manager, she put her faith in Greg to temper the speed of her star's rise. "You're right. But there are tricks I can use to keep a lid on things. At least that's what Greg told me." She grinned, remembering their conversation. "Funny, but I really like the guy. In some ways, he reminds me of my father."

"Do you trust him?"

"Ah, that's the question, isn't it?"

"For you, absolutely."

"Then yes. I think I do trust him." She picked up Brad's hand. "And I trust you, too."

He gave her hand a squeeze. "Even after all I've done?" The apologetic tone of his voice made her very happy. The man was finally getting what she was saying.

Maybe they had a future after all. Although she was a bit concerned that he'd said next to nothing about her declaration of love... Perhaps it was simply too soon for him?

She could only hope.

"Yes," she said with a nod. "If you want to keep that trust, there's one simple thing you can do."

"Keep my promise to be honest."

"Exactly."

CHAPTER TWENTY-ONE

Life fell into a comfortable routine, and Savannah found herself in a place she'd never expected to be—in a mature relationship with a great guy and just plain happy.

After three months of performing at Words & Music, she'd developed a loyal local fan base, had signed with Allied for an album release, and had fallen head over heels in love with her boss.

Brad had followed through on his promise to let her make her own decisions, although there were times she could tell how hard he champed at the bit. He liked to be with her whenever she and Greg had meetings, no matter how brief. Since Greg usually came to her at Words & Music, it would have been difficult to exclude Brad. Not that she wanted to. His experience was invaluable. Yet she couldn't help but worry that he still wanted more for her than she wanted for herself.

At their last meeting, Greg mentioned that Allied would like her to tour.

Although she loved their faith that she could sell out big venues, not only did she disagree, she simply didn't want that kind of grinding concert tour. There was also no way she'd leave Caroline that long, or worse, drag the poor girl from city to city. Thankfully, Greg offered a counterproposal, a plan of smaller and more personal settings, which made her comfortable. What could be worse than being booked into a huge arena and step onstage to find only a quarter of the seats occupied? No, better to play places where she could see every pair of eyes in the audience and give them a great show.

Brad let the plans proceed exactly as she wanted. Out of the blue, he'd also given her a raise, something he claimed she'd more than earned by keeping Words & Music packed every night she performed. Although she was still technically the opening act, he'd told her she far outshone the groups that had their turns following her.

As she'd promised herself, she put half of her earnings into savings and spent the other half fixing up her house. Her only indulgence was buying a reliable car. In his typical generous fashion, Brad had offered to buy her something, even going so far as to take her to a car dealer on one of their dates. The salesman was an old friend of his and had offered her a deal that she immediately knew was too good to be true. She'd quickly figured out that Brad had made the financial arrangements ahead of time. Instead of being perturbed, she'd led them both to a nice used CR-V that had fit both her needs and her budget.

There was only one sticking point in her wonderful new life, and she felt a bit petty for letting it bother her so much.

But it did.

Brad had done nothing more than acknowledge her opening her heart to him. She loved him. More deeply each day. And she loved him for who he was—bossiness and all. Now she needed him to find the courage to say those three important words aloud...

Unless he didn't love her.

His deep voice cut through her post-performance reverie. "Hey, love. You ready to go?"

Love.

That was telling, and the more he used the endearment, the more she yearned to hear it again. She nodded, reaching for her guitar case.

His hand brushed hers away. "You're still good with going to my house tonight?"

"Yep. Caroline was so excited to spend the night at Bri's. Besides, you deserve to sleep in your own bed for once. I'm sure my old mattress must be killing your back."

"Doesn't matter which bed I sleep in so long as you're in it."

Words like that always made the hope that he loved her soar. "That's sweet."

He shrugged and led the way to his Escalade.

Her phone rang right after she buckled her seat belt. She plucked the cell from her jacket pocket. "It's Greg."

"Aren't you going to answer it?"

She was, although she briefly considered letting it go to voice mail. One of the things she'd promised herself was that she'd allow her time away from the club to be private. It wasn't an easy policy to follow since her singing career was so important, but had Caroline been there, she might not have answered. Her daughter always deserved Savannah's undivided attention. Greg knew not to call her this late unless it was important.

"Hi, Greg."

His gravelly voice rumbled in her ear. "Hi, dear. Sorry to bug you after office hours."

"It's fine. What's up?"

"I need to find out if it's possible for you to attend a reception Allied is hosting."

"It depends on what night," she replied. Since Brad was straining to listen to the conversation, Savannah took pity on him. "I'm putting you on speaker. Brad, there's some kind of party that Allied wants me to go to. When did you say it was, Greg?"

"About that... What if I said it was tonight? Now, as a matter of fact."

She checked her watch. "It's nine already. If it's too far away..."

"You're just leaving the restaurant, right?"

"Yeah, but..."

"It's not far," he assured. "Do you know where the Continental is?"

"The Continental?" Brad asked. "That's the renovated hotel on Church Street, right?"

"That's the place," Greg replied.

Savannah had read articles about how some local group had bought and restored the Prohibition-era hotel. The place was far too swanky for her jeans and casual top. "I'm not dressed for—"

"What you're wearing doesn't matter," Greg insisted. "Listen, I know you hate to do stuff like this, but Marie Allen was rather insistent that you be there if it was at all possible. I told her I'd pass along the information but that you prefer to be home with your daughter after performances. She asked me to push you to attend."

Marie had been easy to work with, so to hear she was practically mandating that Savannah go to the reception was odd. "That doesn't seem like her style, to *demand* that I do something."

A chuckle slipped from Brad. "Marie has been on her best behavior with you so far. Am I right, Greg?"

"Absolutely," Greg replied. "Just between us, some of us call her Hurricane Marie. When she wants something, she tends to move heaven and earth to get it. Tonight, she wants you there."

* * *

"Which is why Savannah needs you, my friend," Brad said. His thoughts were in overdrive as he worried that Marie Allen had some trump card in her hand she'd yet to play. That, and he was nearly paralyzed with worry about how he'd handle being at that kind of Nashville party. The "users" would be on parade. He'd be on guard to keep any leeches away from Savannah.

Maybe he was worrying for nothing and could get the two of them out of this. "Do you know why Marie wants her there?"

"I'm afraid not. I went fishing but came back with an empty line."

"Damn."

Savannah let out a sigh. "So do we go?" she asked Brad.

He nodded, knowing Greg was right about Marie. She'd start hounding Savannah if they didn't show up at the Continental tonight.

"What's the verdict?" Greg asked.

"We'll go," Brad replied. "But Marie's getting us come-as-we-are. Jeans and all."

"Well, then. I'll try to get away and join you, but I have other business to wrap up first. Please keep me informed about anything that's discussed, and I hope to see you there."

* * *

Déjà vu.

There had been so many receptions exactly like this one that Brad had attended, both before and after his marriage. The Hitman knew how to party hard. The memories made him squirm in discomfort, especially since he'd met Katie at one of these shindigs.

There was nothing he could do to change the past, so he

tried to let it go. Savannah needed him to be strong and to help her figure out exactly what Marie Allen wanted by demanding she come to this gathering.

"I don't know anyone here," Savannah said, her voice quavering. Then her eyes grew wide. "Unless that's... Oh Lord, that's Perry Sheldon, isn't it? And Marta Kasey?"

"You know them both?" Brad teased, hoping to relieve her anxiety at being in a room full of Nashville's finest. Not only were newer performers like Perry and Marta in attendance, but so were Grand Ole Opry old-timers, celebrities who were old enough to have been friends with Ethan's parents. "Then we should go say hello so you can introduce me."

She swatted his upper arm and gave him a wan smile. "Do you see Marie anywhere? I'd like to get this over with."

"You mean you aren't loving being the newest rising star in the Allied stable?" Since he was every bit as inclined to get out of there, Brad craned his neck to try to find their hostess. "There she is."

He put his hand against the small of Savannah's back and steered her through the throng, targeting Marie, who was waving to them from the farthest part of the enormous ballroom. Passing people he knew from his wild days— almost all of whom expressed surprise at seeing him—he finally got the two of them standing in front of Marie.

Taking Savannah's hands, Marie started gushing over her. "I'm so glad you could make it. I need to talk to you, so I practically begged Greg to convince you to come by."

She directed her gaze to Brad. "Could I please have a few minutes to talk to Savannah?"

He stared at her, feeling his jaw clench. Had it not been for his help, Marie might not have known about Savannah's talent until a long time after another label had signed her. What made her think she had the right to ask him to bow out of any discussion that might impact her career—especially since Greg wasn't there yet to protect her interests? "Pardon?"

Despite a rather panicked look on her face, Savannah said, "It's fine, Brad." Then she glanced at Marie. "We won't be long, will we?"

"Not long at all," Marie replied. "Promise."

Still not comfortable with leaving Savannah alone with Marie, Brad frowned. "Are you sure?"

"It's fine," Savannah repeated.

Marie nodded toward the bar that had been set up on the left side of the ballroom. "Why don't you go have a drink? I made sure there's Belle Meade. That's your brand, right?"

He'd always preached to people that they should buy local. Then he'd always follow his sermon up with his opinion that Belle Meade was the finest native bourbon.

With a flip of her hand, she waved him away. "Go. Have a drink on us. I'll get Savannah back to you in two shakes."

Feeling dismissed and a bit annoyed that Savannah hadn't fought to keep him at her side, he retreated. There was an empty table close to the bar, so he dropped into a chair to wait. *Five minutes*, he promised himself. Then he was heading back over there.

This time, Marie beckoned someone to her right. A tall, muscular blond guy wearing jeans snug enough that he could sing soprano joined them. They looked so uncomfortable that Brad gave his own jeans a quick adjustment.

The guy was about Savannah's age. He nodded and grinned at everything Marie said. Damn if Savannah wasn't smiling right back at him. After a few minutes, a waiter walked past them with a tray of flutes filled with what appeared to be champagne. Marie stopped the waiter and took two glasses, which she handed to Savannah and the guy, before grabbing one for herself. Her mouth kept moving until she finally raised her glass, which made the other two mimic her. Three flutes clinked together.

Brad scowled. What in the hell were they toasting? And if it was that important, why hadn't Savannah urged him back to her side to ask his opinion before she'd clearly committed to it?

His anger rose swiftly. Severely.

Jealousy? Over a twenty-something guy in jeans that all but crushed his junk?

Perhaps.

He didn't like how Savannah was reacting to the kid. Was she flirting? Was she putting on a mask the same way Katie had? Scenes like this—fame like Savannah was enjoying—changed people. The thought that she was using him just to get ahead crossed his mind.

No, not her. She didn't want the kind of fame he could help bring to her. She wasn't the user his wife had been.

A hand settled on Brad's shoulder. "I see that you made

it," Greg said as he came to stand at Brad's side. "And where is our Savannah?"

Brad inclined his head toward her. "She's with Marie."

"I see. I take it you don't know the young man Savannah keeps trying to move away from."

Move away from?

Now that Greg mentioned it, Brad took a better look and could see that her body language screamed discomfort. Posture stiff as a board. Arm hugging her waist. Fingers clenching the champagne flute. Her head was inclined away from the guy, who seemed intent on keeping her anchored near his side.

"You don't know him, either?" Brad asked.

"I do not. But I have every intention of finding out what mischief Marie is inflicting on our girl. Shall we go over there and rescue her?"

"Marie told me to take a hike, that she wanted to talk to Savannah."

"I'm not the least bit concerned with what Marie wants. I am, however, concerned that Savannah understands all that Marie might be telling her." With a sly smile, Greg said, "Are you joining me as I crash her private little party?"

"Let's go."

CHAPTER TWENTY-TWO

"Then we're all set?" Greg asked.

Savannah still leaned against Brad's SUV, where she'd been since Brad and Greg had finally come to rescue her from Marie Allen. They'd talked business for only a few minutes since Savannah had already agreed to Marie's proposal. "I think so."

"You really don't mind a duet on your album?" Brad asked.

Although his earlier anger seemed to have dimmed, she couldn't help but think that something was still bothering him. Funny thing was that his irritation didn't seem to be caused by her decision to allow another artist to sing on her album. She just couldn't seem to figure out exactly what burr was under his saddle. He'd been brusque with Marie, but when he was introduced to Tony Plunkett, he'd been downright hostile.

The kid was only twenty-one, and he'd been runner-up

in some popular singing show—although she couldn't remember which one to save her life. Allied Sound had been one of the sponsors, and Marie had seen something special in Tony. So she'd asked if Savannah minded making room on her album for one duet. To sweeten the deal, Marie had given her freedom to pick the song—although she'd explained that she had a songwriter or two in mind and would prefer the duet to not be a Hitman song. She'd claimed that the album needed a bit of diversity, which made sense.

Since it seemed like such a small thing, Savannah had agreed. What harm could it do? Tony clearly had talent, and should they prove incompatible when they hit the recording booth, Marie was sure to pull the plug. Plus there was no guarantee that Brad could even write enough songs to fill all the tracks in the short time before Marie wanted to get in the studio. Why stress him out over such a tight deadline?

"A duet's fine," she finally replied. "If we don't click, then I'm sure we can scrap that plan."

"Oh, my dear," Greg said. "If only it were that simple."

"If what were that simple?"

Brad was shaking his head as Greg continued. "If you knew Marie the way we do, you'd realize she's already made up her mind. Since you agreed, this is going to happen."

"Wouldn't matter if he sounds like a scalded cat," Brad added. "You're stuck with the jerk now."

Greg shot a rather withering scowl at Brad. "You're being a bit hard on our girl, Brad. You and I have both acquiesced to Hurricane Marie and her rather persuasive manner at one time or another. Why should you expect any less of Savannah?"

No response from Brad, which only confused Savannah. She could only guess at the cause of his anger and felt at a distinct disadvantage. "It's only one song. One stupid song. And I told you she won't use the songs you've written for me. Who cares if the duet isn't one of your songs?"

Greg kept shifting his gaze between the two of them as though trying to solve some puzzle. Then understanding dawned as a knowing smile filled his face. "Now I see..."

"That makes one of us," Savannah drawled since she didn't understand at all what was happening. "Maybe you can explain it to me, 'cause I don't get how my agreeing to sing a duet started all this. Are you guys upset because I didn't run it by you first?"

Shaking his head, Greg replied in his ever-elegant way, "My dear, I am merely your manager. As I told you when we first spoke, I am here to assist you, not run your career or your life. I will never fault you for any choice you make. My job is to try to give you exactly what you want for yourself as a singer."

Brad didn't look appeased, seemingly lost in whatever thoughts were still plaguing him.

She was fed up—not with Greg, though. No, he had quickly become an ally. At that moment, her exasperation was focused directly on Brad. "Then what's got everyone so riled up?"

"Not *everyone*," Greg corrected. "A duet means little in

the long run, and I chalk it up to a typical Marie maneuver. She sees the potential in you. In fact, she saw it from the start, which only goes to show her talent at finding talent." He let out one of his little laughs, probably at his own play on words. "I can't think of a better way for Allied to strengthen their investment in this Plunkett boy than to hitch his wagon temporarily to your rising star."

"I get all *that*," Savannah said.

Greg stared at Brad. "Then I believe the only problem here is *you*."

With narrowed eyes, Brad folded his arms over his chest but continued to say nothing.

"Brad?" Savannah asked. "How is Brad a problem?"

Shaking his head, Greg revealed his usual aplomb. "Of all my talents, I'm afraid there is one I have never mastered. I cannot—nor will I ever *try* to—solve problems between two people in love."

* * *

Brad couldn't help but think everything in his life was rapidly going straight to hell. The problem was that the only person he could blame was himself.

He'd been fine. Better than fine. His work at Words & Music had been satisfying. He enjoyed the people he employed and was good at what he did. The music was no longer taking over his every thought, and he'd made peace with himself.

Then Savannah Wolf had sung for him.

No, not for *him*. That was bullshit, and he knew it. She'd stepped onto his stage to share her gift with the world— a gift that deserved to be enjoyed by everyone. Although she might not have set out to do so, she'd captured him as neatly as any trap ever designed. Completely. She'd become his muse. His lover.

And she'd stolen his heart in the process.

Brad had known it for a while, although life had been much easier to manage if he compartmentalized his feelings. Each time Savannah murmured how much she cared for him, his heart knew he felt the same. While he cherished her, not once had he found the courage to say the words. What was he waiting for?

Chicken shit.

Of course he was afraid. Love was scary. *Fucking terrifying, actually.* Having never truly felt it this intensely before, not even for Katie, he had a hard time putting a name to exactly what emotion had filled him each time he'd been with Savannah.

He'd called it desire. Plain old lust. But she was magical. Different.

What had forced the word "love" into his brain had been nothing special, nothing revelatory. Savannah had helped him realize he loved her just by being herself.

What in the hell was he going to do now?

Marry her, his thoughts whispered. *And do it right this time...*

Hard to allow that notion to blossom when jealousy was running roughshod over him. When he'd seen that pretty boy put his arm around her shoulder, Brad could barely hold back the need to march across the ballroom and punch the trespasser in the nose. While he was at it, he'd consider telling Marie to go screw herself since it was clear she'd dragged the boy into Savannah's path.

It's just a duet. One damn duet.

In which Savannah would sing a song that wasn't his.

"I'll be on my way now," Greg said. "Then you two can chat in private."

She gave him her customary kiss on the cheek before he strolled across the parking lot to his car.

Quiet descended until Greg's taillights had faded.

Savannah still stood with her back pressed against Brad's SUV, nibbling on her lower lip and looking too defeated for his taste, especially since he'd been the one who put that expression on her face.

Stepping up to her, he put his hands on her waist. "Sorry," he mumbled.

She stared up at him with those hypnotic eyes. "For what, Brad? I still don't understand, and all Greg's supposed explanation did was muddy the water."

"I overreacted, okay? To the duet, I mean. Like you said, it's only one stupid song. I guess I was..." He shrugged. "Jealous. I was jealous."

Her eyes searched his. "Jealous? Because I'm singing a song you didn't write?"

"That's part of it." He'd apologized and given her an explanation, half-assed though it was. Why did she keep pressing him?

For the same reason he would be doing the same thing. Not only was she astute, but she also always seemed to be able to pick up on his emotions, even his thoughts. But it didn't take a genius to see he'd been acting like a grizzly bear that had been poked with a stick. In the eye.

"I didn't like seeing that guy touching you," he finally admitted, which wasn't easy. Jealousy was new to him.

As new as love.

This relationship stuff was a pain in the ass.

"Being close to him was…agonizing," she said with a crooked grin. "The kid must've been wearing a whole bottle of cologne. Why do boys do that? Bathe in stinky, cheap cologne?"

Kid. She'd called him a kid.

Brad grinned. "They're too young to know better. Trust me, some girl's gonna come along and straighten him out."

A yawn slipped out, and she tried to smother it with her palm. "Sorry. I'm a bit tired. Are you ready to head to your place?"

Tired or not, she was beautiful. Moonlight shone down on her, and his heart tightened merely looking at her. He couldn't stop himself from kissing her.

The moment his lips touched hers, he realized exactly how right things were between them and decided the time to hesitate was past.

He loved that she sighed when he ended the kiss.

"I want you," he said with a growl of need. "I want to be inside you so bad."

"Then take me to bed."

Nuzzling her neck and breathing in her sweet scent, Brad smiled. And took a leap of faith. "Oh, I will. I need to make love to the woman I love."

"You love me?" Tears pooled in her eyes.

"I do. I have for a while."

"Oh, Brad." She threw her arms around his neck and hugged him tight. Then she kissed his ear and whispered, "I love you, too."

* * *

Savannah couldn't remember the drive to Brad's house. For all she knew, they'd floated there on a cloud. Despite her hopes and dreams for a happily ever after, she'd never expected him to blurt out those three little words.

But he had, and her heart soared. Her libido was every bit as elated. All she could think of was getting him alone.

The yawning she'd been unable to suppress back at Words & Music had been pushed aside with the rush of her desire. She was in such a hurry to get him inside and naked that she fumbled with her seat belt latch and felt stupid when Brad finally chuckled and gave her an assist. The cocky grin on his face meant he knew she was rattled.

Of course she was rattled. He'd told her that he loved her, and she'd confessed her feelings as well. She wasn't sure her heart would ever settle back into a normal rhythm. "Thanks," she murmured before she crawled out of the Escalade.

He caught her right inside the kitchen door and tugged

her into his arms. His kiss made her toes curl, and she returned his ferocity with all of the emotion coursing through her. Their tongues mated as their hands removed any barrier between them.

Somehow they made it to a couch, where the trail of their discarded clothing finally ended. Tumbling onto the cushions, Savannah ended up under Brad, which was exactly where she wanted to be. When he latched on to one of her nipples with his teeth, she tunneled her fingers through his thick hair and closed her eyes.

This was what she'd always wanted, what she'd always needed. Heat and desire and love. The full package.

Rocking her hips up, she whispered how much she loved him and how desperately she needed to feel him inside her.

* * *

For the first time he could recall, Brad lost all control. He roughly separated her thighs with his knee and rubbed his cock against her, hoping to hell she was ready for him. He found a wet welcome that he took greedy advantage of as he plunged inside her tight heat.

Savannah wrapped her legs around him, lifting her hips each time he thrust. Each of her moans, each time her nails scraped his back, he was sure she'd push him over the edge. But he wanted this to last forever. "I love you, Savannah," he ground out, hoping the words hit her every bit as hard as her declarations always got to him.

"I love you, Brad."

Then there were no more words. Only the feel of her soft skin. Only the alluring scent of her hair. Only his body joined with hers.

He couldn't stop the climax that pounded through him, and she cried out in release a moment later.

Happy to stay where he was for the rest of his life, Brad wondered how he got so damn lucky. Savannah deserved better, but he wasn't about to let her go.

"We shouldn't have done that," she said.

"What?"

"We shouldn't have done that," she said again. Then she tapped his shoulder. "You're heavy."

"Sorry."

They dressed in quiet until his curiosity could take no more of her silence. "What shouldn't we have done?"

"We didn't use a condom."

The absence of birth control had crossed his mind—for a nanosecond—before he'd let the thought go. "I'm clean. I got tested earlier this year."

She cocked her head. "You're not worried about whether I'll give you a—"

"Not a bit."

"And what if I get pregnant?"

That question didn't frighten him the way he figured it should. He simply shrugged. "Then we have a kid. Caroline would like a sibling."

"It's the wrong time," Savannah insisted.

After sitting on the couch, he patted the spot next to him. She heaved a sigh and plopped beside him.

"I love you," he said again, finding it easier to do each time the words fell from his mouth.

"I love you, too. Let's just hope I didn't get pregnant. We'll be more careful from now on."

Taking her hand, Brad fought against his yearning to ask her to marry him. Part of him wanted to bind her to him, to hear her take those vows to love, honor, and cherish that he used to think were so damned silly. He wanted those promises from Savannah, and he wanted to give Caroline a man in her life—someone who was growing to care for her as he cared for her mother.

"Move in with me," Brad blurted out. "You and Caroline. Come live here with me."

Savannah's blue eyes widened. "That's really sweet, Brad, but...I haven't changed my mind."

He bristled. "Things are different now. Okay?"

"How are they different?"

For a moment, he closed his eyes and let his head drop back against the cushion. This love stuff wasn't easy; talking about his feelings was even worse. Raising his head, he turned toward her and cupped her face in his hands. "I love you, Savannah. And I love your daughter. I want you both here with me. Every day. Will you at least think about it?"

Her eyes searched his before she nodded.

"Yes, you'll move in?"

"Yes, I'll think about it."

CHAPTER TWENTY-THREE

How about one more take on that?" Marie might've phrased it as a question, but Savannah had quickly learned the woman always got her way.

"Hurricane Marie" was right.

Her voice weary, Savannah nodded. A glance to the clock showed that they were closing in on midnight. She'd missed reading Caroline a bedtime story and tucking her in, which made her sad. But she reminded herself that marathon recording sessions wouldn't happen all that often.

Marie—and Raul Martinez, the producer—were demanding, so Savannah sang her heart out. Thankfully she had the next two days off from Words & Music. Her voice would need all that time to recover.

Brad had been in the control room the whole time, even through the ten takes of the duet with Tony, four of which had been nothing more than chances to get the kid to loosen up. Before the fifth take, she'd finally told him a dirty joke, and that seemed to do the trick. When he'd started laughing, Brad had started frowning. Evidently he hadn't gotten over his jealousy, but she found that not only quaint but reassuring.

He loved her. He really did.

The only time he'd come forward to bug Marie and Raul was when she'd done takes of his songs. Marie had allowed three of them even though Brad had written two others in the past handful of weeks. She'd insisted she wanted to save them for the next album. *If* there was a next album...Everything rode on the success of the tracks she was laying down now.

Taking sips of lukewarm honeyed tea, Savannah watched as Brad went to stand by Marie. From his rather animated gestures, he appeared to be disagreeing with her. Probably over the time, since he kept pointing at the clock behind them. Marie kept sipping a glass of wine she'd just poured and shaking her head.

She wasn't the only one with alcohol. Other drinks were readily available in the friendly setting of the Allied recording studio. The backup musicians were all drinking. The odd thing was that the more whiskey they poured down their throats, the better they played. She preferred minimal accompaniment—a guitar or two, a keyboard, and Leah and Maggie. Marie had disagreed and had a full band in attendance to lay down tracks for each of the album's songs. They all reeked of cigarette smoke and Jack Daniels.

Her thoughts drifted to the big change soon to come in her life. Her town house wouldn't be her house much longer. Greg had presented her with the first advance from Allied—minus his commission, which he'd more than earned—and she'd immediately begun the search for a new home. A nicer home. Caroline deserved a great place with really good schools.

Savannah hadn't mustered up the courage to tell Brad. He'd been so insistent that they move in with him. She'd have to break it to him soon, especially since the realtor Greg recommended had several places lined up for her to tour. Once that "For Sale" sign popped up in the front of her row house, he was sure to notice.

No matter how tempting it was to go ahead and accept Brad's invitation and live with the man she loved in that gorgeous house, she just couldn't. The words of acceptance wouldn't come.

Why?

Because this isn't forever...

Having made that mistake once—pitching her life in with a man's—she wasn't about to get burned again. It always ended disastrously. Brad wasn't a guy who would ever settle down. Not permanently. Oh, he might play house with her for a while. A few years or so tops. She wasn't about to put herself in the position to have him ask her to move out. Her heart couldn't bear it, nor would she put Caroline through that kind of ordeal.

Better to keep a modicum of separation between them in the form of separate addresses.

Getting out of this relationship, which would eventually happen regardless of how much she loved him, wouldn't wreck her whole life.

It would only break her heart.

"Ready?" Marie's voice sounded in Savannah's head-phones.

Savannah nodded as the musicians set aside their drinks and started shuffling the pages on their music stands.

The song had a melancholy key and verses that spoke of love and loss. Her tumbling emotions were easily poured into this take, and when the music ended, tears stung her eyes.

* * *

Savannah patted her face dry and set the hand towel aside. Staring at her reflection, she sighed. There were dark circles under her eyes, and her skin was pasty.

She was exhausted.

Marie had kept her in the recording studio at Allied past two in the morning for three days running. At least tonight they'd wrapped up at ten, so Savannah was finally able to look forward to a good night's sleep.

Flipping off the light, she headed to her bed and pulled back the sheets, only to hear the front door open and close. Even though they spent almost every night together—usually at her place—Brad had stayed at his house the last two nights. He'd evidently used the key she'd given him and decided to join her again.

Instead of going downstairs to greet him, she decided to wait for him in bed. After that first night, he hadn't come to the recording sessions. He'd given her space to get the recordings done, telling her that his hovering was probably making her crazy.

She had to admit those evenings had gone smoother than the first time she'd sat in that booth, probably because she was able to focus on the music and not worry about Brad's reaction to each and every little detail of her performance or the changes Marie made between takes.

When Savannah heard the typical creak of footsteps on the stairs, she had a moment of panic that it wasn't Brad coming to her room. Instead, some serial killer was making his way through her house to come and murder her in some grisly manner.

Stop being silly. Of course it was Brad. She'd heard him arming his familiar car alarm. The frightening thought had merely been the same that probably plagued any woman living alone with a child who depended on her for safety.

"Savannah?"

"In bed, Brad."

He breathed in sharply as he stepped into the room. "That sounds promising."

"Probably not as promising as we'd like," she said.

In the dark room, she could just make out his form as he whipped his shirt over his head, jerked off his boots, and then went to work on his pants. "What's that mean?"

"I got my period."

"Oh..." Having kicked aside his pants, he stood there in his briefs. "Then you're not pregnant?"

There seemed to be a touch of sadness in his voice, which was totally unexpected. "I'm not pregnant."

"I wondered...I mean, if you had been..." He came to stand next to the bed. "Never mind."

She lifted the cover and patted the mattress. "Come to bed."

After he slipped between the sheets, she rolled toward him, loving how he wrapped his arm around her and pulled her closer so she could snuggle against his warm body. "Would you have been mad?" she asked as she threw a leg over his thigh.

"You mean if you were pregnant?"

"Yeah."

"No. Not mad."

As usual, Brad answered her in an enigmatic tone. The problem was that she desperately wanted to know what he was thinking. "Did you *want* me to be pregnant?"

He took a long time thinking it over. "Maybe...a little."

Another surprise. "You want kids?" she asked.

"I hadn't really thought about it before," he replied.

"Did Katie—" Savannah stopped herself from asking the question crowding her thoughts. They'd agreed to leave the past in the past, but there was so much more she wanted to know about his marriage and his late wife—anything that could give her insight into the puzzling man.

He answered her anyway. "She didn't want kids."

"Did you?"

"Like I said, I hadn't thought about it. She told me she didn't want kids. Because of the lupus, she couldn't have 'em anyway, so I let it drop and didn't think about it again."

As if things between a couple could be that simple.

He let out a yawn. "Since making love is out, we should get some sleep."

Which meant the topic was closed. "Yeah. We could both use some rest."

"Love you," Brad said, kissing her forehead.

"I love you, too. With all my heart."

* * *

Brad awoke with a start, a vivid dream still stuck in his head. Not since high school had such erotic images filled his mind...and his body. A moment later, he realized the dream had been born in the reality of Savannah's sweet attention.

Lying facing him, she had her fingers wrapped around his cock as she gently stroked him. "You're awake?" she whispered.

"Oh yeah..." Hard as rock, all he wanted to do was flip her on her back and make love to her. Then he remembered the obstacle to that plan and wondered what she was thinking by getting him so aroused. "Savannah, what—"

"Shh." She released him and pushed his shoulders against the mattress. "Let me play." Then she started to kiss her way down his body, licking each nipple before moving lower.

While it was probably stupid to argue with her, he couldn't help but comment, "You don't have to—" Whatever he'd been about to say scattered in his thoughts like autumn leaves in the wind when she took him into her hot, wet mouth.

Brad fisted his hands in the sheets, trying hard to hold on to his self-control. She was so giving, so thorough in her attention, that he could hold nothing back. The woman seemed to know how to keep him teetering on the edge of release and then ease back to allow him to catch his breath.

He'd always assumed she had limited sexual experience judging from how badly she'd been burned. A woman hurt that gravely tended to stay the hell away from men. The way she used her tongue, her teeth, had him so aching and full that he wondered if he'd been wrong.

No, his pleasure was not from how talented she was, although she was pretty damn good. His love for her made everything she did feel as if she was touching his soul.

When she finally granted him release, his climax consumed him. Only when his senses began to return did he worry that he'd given her the wrong impression. "I'm sorry," he mumbled. It was a sincere apology, although the orgasm had been beyond belief.

"Sorry?" Savannah frowned. "For what?"

"That was selfish of me."

"Selfish?" She let out a chuckle. "*I* give you a blow job and that makes *you* selfish?"

"I can't...you know...return the favor. Unless you want to wait a few minutes for me to bounce back and make love to you."

Her frown returned. "You'd do that? Even with my period?"

"Of course I would."

"I thought all guys hated that."

He shrugged. "Evidently not all guys. Wouldn't bother me."

Leaning in, she brushed a kiss against his cheek. "That's sweet, Brad. But no. I'd rather wait 'til it runs its course. You okay with that?"

Although he nodded, he was wide awake now and had no desire to go back to sleep. He'd stayed away from her for two long nights and had missed holding her. His bed had felt too big and far too empty.

"How did the sessions go?" he asked.

Flopping back against her pillow, she let out a loud sigh. "We're done. Thank God."

"Marie was finally satisfied?"

"For the most part. She said she might need me to come back in for a few 'tweaks,' as she called them. At least this was the last big night in the studio. I should be able to perform tomorrow." A glance at the clock. "Today, actually."

"I wasn't asking because I worried about you being at the restaurant," he said, thinking she'd misunderstood the motive behind his question. Sure, the crowds the last two nights were disappointed, but Brad had arranged for a couple of decent opening acts to fill in while she was away, and he'd thrown in free appetizers.

"I should've told Marie we needed to record on my days off," she insisted.

"You *did* record on your days off. You just needed a little more time. It's no big deal, love. I handled things at Words and Music."

She turned her head to stare at him. "Is that why you weren't at the studio? Because you needed to be at the restaurant?"

"Yeah, I was there. That, and in all honesty, I've been working on hunting down Michael." A nervous chuckle slipped out. "Marie also drives me right up a tree."

Eyes wide, Savannah sputtered. "But . . . but . . . why?"

"For Caroline," he calmly replied. "And for you. Your daughter deserves nice things—books, dance lessons, whatever her sweet little heart desires." He held up a hand to halt her when she tried to speak again. "I know you can pay for all that now, but the man has a responsibility he walked away from. Two responsibilities."

"Have you found him?"

Brad shook his head. "When I do, you know that I would never do anything with the information except hand it over to you so you could decide what you wanted to do with it. I just want you to have the option to go after him—if *you* want it. I know that your relationship with Michael ended badly, so if you want some sort of closure, then I'd like to give that to you."

It came as a nice surprise to discover that she trusted

him, that she trusted his intentions. This wasn't Brad trying to force his will on her; this was Brad giving her
options to make her own choices.

"Thank you," Savannah said. While she wasn't positive
that stirring up any hornet's nest involving Michael would
be wise, she was grateful in the ease developing in her relationship with Brad—a nice give-and-take.

"I love you," she said.

He rose, picked up her hand, and kissed her palm. "I
love you, too."

CHAPTER TWENTY-FOUR

Joslynn shot Savannah one of her patented stern frowns—
the type that probably kept unruly patients in line. "What
do you mean you haven't told him? You're looking for a
new house and you haven't taken the time to mention it to
your boyfriend?"

All Savannah did was grumble and stir her coffee. She'd
asked Jos to meet her at Shamballa, their favorite coffee-
house, for a cup of brew and a friendly chat. Instead, she
was getting a rather heated lecture.

"Look," Joslynn said, "I know relationships aren't exactly my...um...area of expertise, but I'd think making a
major life change like searching for a house might be something that you'd want to discuss with the man in your life."

Perhaps what Savannah had truly brought her friend
here to do was to talk some sense into her. Because Jos was
right—Savannah shouldn't hide something so important
from Brad.

A smile eased Joslynn's features. "If I'm judging your expression correctly, you're starting to see the light."

Savannah nodded.

"So you'll tell him?"

"I'll tell him."

After a curt nod, Joslynn sipped her coffee.

"He won't be happy about it," Savannah couldn't help but point out.

"Why not? He's the one who wanted you to be a star. I'd think he'd be happy for you that you've earned enough money to afford a nice place. This is good for you. And for Caroline. Didn't you say you were looking for a house with a pool for her?"

"He won't be happy because he still wants us to move in with him."

"Ah . . . and you told him no."

"It's too soon for us to live together," Savannah insisted.

Jos held up a hand. "You don't have to convince me. Shit, even if I ever got married—which is about as likely as a woman walking on Jupiter—I'd probably keep my own place. I can't stand the idea of sharing a house with some guy who leaves the toilet seat up and kicks his shoes off wherever he wants." She shuddered for effect.

Since Savannah was well aware of how fussy Joslynn was about her home, that revelation wasn't a surprise. "You don't let . . . what's that doctor's name, the one you're dating?"

"Douglas."

"You don't let Douglas spend the night at your place?"

"Nope." Joslynn let out a chuckle. "Besides, he's not my boyfriend or anything. He's just a booty call."

Savannah let out a snort. "Any guy dating you is just a booty call."

"What can I say?" Joslynn shrugged. "I like sex, and I enjoy my independence."

In all the years the two of them had been friends, Savannah had never known the woman to even *consider* a serious relationship. Joslynn's dealings with men were more typical of how a man might treat a woman—as an escort for an important event or as a convenient bed partner. Although she might date one guy for a while, she always broke it off if he tried to tie her down.

Savannah admired her friend's adamant refusal to let her life revolve around a man, to take total charge of her own happiness. But at the same time, she wondered if Jos knew how much she was missing. Savannah had found such comfort in sharing her world with Brad. Although they might've had a rocky start, their relationship was now sailing along smoothly.

Unless she screwed it up by keeping important secrets...

That realization prompted another—Brad wanted honesty, which she'd promised, yet she wasn't being truthful with him. Searching for a house without telling him was every bit as bad as his making grand plans for her singing career without consulting her.

"I'll tell him," Savannah said. "Next time we're together."

* * *

Brad came jogging over to the fence when he saw that Savannah and Caroline had arrived. When he'd asked Savannah if she wanted to play softball with the Words & Music team, she'd declined, claiming she had absolutely no athletic ability. Instead, she'd offered to bring Caroline so the two of them could cheer for Brad and his friends.

He grinned at Caroline, who was dressed in the Words & Music T-shirt he'd given her. "Hey, pumpkin. Come to watch me do my Greg Maddux imitation?"

The girl cocked her head. "Who's that?"

"He's an awesome baseball pitcher."

"What's a pitcher?"

Savannah put her hand on Caroline's shoulder. "We don't watch sports."

"We watch dancin' shows," Caroline announced.

"Well then," Brad said, "I'll teach you about sports, and you can teach me to dance." He shifted his gaze to Savannah, who was also in a Words & Music shirt. "Glad my girls are here to cheer for me."

"Are we still going for ice cream after?" Caroline asked her mother.

"Sure are," Savannah replied. When she looked at Brad, her smile faded. "I need to talk to you about something."

That sounded too ominous for his peace of mind. He slid his hands in his back pockets. "Uh-oh." A glance at where the players were taking the field. "Want me to skip the game?"

"No, it can wait. No biggie."

While he wanted to find out exactly what was bothering her and to find out right now, his team was counting on him. "We'll talk after the game?"

She nodded. "Go on. Go have fun."

As if he could concentrate on the game now.

"Brad!" Russ called. "You coming or what?"

Since Russ treated each softball game as though it were every bit as important as his NFL forays, Brad nodded and went to await his turn at bat. His gaze kept shifting to where Savannah and Caroline were sitting in the bleachers.

Things had been going great lately, and he couldn't think of a single thing she might need to tell him that would've made her frown so fiercely. Unless...

She's pregnant.

Now he was just being stupid. She'd just had her period. His imagination was working overtime, and he startled when Ethan kicked his foot. "What?"

"You're up next. Grab a bat."

Before Brad even had a chance to search for his bat, Russ handed him the right one. "Where's your head today?"

Brad stepped back and gave the bat a couple of swings without answering.

"You know how much I hate to lose to Black Mustang."

Taking another swing to loosen up, Brad tried unsuccessfully to stop worrying about whatever it was that Savannah needed to tell him.

Russ folded his arms over his chest. "I thought you hated Robbie Campbell as much as Ethan and I do."

Brad let the bat rest on his shoulder. "We'll beat him."

The crack of a bat soundly connecting with a ball made them both turn to watch head waitress Cheyanne send a ball sailing toward left field. Despite the outfielder diving to catch it, the ball landed on the grass, taking a funny bounce that allowed Cheyanne enough time to take second base.

"You're up. Send her home," Russ said, cuffing Brad on the shoulder.

As he stepped toward the box, he caught his name floating from the bleachers. A quick glance found Savannah and Caroline on their feet, cheering for him exactly as they'd promised.

Not being a man prone to sentimentality, he was taken by surprise with the way their support touched his heart. In that moment, he realized that he would move heaven and earth to keep the two of them safe—would do whatever he could to make them happy.

They were his family.

"Batter up," the umpire barked.

Russ got Brad's attention and gave the sign to bunt and try to advance the runner.

Just to be contrary, Brad let a big grin fill his face as he pointed at the fence as though he were Babe Ruth. Cheers—and a good number of jeers from the Black Mustang crowd—filled the air. A glance at Savannah and Caroline made his smile broaden. They were whispering to each other with grins on their faces, which meant they understood exactly what he was doing.

His girls knew him well.

After shooting Brad a scowl, the pitcher tossed one right at his head.

Brad dropped, sending dust flying up around him. All he did was smile in retaliation as he got back to his feet and gave the bat a couple more practice swings. Russ wasn't the only one who wanted to knock Robbie and his Black Mustang team down a notch or two.

Back in the box, he pointed at the fence again. Then when a more reasonable pitch came, he laid down a smooth bunt that took them all by surprise, so much so that he made it to first base as Cheyanne scored their first run.

Robbie was first baseman, and his kicked a cloud of dust at Brad, who stood firmly on the base. "You're an asshole, Maxwell."

Not at all intimidated, Brad smacked some of the dirt off his pants. "An asshole who just faked the hell outta your pathetic team, Campbell."

A glance back to the stand found his girls waving at him, so he waved back.

All was right with his world.

* * *

Brad handed the cup of strawberry ice cream to Caroline, then he passed the hot fudge sundae to Savannah. As he paid the server and grabbed his own sundae, the gals went to find a booth.

They slid down the benches on opposite sides. When he

joined them, he gave Caroline a flip of his hand to get her to scoot over a few more inches so that he could sit next to her.

Instead of diving into his strawberry shortcake, he jumped into Savannah's earlier and rather ominous declaration. "What did you need to tell me?"

Playing with her plastic spoon, she dragged the drippy fudge over the top of the mound of ice cream. "I'm going house hunting this afternoon."

"What?" Seemed like that word popped out often when he was with her. She always kept him guessing, always surprised him.

Just one of the reasons he loved her so much, although he wasn't happy with this particular announcement.

"I'm putting the town house up for sale," she calmly proclaimed. "You know that I need to look for something bigger for Caroline and me."

Was she trying to goad him? He'd asked her to share his house more times than he could remember, and he still wanted that, despite her casual dismissal. "I asked you to move in with me, and you're talking about getting yourself a new house?"

She reached out to lay her hand over his. "It's just too soon for us to move in with you." Then she inclined her head toward Caroline. "We need time, baby. That's all. Let us adjust to all the changes, then we can revisit the idea of sharing a home later."

Baby. She'd never had a pet name for him before. For some weird reasons, hearing it felt like a victory—like a deepening of her affection.

Then why the planned home search? Savannah and Caroline would have everything they needed at his place. He'd even offered to sell it and buy something else for the three of them if Savannah was hesitant to share a home he'd lived in with Katie.

"There's no way I can change your mind about this, is there?" Brad shook his head with a small sigh.

"I need my own place."

Despite his hurt, he gave in. "You win. For now."

"I get a pool!" Caroline announced, her lips covered with pink ice cream.

Savannah plucked a napkin from the dispenser and handed it to Caroline. "If we can find one."

With a smile, he said, "If you find the perfect place and it doesn't have a pool, you can always come swim at my place, pumpkin."

As they ate in silence, he tried to remind himself to be patient. Savannah had been through hell with Michael, and with time, she'd find that she could depend on him. In the meantime, he was turning over every rock, trying to learn more about Michael in hopes that some of what she'd lost—what Michael had stolen from her. So far, nothing had surfaced. But Brad was determined to keep looking.

A teenage girl with purple hair came hesitantly toward the booth, smiling nervously as she stared at Savannah. "Um...hi."

"Hi," Savannah said in return.

All the teen did was stare as she fiddled with her bejeweled phone.

"Is there something you wanted?" Brad asked.

Without taking her gaze from Savannah, the girl said, "Um...yeah. I mean, are you...um...her? Savannah Wolf?"

Eyes wide, Savanah nodded.

Brad couldn't help but chuckle. "She sure is. Savannah Wolf. In person."

Leaning closer, Caroline acted as though she were going to whisper in his ear, although the volume was loud enough that he almost winced. "Who's that?"

He cupped his hand to her ear and said softly, "That's one of your mom's fans."

"What's a fan?"

"She likes the way your mom sings."

"Oh..." Caroline cocked her head. "I like the way Mama sings."

Brad kissed her cheek. "Well, then. You're a fan, too."

The smile on Caroline's face made him smile in return.

"Wow," the teen said, a bit breathless. "You're really *her*."

All he could think was how great it was that Savannah was having her first "fan" moment and he was privileged to witness it.

She seemed to handle it well, a blush spreading across her cheeks as she smiled at the teen.

"Can I...um...take a selfie with you?" the teen asked.

"Of course," Savannah replied before posing with the fan, their heads close together as the girl captured the moment.

After they were again alone, Brad reached for Savannah's hand. "You handled that very well."

"How weird was that?" she asked, still appearing a bit bewildered at the attention.

"Not weird at all," he replied. "You're a great singer. You're gonna have a lot more moments exactly like that."

Caroline popped up to stand on the bench, waving at another little girl. "That's Kailey! Hi, Kailey!"

The girl waved back as she and her mother took seats a small nearby table.

"Mama, can I go see Kailey? I wanna tell her you got a fan."

Savannah locked eyes with Kailey's mother, who nodded. "Just for a few minutes, okay?"

Picking up her ice cream, Caroline scooted closer to Brad, who got to his feet to let her out of the booth. "Thanks, Mama!" She ran off without a backward look.

Now that they had a moment of privacy, he sat back down and returned to their original topic. "Fan girl aside... I wanted you to know that I understand you wanting your own place."

"You do?" She eyed him skeptically.

He nodded. "Would you like some help finding a place? Who knows, I might even look."

"Why would you want to move? Your house is... phenomenal."

"My house is a pain in the ass. It's too much for just me." A subtle hint, but he couldn't help himself. He wanted his girls home with him.

They'd spent so much time in the big house that, whenever he was alone, he saw them everywhere. In the kitchen, making lunch together. In the basement studio with Caroline smiling as her mother sang to her when she laid down practice tracks for new songs. In the family room, where Brad now kept a wooden toy box full of things he'd bought for Caroline to play with whenever she visited as well as the toys she'd left behind.

A marriage proposal was on the tip of his tongue. He wouldn't let it slip out. Not now. Not yet. If she already felt that he was pressuring her to move in with him too quickly, then she'd surely think a proposal was entirely out of the question.

But he wanted to ask her to marry him almost as badly as he'd ever wanted anything. The more time he spent with Savannah—and with Caroline—the more he was convinced they belonged together.

Now he just needed to convince her. And Brad vowed that this was a battle he would win.

CHAPTER TWENTY-FIVE

Savannah walked into rehearsal feeling as though she were floating in on a cloud. Thanks to her realtor, she'd found the perfect house for her and Caroline. Not only was it the perfect size, but it also had the character only an older home possessed. The owners had renovated the kitchen and baths, and the place had modern conveniences without losing any of its quaint charm. The cherry on top was that it was less than five miles from her parents' house. Brad had even loved it right down to the wainscoting, and he'd given her some great advice when she'd written the offer.

Now she only had to wait and hope the sellers accepted.

She pulled her guitar from the case and strode to the stage. Only one of the musicians had arrived, but Leah and Maggie were already in their spots. It took Savannah a moment to realize they were both twittering like a couple of teenagers and frowning as they stared at the screen of a cell phone and whispered to each other.

After setting her guitar on a stand, she went to them, wondering what bad news had hit and wanting to see if she could improve their moods. Allied had chosen another song for her, and she wanted to debut it later that night. It was time for them to quit playing with their phones and get down to business.

"What's up, ladies?" she asked.

Their expressions swiftly changed, morphing to . . . pity?

Not sure what to say, she held out her hand. "May I look at what's got you both engrossed?"

Maggie gave her the phone and nibbled on her lower lip as Leah looked away.

Savannah's first glance at the screen made her stomach lurch. "What the . . ."

There was a picture of her and Brad standing hand in hand as he gave her a rather tame kiss. She remembered the moment well. They'd been in front of their favorite restaurant, waiting for the valet to bring Brad's car around. The headline read: "The Hitman's New Songbird?"

Scrolling down the screen, she quickly read the article, wondering how someone could be so cruel. The write-up talked about her meteoric rise and how Brad had orchestrated it. There was speculation that she was the muse for his new songs as well as his latest fling, one at the end of a very long line. Just reading the names of the famous and near-famous women who'd been in and out of his life made tears blur her vision.

How many of those women had he said the same sweet things to? How many had he told that he loved them? How many had he made love to?

Jealousy was a sickening feeling, but Savannah couldn't push it aside no matter how hard she tried. Instead, she burned with it even though she hated the pain that accompanied it.

Her hands trembled when she handed the phone back to Maggie. "Where did you find that?"

Leah was the one to reply. "It's a big website called *Nashville Watchdog*. Everyone in Nashville visits it."

"Not *everyone*." Brad's voice was filled with barely leashed anger. "A lot of people hate that shit." He strode across the stage as the ladies scurried in the other direction, no doubt avoiding his anger. He set his hand on Savannah's shoulder. "I was coming to tell you about it. Greg called me."

"Why didn't he just call me?"

"He figured I could break it to you before you saw the story," he replied. Then he shot a nasty glare at her backup singers. "He wanted me to prepare you because he knew it would upset you."

She let out an inelegant snort. "Too late."

"Obviously," he drawled. With a frown, he added, "There's more..."

"More stories?"

He shook his head. "More Greg wanted me to tell you."

When he didn't elaborate, her temper ignited. "Out with it."

"There are three different people begging to talk to you."

Savannah bristled. "Reporters?"

Brad nodded. "One magazine, one local TV station, and someone from...get this...CMT."

Since when did anyone at CMT even know she existed? "Did you do this?" she snapped.

"Did I do what?"

"Did you contact all of them to tell them to interview me?" The nerve of him!

He looked surprised. "Why in the hell would I do that?"

"For the same reason you put me on YouTube or made me get a manager or got me singing for Allied. Because you still think I'm going to be some...*star*."

Folding his arms over his chest, he drew his lips into a stern line and scowled at her. Her face heated in response, but she didn't glance away, meeting his eyes and holding them.

"I seem to remember," he finally said, "that I made you a promise not to do anything else without your permission."

"Yeah, well..." Savannah bit her tongue. They were both angry, and if she didn't guard her words, she'd be saying things she couldn't take back.

Brad's expression softened. "Look, you're upset. Stories like this come and go. I've learned to let stupid stuff from the press roll off my back."

"Probably because you've had a lot of experience." Damn, she hadn't meant to say that, nor had she intended the double meaning. Her mouth seemed to be a few seconds ahead of her common sense.

His eyes narrowed, telling her she'd hit a nerve. "You'll get thicker skin with time."

The tense scene was interrupted by the ringing of her cell. The only reason she didn't ignore it was the familiar ringtone—"Holding Out for a Hero." Fishing the phone from her pocket, she answered. "Hey, Greg. Just got the 'good' news from Brad. Now what?"

"And good morning to you, too."

The man had impeccable manners, and she'd violated one of his cardinal rules by not greeting him properly. "I'm sorry. Good morning. What can I do for you?"

He let out a small sigh. "I'm sorry, Savannah, but I've failed you."

"Sorry? Why would you be sorry?"

"I've tried hard to keep publicity low key, but I fear we can no longer hide in plain sight."

"I'm confused," she admitted. "What exactly are you talking about?"

"I have had calls from two national morning shows asking for you to appear."

Everything was spinning too fast for her to catch her breath. "I don't understand. Why all this attention? Why now?"

Greg's voice continued to buzz in her ear. "You've gone viral. That's all there is to it. The YouTube videos. The Allied publicity push. The word of mouth about your performances at Words and Music. It's all multiplying. Add that you're in a relationship with Brad, who's been out of the public eye for years. You've become the celebrity du jour."

* * *

Brad was tired of being on the outside of whatever was happening to the woman he loved. The *Watchdog* story had been a blow to his pride, probably because seeing all those names compiled like a team roster was humiliating. He could only assume Savannah was as disgusted with him as he was with himself. Had he kept his pants more firmly zipped, not only would he not have to see her looking at him with such sad eyes, he also wouldn't be the laughing-stock of Nashville.

"What did you tell them?" she demanded.

Brad couldn't wait a moment longer. "That's Greg, right?"

She gave him a curt nod.

"Put him on speaker."

Although she seemed miffed, probably at being ordered about, he didn't care. If he didn't know what was happening, he couldn't help solve her problems.

She did as he asked, holding the phone out so they could all participate in the conversation.

"You're on speaker, Greg," Savannah announced.

"Ah, then Brad is now listening in."

"Damn right," Brad replied. "Get me up to speed, if you don't mind."

"Please," Savannah added with a scolding gaze.

"Please," he parroted back.

"I was just telling Savannah," Greg replied, "that she is going to have to ride out this wave of publicity. So are you, my friend. The waters could get pretty choppy."

"I can handle it." Even as he said that, Brad wondered exactly how bad things were going to get. The press was already using his tawdry past against Savannah, and the more response they got from that tack, the more sensational the stories would grow. Not that they needed to be embellished. He'd given the press more than enough to work with.

Wallowing in self-pity wouldn't help her. He couldn't change his past, and he couldn't call off the dogs. Greg was right—Brad and Savannah would have to hold tightly to each other to get through this. Apologizing wasn't going to make anything change, so he focused on damage control. "Tell us what to do, Greg."

"Nothing," Greg replied. "Live your lives and don't talk to any reporters. I'll decline the offers—for now."

"Offers?" Brad asked.

"That's what I was explaining to Savannah. There are a couple of national news shows asking for interviews. I'll put them off until we need them."

"Why would we ever need them?" Savannah asked.

"If push comes to shove," Greg replied, "we might be able to put them to good use."

* * *

A week later and Brad began to understand what Greg had meant about putting the news shows to good use. Publicity had escalated. Evidently the combination of a man-whore songwriter and a mysterious, talented singer was irresistible. He was sick and tired of hearing about his past love life, but the stories just kept coming.

Greg had finally gotten fed up and decided it was time for Savannah to go on the offensive. An appearance on a national show could turn the tide in her favor. He'd booked an interview on *Wake Up, America*. Although Brad wanted to be at her side, Greg insisted she'd be better off on her own. Her petite size and vulnerable air would make it seem as though the paparazzi were ganging up on a poor little single mother. If Brad was there, his presence would invite the reporter to shift the attention to him and his past stupidity, something Greg wanted to minimize.

Brad was now nothing more than an anchor around her neck.

With a shake of his head, he turned his attention back to rehearsal. Savannah was struggling to find focus, and the song kept coming out wrong. Of course it was one of his songs—the last one he'd written in nearly a month. The gamut of emotions caused by the craziness in their lives had silenced the music in his mind. All that remained in his head was one thing: his love for Savannah.

"It's still not right." She set her guitar aside and looked back at Leah and Maggie.

They both protested, insisting she was fantastic, until her raised hand brought their false praise to a stuttering halt. "Brad?"

He went over to her and took her hand in his. "We'll work on it."

A world-weary sigh slipped out. "I appreciate the honesty."

"It'll be fine, love." Her phone rang right as he brushed a kiss on her lips. "Wind Beneath My Wings" told him her mother was calling. "You better get that."

Savannah answered, and in a matter of moments, she'd fallen into a panic. "Is she okay? Where are you now?" After listening for a few tense seconds, she nearly shouted, "I'm on my way!"

Brad steadied her by gripping her shoulders. "What's wrong?"

"Someone attacked Caroline."

CHAPTER TWENTY-SIX

Caroline handled things much better than her mother. Savannah couldn't help but admire her daughter's ability to cope with what had happened.

"Attack" had been too harsh a word. The men hadn't truly harmed Caroline. But at her tender age, having three photographers stalking her, shooting picture after picture as she walked in the park with her grandmother, had been frightening and was still giving Savannah nightmares.

The press had become relentless. Everywhere she and Brad went, they were hounded. The dark side of fame had descended almost as quickly as the fame itself. She could handle it touching her. Having that darkness reaching out to envelop Caroline?

That, she couldn't allow.

Brad fit his legs against hers as he snuggled up to her back. They often spooned as they slept. When they slept. His insomnia had become as bad as her own.

"You okay, sweetheart?" he whispered.

"Fine," she replied, trying not to grumble at him. The question, which he asked multiple times a day, had begun to fray her already taut nerves. Each new day found her on the verge of a panic attack, and she felt a little more of her self-control slipping away.

One more thing would surely push her over the edge, and God help whoever was in her way when that happened.

"Are you going to talk to *People* magazine?" he asked.

"Greg thinks I should. He knows the reporter and thinks she'll give the story the right spin—maybe get some of these bloodsuckers to lay off." *As if...* Now she understood why so many celebrities chose homes far away from the city. They needed their privacy. She was beginning to miss hers.

"Are you ready for *Wake Up, America?*"

Hardly. Savannah dreaded that appearance with every ounce of her being. But the day was fast approaching, and she had less than a week to brace herself. This interview was supposed to be her chance to deflect attention from her relationship with Brad and shift the focus to her music. That was Greg's plan, but she wasn't as confident of success as he and Brad were. "I'll be fine."

"'Fine.'" He scoffed. "Is that the only word you know lately?"

She craned her neck to glance back at him. "What do you want me to say?"

"Tell me the truth."

"The truth? I just wanted to have a nice steady job

singing. That was all. Instead..." She let her head fall back to the pillow. There wasn't anything Brad could do to repair the damage. Besides, he'd had only the best of intentions, even if he hadn't shared any of his plans with her to see how she felt. He'd gone right ahead and... "Sorry. I really am fine, baby. Okay?"

* * *

No, not okay.

But what was Brad supposed to do? He'd fucked up. There was no other word for it. In his desire to make her a star, he'd done exactly that.

And destroyed her life.

"I'm sorry," he said for what seemed like the millionth time.

"I know."

Waiting to see if she would tell him anything more, he struggled for the right thing to say, for the right thing to do. How could he make this better?

He couldn't. That was the problem. The genie was out of the bottle and he wasn't going to be able to stuff it back in. Greg was doing a good job of damage control, but no matter how much positive light he tried to shine on Savannah's career, the tabloids came back to one thing.

She was dating the Hitman, and he was the scum of the earth. A womanizer. None of the reporters bothered to talk about how he'd nursed Katie through that horrible time when she was dying. Highlighting anything that might paint him as a good guy wasn't nearly as important as finding names of his past sexual conquests.

Funny, that list was a lot longer than the true tally of the woman he'd actually been with. Wannabe singers were popping out of the woodwork to get their fifteen minutes of fame by talking about their torrid affairs with the Hitman. Their stories were at best exaggerated, at worst out-and-out lies. Lord knew she had enough on her plate at the moment.

Savannah's breaths became deep and even, meaning she was finally getting some sleep. Each day seemed to drain her a little more, and he was worried. He knew she was getting sick and tired of him asking how she was, but he couldn't help himself. She'd lost a little weight, something such a petite woman couldn't really afford. There were dark circles under her eyes. But the most obvious sign of her distress was in her voice.

When she sang, she'd lost some of the luster, some of the sparkle that made her so damned special. Her performances were mechanical. They were technically proficient, and yet they lacked the polish that had her first single selling like crazy. Ethan's opinion of her performance that night was that Savannah was "phoning it in." Brad agreed, but she was stressed enough. He wasn't about to tell her she needed to do something to get her groove back when he'd been the one to knock her down.

Savannah would be better off without me.

He wouldn't leave her. Oh, no. That would only be fuel on the fire. Nor would he push her away. He loved her too much to ever hurt her like that. So the poor woman was stuck with him as her albatross until she wised up enough to walk away.

* * *

Russ stormed into the office and tossed a paper on the desk. "Number twenty! Can you believe it?"

Brad picked up the paper. "*Billboard*?"

"Yep." Plopping on the couch, Russ grinned. "Maybe that'll put a smile back on our girl's face."

Since Russ refused to quit calling Savannah "our girl," Brad had given up trying to get him to stop. Had she been Russ's girl, she wouldn't be in the middle of this mess. But then again, she wouldn't be number twenty on the country chart with a bullet, either. "Maybe."

After the surprise Russ had just dealt him, Brad was ready for the day to settle down. Instead, Ethan came strolling in. "What are you doing here?" Brad asked.

"Isn't *that* a nice greeting?" Ethan shot him a glare. "Did you forget the monthly partners' meeting?"

A frantic glance to the desk calendar made Brad groan. "It's the first."

"Yep." Ethan took a seat next to Russ. "Time for our meeting. I call the three of us to order. Any new business?"

Russ jokingly raised his hand.

"I recognize the *junior* partner," Ethan quipped.

"I move that we promote Savannah to our headliner."

"Hmm." Ethan rubbed his chin. "I second. She's more than earned it."

Brad shook his head. "The last thing she needs is more pressure."

"What pressure?" Russ asked. "She's our headliner in everything but name only. She brings in the crowds. We might as well acknowledge it. And while we're at it, we could give the woman a raise appropriate to the amount of business she's brought to the place."

"If we do that," Ethan said with a wink, "we'll make her rich."

"She's going to be rich anyway." The words fell out in a grumble that Brad hadn't intended. He couldn't shake the guilt that great things were happening for Savannah because of him, but she hadn't wanted any of them.

Her intent had never been to make a fortune. She'd never wanted to be in *People* or on *Wake up, America*. Not once had she ever thought she'd be famous enough that the paparazzi would stalk her or her daughter. Yes, great things were happening—if a person wanted to surrender her privacy, her whole damn life, to the media.

"We're not doing anything without her consent," Brad insisted. A knock on the office door drew his attention. "Come in!"

Savannah was the last person he'd expected to see. When he'd left her that morning, she was intent upon driving Caroline to her parents' place and lying low for the day. The wan cast to her face made him pop to his feet. "What's wrong?"

With a trembling hand, she held out a packet of stapled papers that had once been folded like a business letter. "I can't believe this," she said, her voice as thin as a reed.

"Can't believe what?" Brad took the papers and tried to read the first page, but the words wouldn't register. "What the hell is this?"

"Michael is suing me. Says that I owe him agent fees for everything I've done since he walked out."

"*What?*" He started flipping through the pages as his anger climbed.

Ethan and Russ both rose and came over to see what Brad was reading.

"That bastard." He handed the papers to Ethan, who held them so both he and Russ could read the first page.

Ethan shook his head. "What a prick."

"The guy's got balls," Russ added. Then he smiled at Savannah. "Don't sweat this, honey."

"When this plays out, he'll be paying you back," Ethan said. "With interest."

"Or I could just break his legs for you," Russ offered with a goofy grin, although he was probably partly serious.

Unable to stand there and do nothing, Brad went to Savannah and pulled her into a hug. "It'll be fine, love." While there was no doubt any lawsuit brought by a man who'd stolen his client's money and abandoned his kid would be tossed right out of court, this was going to pile even more stress on her. Her slender shoulders were clearly overloaded as it was. "I know some really great lawyers."

"I already called Greg," she said, pushing away from him.

"Good," Brad said with a nod. Greg was well aware of Michael's checkered past. His advice, as always, was sure to be stellar. "What did he say?"

"He said his brother's a lawyer who has a lot of experience with entertainment law. I'm supposed to meet with them both after lunch."

"Good," he said again. "I'll get things done here and be ready to go with you."

"No, I can handle it," she insisted.

Of course she didn't need him. He'd caused her nothing but misery from the moment she'd stepped onto his stage. "I'd like to go with you, Savannah."

"I just figured . . . " Savannah shrugged. "It's fine if you're too busy."

"I'm never too busy for you, and you damn well know it." He was practically shouting. Both Ethan and Russ shot him scowls, which meant that his anger was obvious. "I've still got people trying to learn everything they can about Michael. It's been mostly blind alleys so far, but maybe something will pay off soon. Then we'll have more ammunition to use against the jerk. I'm doing everything I can to help you, Savannah."

Although her expression was resigned, she nodded.

"Do you want me to go?" he asked.

She thought it over for a few moments. "Your temper might get the better of you. Let me handle this one alone. Okay?"

He gave her a reluctant nod, and she quickly left the office.

After she was gone, Ethan went to the door she'd left open and closed it. Then he faced Brad. "What can I do to help?"

Since Brad had expected Ethan to scold him, he wasn't sure how to respond. He was still reeling from Savannah's choice to handle her ex by herself. He tried to rationalize her actions by attributing them to her being thoughtful of his need to be at Words & Music. "Not sure, but I'll let you know."

"Same here," Russ added. "I wanna help."

"The guy's a fucking moron," Brad said. "He steals her blind then thinks he can score more now that she's getting a name?"

"Not to mention all the back child support he owes her," Ethan added. "Not sure why he'd open that Pandora's box. I'd say his lawyer's a fucking moron, too."

"Some judge will throw it out," Russ insisted. "It'll never hit a courtroom."

While Brad was inclined to agree, he couldn't help but keep his cynicism. "Never say never."

CHAPTER TWENTY-SEVEN

The appointment went well, but Savannah couldn't seem to get her runaway anxiety under control. Greg's brother, Geoffrey, was every bit as composed and focused as Greg, and she had no doubt he was a good attorney. She'd given her trust to Greg, which meant she would offer it to his brother. Her only hope was that Michael might come to his senses before things got out of control.

She felt cornered. Trapped.

Greg put his hand on her shoulder. "This will work out, my dear."

"I sure hope so."

He gave her a squeeze before his hand dropped away. "I'm not saying this won't get a little...messy. But I do promise you that Geoffrey will not only bring an end to this frivolous civil suit, he will make Michael sorely regret harassing you."

While that sounded wonderful—to see Michael squirm—

she couldn't help but worry that anything that pissed him off might make him retaliate by interfering in their daughter's life. The last thing Caroline needed was that jerk hanging around confusing her. The girl had accepted her grandfather as the man in her life, the father figure she needed. If Savannah let her lawyer push Michael's buttons with threats, would he try to insert himself into Caroline's world?

Why would he? With Caroline came financial responsibility. The man was too damn greedy to share anything he had with anyone, let alone the daughter he'd abandoned. Savannah would just have to trust that Geoffrey would know the right thing to do, and maybe he could force Michael to crawl back under whatever rock he'd been using to hide. The man was never one to rise to a challenge. He was all about the quick score and moving on.

Brad would be waiting for her to check in. Her embarrassment had kept her from having him at her side. Every time she even thought about how naïve she'd been with Michael, she wanted to scream. No way she'd relive all that foolishness with the man she loved.

She waved farewell to Greg and settled in the driver's seat. Pulling her phone from her purse, she tried to think of what to text. The press had turned relentless, becoming almost crueler to Brad than to her. She'd had to go to great lengths to keep her life private, which meant in turn that he was hounded as well. Neither of them seemed to have a moment of privacy.

On Greg's advice, she was able to get her finances in good order. Her new home wouldn't be in her name, which would make it next to impossible for anyone to tie her to it. That house would be her haven, her place away from prying eyes. She, Brad, and Caroline could enjoy peace and quiet there.

At the moment, there was no peace. No quiet. There was only fear. Fear of whether Michael could truly slither back into her life. Fear for her daughter's well-being. And fear that this love she shared with Brad might come to an end. Not because she'd stopped caring for him. Far from it— she loved the man more every day. But her life was rapidly spiraling out of control, and she wouldn't allow him to be dragged under because of her.

If push came to shove, Savannah would walk away from Brad if it meant the firestorm of bad press about his past would follow her and not him. If he were no longer in- volved in her life, the reporters would tire of writing the same disgusting stories about him. They could focus on her—or maybe on whatever newest entertainer had some- thing juicy to report. The time might come when she had to leave him to save him, no matter how much it hurt.

Perhaps that time was drawing near...

* * *

When Savannah didn't text, Brad couldn't help but worry. She'd promised to send him a message as soon as she met with the lawyer. Although he'd wanted to be at her side, she had insisted that Michael was her problem. What she didn't seem to understand was that

Brad's love for her made her problems his problems.

Why couldn't he convince her of that?

Probably because she was disgusted with him—because of his past, which kept popping up in every story about her.

Brad couldn't shake the feeling that *he* should be her savior, her knight in shining armor. Instead, Greg and his brother were the ones leading the charge against her asshat ex while Brad spun his wheels, turning over every rock to try to find some dirt on Michael. Worse, Savannah seemed to need him less and less. And that hurt.

His phone chimed a text from Savannah.

Meet you at W&M

Twenty minutes later, he pulled his Escalade up next to her CR-V. It was the only thing she'd bought except for the house. Just another sign of her maturity. Most people, especially performers who came into a chunk of money, would probably blow it on things they didn't need. Frivolous things. Ridiculous things. Not Savannah. She worked closely with Greg to protect the funds she'd received as though she feared there would never be more coming her way. Brad admired that.

He got to her car fast enough to open the door for her. As soon as she was on her feet, he gave her a quick kiss that he wished could last longer. Not in public, not when there could be cameras pointed in their direction. He wasn't about to give them anything they could use against her.

Once inside, he led her to the office, hoping she'd open up about what had happened when she'd talked to Greg's brother, Geoffrey. What he got was silence as she sat on the couch, focused on her phone, and furiously texted someone—probably Joslynn.

"Savannah," he finally said.

She glanced up, frowning. "What?"

"Are you ever going to tell me what happened?"

"Sorry. I'm still a bit preoccupied. Geoffrey thinks a judge will throw out the lawsuit." A glance down to her phone. "He's hoping this won't last that long, though. He's talking to Michael's lawyer right now about a settlement."

"Your lawyer's texting you?"

"His secretary."

Things were happening much faster than Brad had thought possible. Maybe the storm he'd anticipated would end up being nothing more than a passing shower. Lord, how Savannah deserved a break. She barely slept now, and if she had to keep dealing with her ex, she was going to stress herself sick.

He wanted to share this burden. If only she'd let him...He took a seat next to her and draped his arm over her shoulders. "What can I do?"

She shook her head. "Geoffrey's taking care of it."

"For you, sweetheart. What can I do for *you*?"

"I'm fine."

If he heard that word one more time, he was going to blow his top. She was about as far from "fine" as she'd been in the whole time he'd known her. "How about we have friends over tonight?" he suggested. "Ethan has been wanting to cook for us."

She shook her head again, although she leaned a little closer. "I just wanna go home after the show."

"It's Tuesday, Savannah. There's no show tonight."

"Tuesday?" A frown bowed her lips as she gave him an incredulous frown. "Really?"

He nodded.

A forlorn sigh slipped from her lips. "I . . . I lost track."

"So we've got the night to ourselves," he said. "Let's do something that will make you smile again. Take Caroline swimming? Go catch a movie?"

Easing away from him, she got to her feet and shook her head. "Nothing's going to make me smile again until Michael goes away."

Even though Brad doubted a snake like that would simply disappear, he held his tongue. He'd never seen her so resigned, and he wasn't going to let his doubts add to her worries.

"If it's okay with you," she said, "I'd really like to go home and spend some time with Caroline."

"That sounds great. We can take her to—"

Before he could even tell Savannah his idea, she was already shaking her head. "I'm not going anywhere with her. There might be photographers."

"You can't live your life like a hermit."

She flashed him a glare. "Protecting my daughter doesn't make me a hermit."

"You are if you allow those bastard reporters to make you a prisoner in your own home."

"It's safe there."

"Safe? From what? A couple of stupid pictures? Who gives a shit?"

"*I* do," Savannah insisted. "*I* don't want Caroline to have any contact with the press."

"That's not going to be possible. You're a celebrity now, like it or not."

Folding her arms over her chest, she narrowed her eyes. "Oh, I *don't* like it. I don't like it one damn bit."

Ah. So that's the way of it.

The blame was plain in her angry tone, and the fight they'd been sidestepping ever since that first story had appeared threatened again. "And it's all *my* fault," he drawled as he stood up. "You're rich and famous because I'm an asshole and made you that way. What in the hell was I thinking?" He waited a beat for emphasis. "Oh, I remember. You wanted to be a singer and I had the audacity to let people know you were a talented one. Damn me to hell for that."

"Stop it."

Brad's temper was rapidly rising. "No, I won't stop it. I'm tired of stopping it. We need to talk about this or we're never going to get past it. I can't keep apologizing forever. Either you need to forgive me and accept that what's done is done or I need to—"

"To what, Brad? To leave? Like Michael?"

"I didn't say that," he insisted, folding his arms over his chest.

"Not yet."

"Not ever. I love you, Savannah."

"But..."

"But I'm tired of being punished for doing what I thought was the right thing." He splayed his fingers through his hair before putting his hands on his hips. "I made a lot of mistakes. I assumed too much. I should've asked you what you wanted before I went balls out to get you noticed. It's all water under the bridge now. I can't change any of it."

The more he thought about her situation, about her career, the more he saw her becoming famous as inevitable. How could a woman with a voice like hers ever expect to be nothing but a warm-up act? Or sing commercial jingles? Or back up some other singer who wasn't as good as she was? Everything that had happened in her career had been bound to happen someday. All his songs and efforts had done was to propel her into the spotlight sooner rather than later.

* * *

Savannah closed her eyes and let her head fall back. She was being unreasonable. While she wanted to blame Michael, for the first time, he deserved no blame. This was her own doing. Things were out of control, and she was taking her frustration out on Brad.

She'd forgiven him a long time ago. So why was she picking a fight about something so ancient?

Fear. Plain and simple. Michael terrified her. She couldn't help but worry that there was more to his return than wanting money from her.

She breathed a heavy sigh. "I'm sorry. I didn't mean... I'm just...frustrated."

His frowned eased. "As you have every right to be."

A text came in, startling her. She checked her phone. Geoffrey's secretary was texting her again.

Finally got info. Call when you can.

In a panic, she dialed Geoffrey's office. Penelope answered. "Savannah! Thanks for getting back to me so quickly. Geoffrey needs you to come back to the office at five."

"Why?"

"Like I texted, I've got some info for you. My boss had a rather lengthy chat with opposing counsel. Your ex hired Tom Cummings. Not the brightest crayon in the box, according to Geoffrey. But it seems as though this lawsuit can disappear if you'll just do one thing."

Typical Michael. Divert attention from his true purpose. "And what exactly is this 'one thing'?"

"He wants to talk to you face-to-face."

A foreboding chill raced the length of her spine. "Why?"

"That," Penelope replied, "I'm afraid I don't know."

"But we'll be with Geoffrey, right?" Savannah asked as she held up a hand to Brad, who was hovering over her. "I won't be alone with that son of a...with Michael."

"That's my understanding."

So he just expected her to show up to a meeting and that would be the end of his lawsuit? Things were never that easy with him. Ever.

Yet if there was a chance, even a slim one, she had to act. "Fine. What time did you say?"

"Five. If you're sure..."

"I am. I'll be there." She glanced at Brad, realizing that she needed him by her side. "And I'm bringing Brad."

"I'm really sorry, Savannah, but you can't," Penelope insisted.

"Why not?"

"You're allowed to have Geoffrey because he represents you, but Cummings was adamant that you not bring Brad. He said Michael would walk out if Brad's there."

Figures. When she needed Brad's support the most, Michael was going to make sure she'd be defenseless. "Fine. I'll let him have his way. See you at five."

"We'll see you then," Penelope said.

Savannah ended the call before she could change her mind.

Still looming over her, Brad asked, "Where are we going?"

She faced him. "I have to go back to see Geoffrey at five, but you can't go."

"Why not?"

"It's Michael. He wants to talk to me. Alone. Evidently, this meeting might make all this lawsuit crap disappear." Not that she was convinced the man was telling the truth. Why would he start now? "We'll have to skip tonight."

Brad shook his head. "I'm going with you," he insisted.

"I want you there, I do, but Michael said if you come, the meeting's off. If there's a chance to make this all go away, I need to take it."

"I'm going with you," he said through gritted teeth.

"Please don't get mad." She made a point of checking her watch. "I need to go. I want to see Caroline before I head back downtown."

"Look, can I at least wait in the lobby?" As usual, he was going to be obstinate.

"You'll just piss him off," she insisted.

He let out a snort. "Like that would bother me."

"Brad..." It was hard to be stern when she really wanted him at her side.

"I'm going, Savannah. I'll stay out of the meeting and sit in the lobby like a good boy. But I'm going. And that's the end of the discussion."

She found her first smile of the day. On tiptoes, she kissed him to let him know how much his stubbornness pleased her.

CHAPTER TWENTY-EIGHT

Savannah took a moment to compose herself. The man who'd tried to ruin her life waited behind the door she was poised to open. She would face him.

Then she would drive him back to wherever he'd come from.

She was so damned tired of always giving Michael exactly what he wanted. Not anymore. A hand settled on her shoulder, and she remembered she didn't have to wage this battle alone. She glanced back to see Brad offering a weak smile. Behind him, Geoffrey, with Greg at his side, conferred with Penelope at her desk.

"You ready for this?" Brad asked, his voice soft.

Once they'd arrived, she'd made up her mind that he wasn't going to be left behind during the meeting. No, Brad would be with her when she needed him most. She fired her first shot in the battle. "I've decided I want you in this meeting with me."

"That could cause some trouble," Brad pointed out.

"God, I hope so." Despite the show of strength, she shivered, rubbing her upper arms.

"He's only a man, love. Nothing more."

"Meaning?"

Brad squeezed her shoulder. "Don't build him up to be more than he is. That man stole your money and abandoned his kid, but he's not some supervillain. He also isn't very smart."

"How do you know that?"

"First, he gave up something as great as you and Caroline, and second, he thinks this lawsuit is a smart move."

"We'll bury him," Geoffrey said as he joined them.

Greg, who had been waiting in the law office when she and Brad arrived, was only a few steps behind, nodding. The brothers resembled each other enough to be twins, and their mother had obviously instilled impeccable manners in them both. Savannah was beyond grateful to have them on her side.

The confidence in her lawyer's voice and the not-so-gentle reminder from Brad gave her the strength she needed to face the devil.

No, not the devil. *Just Michael.* Michael Hart.

The biggest asshole in the whole world.

She'd been such a fool to be involved with him in the first place. Naïve and young, she hadn't seen him for who he truly was. Instead, she'd listened to his name-dropping and pie-in-the-sky schemes and thought he was experienced and influential when he'd been neither. Swearing up and down that she'd be a superstar, he made her believe that was her destiny. He'd also done a good job of playing the part of dutiful boyfriend—until Savannah had told him she might be pregnant.

Then his mask had fallen away. He left her before she could work up the guts to leave him.

Geoffrey stepped in front of her and opened the door to his conference room. "Ms. Wolf, after you."

The men followed her inside the opulent room.

A large walnut table with heavy, carved legs took up a great deal of the space. At the head waited a wooden chair with velvet padding that was much larger than the other seven. *Geoffrey's seat, no doubt.* At the other end of the table, Michael sat with an older man, judging from his gray hair. She let her eyes meet Michael's.

He hadn't changed much in the six years since she'd seen him. Still lanky, he looked in need of a good meal. She knew the truth, though. He ate like a starving piglet, but he had a fast metabolism. Much as she'd wished his black hair would've fallen out, she had to admit he was still a rather handsome man. Thick hair. Clear brown eyes. A small cleft in his chin. But when he smiled, everything attractive about him faded. That grin was so fake, so slick, she could easily see a forked tongue darting out between his lips.

For some weird reason that image eased some of her worries. Brad was right—Michael was only a man. She'd grown up and learned a lot about the world since she'd last seen him. She'd already let him hurt her enough.

His effect on her life was over.

Michael popped to his feet. "Why is *he* here?" He rudely pointed at Brad.

Before Savannah could reply, Geoffrey put his hand on her shoulder. "If you will kindly sit down, Mr. Hart, we shall explain everything."

"I told you he couldn't come," Michael insisted.

"And I really don't care what you told me. I want him here," Savannah countered. The bravado wasn't easy because of Michael's red-faced anger.

"No. No way."

Savannah glanced to Greg. "Then this meeting is over."

All Greg did was give her a brusque nod, although she caught the hint of a grin.

Michael's lawyer stood and leaned closer to him, whispering a few things. After a few tense moments, the two of them finally sat back down.

"Fine," Michael said. "Have it your way."

Savannah had to bite back a smile.

Geoffrey calmly took his seat at the head of the table as Brad helped her settle in the chair to her lawyer's right. Greg sat on Geoffrey's left, and Brad took the open seat next to Savannah.

Plucking the file that rested on the table, Geoffrey opened it, cleared his throat, and then began. "This meeting isn't a formal proceeding, but I would like each and every one of us to speak as though we were under oath." He effectively arched a gray eyebrow. "Is everyone agreed?"

There was murmuring of promise among the attendees, although she couldn't help but notice that Michael remained silent.

No surprise there. The man didn't have an honest bone in his body. Had he held his hand on a Bible and sworn to tell the truth, she still wouldn't believe him.

"Good. Now..." Geoffrey looked at Michael's attorney. "Perhaps introductions would be the best way to proceed. I am Geoffrey Jorgenson, attorney for the defendant, Savannah Wolf. To my left is Gregory Jorgenson, Ms. Wolf's manager."

"*I'm* still her manager," Michael insisted. "We never terminated our agreement."

Before Geoffrey could respond, Michael's lawyer motioned him closer and a few soft but angry words were exchanged.

His lawyer leaned back and said, "Apologies for the interruption. Please continue."

Although he was frowning, Geoffrey nodded to Brad. "This is Brad Maxwell, an interested party who is here at Ms. Wolf's invitation."

Narrowing his eyes, Michael leaned closer to his attorney again, whispering in his ear. He continued until Geoffrey loudly cleared his throat again. Then Michael's attorney said, "My client is concerned that we have an uninvolved party in this conference. Frankly, we asked when we called for this meeting for him to stay away, and we would like Mr. Maxwell to leave."

Brad leaned back, crossing his arms over his chest.

Savannah shook her head. "He's here; he's staying. He goes; I go."

Geoffrey waved the notion away. "As I said, he's a interested party and—"

"I know all about who he is. He's her *boyfriend*," Michael announced with a sneer.

Geoffrey folded his hands on top of the file. "Quite frankly, if Ms. Wolf wishes him to be here, his relationship with her is irrelevant and of no concern to you. That being said, my client has made her position clear. Do we proceed with this conference, or do we meet again when depositions are scheduled?"

Michael's attorney said something to his client and then cut him off with a clipped, "He stays."

"Now, if we may proceed," Geoffrey said.

"I'm Tom Cummings," the lawyer announced. "Y'all know my client, Michael Hart."

Geoffrey picked up the top page. "I believe we need to hear from the plaintiff on his rationale for filing this rather... unexpected suit." He swept his hand across the paper. "I must admit I'm a bit perplexed at why Mr. Hart believes he's owed anything at all. From my forensic accountant's examination of Ms. Wolf's financial documents dating back to the time she was associated with Mr. Hart, my opinion is that Ms. Wolf has good cause to seek her own suit."

"We had a contract that never ended," Michael insisted, brushing aside his attorney's hasty attempt to hush him. "She's making a shit-ton of money, and she owes me my thirty percent. I'm her manager."

Savannah was poised to launch a verbal attack at him when Greg put his hand over hers and gave her a curt shake of his head.

"As part of discovery," Geoffrey said, "I will of course ask to see the executed management contract."

A flush spread over Michael's face. "We had a verbal agreement."

An easy smile spread over Geoffrey's face. "Ah. A *verbal* agreement. Did that verbal agreement happen to give Mr. Hart the authorization to remove all the funds in the checking and savings accounts he shared with Ms. Wolf?"

When Michael tried to answer, Tom stopped him with a slash of his hand. "We're not here to discuss any personal matters between the parties, which includes funds that both parties had access to and the ability to remove without the other's permission. What we want is what's due my client per their managerial agreement, which is what she's earned in performances and recordings. The agreement he has with Miss Wolf is that he will receive thirty percent of—"

Brad let out a jeer. "Thirty percent? What kind of manager gets *thirty* percent?"

"This one does," Michael replied. "The best."

"Oh?" Brad shook his head with a rueful snort. "Then you're the reason why she's recording for Allied Sound? You're the reason she's rising on the charts? Don't make me laugh."

"Damn right I'm the reason," Michael said. "She got her start in this business because of me." He jabbed his thumb against his chest. "I deserve a piece of the pie."

"Gentlemen, please," Geoffrey said. "Let's keep things civil."

Greg chimed in for the first time. "Thirty percent would be considered robbery by any reputable manager or agent."

"It's what she agreed to," Michael retorted with a shrug.

"Mr. Hart, I would assert that you leaving my client and absconding with all funds available to both parties would bring an abrupt end to whatever verbal agreement existed between you two." Geoffrey shuffled through the papers in the file and pulled one out. He slid it neatly down the table to have it come to rest in front of Michael. "I also believe we need to discuss another couple of issues."

Michael picked up the paper and his eyes widened. "You've gotta be kidding me."

With a rather wicked smile, Geoffrey said, "I never *kid*, Mr. Hart. From my accountant, we've determined that you currently owe Ms. Wolf back child support, including interest, in the amount of—"

"I didn't want a kid!" Michael shouted. "I'm not paying Savannah a dime for any child support! She was careless enough to get knocked up—"

His lawyer interrupted him with an angry glare and a "Stop it" that might have been whispered but contained quite a bit of censure. Then he directed his attention to Geoffrey. "The issue of Mr. Hart's representation and whether he is culpable for child support are unrelated."

"I disagree," Geoffrey retorted. "You're asking for funds

you believe are owed your client; I'm simply returning the favor."

* * *

Brad began to tune out the chess match of negotiations between the two lawyers before his blood pressure skyrocketed. Geoffrey seemed to have things well in hand, and he hadn't even used his trump card yet—the card Brad's research had given him. Instead, he focused on sizing up Michael Hart.

The guy was a prick through and through. What Brad couldn't understand was why Savannah had fallen for him in the first place. The man was arrogant, pigheaded, and seemed to believe that his opinions were fact. Not once did he admit he was wrong in the way he'd treated Savannah. He spoke about Caroline as if she were some unwanted burden, which made Brad's blood boil.

Then he realized what truly bothered him the most. His own personality held far too many similarities. The burst of self-awareness was unwelcome and uncomfortable. Hell, he'd done all the same sorts of things to the poor woman. The career he'd tried to build for her had been his creation, not her own design.

One huge difference made him find some hope. It was plain that Michael never truly loved Savannah. From what Brad could see, the idiot was a narcissist, caring for no one but himself. Brad loved Savannah. He loved Caroline. He would never hurt them. Every dime Savannah earned was hers to use as she wished, and Greg did exactly what she wanted him to do and charged her a reasonable manager's fee. Otherwise Brad would never have introduced them.

I'm not like Michael Hart. I'm not.

Having lost himself in thought, Brad was taken by surprise when Michael shoved his chair back and jumped to his feet. His fist slammed down on the table. "I'm sick and tired of this. I want what's due me."

While Tom tugged at Michael's shirtsleeve, Geoffrey calmly said, "Get a hold of your client or this meeting is over."

Michael brushed his attorney's hand away. He directed a glare at Savannah. "Know this, Savannah. If you don't give me what I'm due, I'm going to make your life a living hell. Think the press is bad now? I've only just gotten them started."

"What are you talking about?" she asked, the confusion plain in her voice.

He jerked his thumb in Brad's direction. "Who do you think told them all the dirt on this moron? I still have lots of friends in the press. Friends who can destroy you. After that's done, then do you know what I'll do, *sweetheart*?"

Geoffrey was on his feet, as were Brad and Greg.

"Stop your threats right now, Mr. Hart," Geoffrey said as he pulled his phone from his jacket's breast pocket, "or I'll be forced to call the—"

Michael kept right on as though Geoffrey were nothing more than an annoying insect. "If I don't get my money, I'll use all that dirt to take the kid away from you. So find a way to pay me what I deserve, or you'll be sorry." Turning on his heel, he strode out of the office, his sputtering attorney following in his wake.

A moment later, Penelope came dashing into the conference room wide-eyed with phone in hand. "Is everyone okay? I'm going to call security."

"No need," Geoffrey replied as he slid his phone back into his jacket. After taking his seat, he gestured for everyone else to do the same. "I believe Mr. Hart will be well away before security could even get here. But thank you, Penelope."

"You're welcome." She closed the door behind her as she left the conference room.

Brad took Savannah's hand in his, angry that she was trembling. "He's all talk, Savannah."

She didn't respond, looking to Geoffrey with pleading eyes that made Brad wish he would have grabbed Michael and punched him in the mouth.

"While I'd like to tell you that he's all talk," Geoffrey said, "we need to do our best to be prepared should he follow through with any of his threats."

"Could he really take Caroline away?" she asked in a whisper-soft voice.

"No, I don't believe so," Geoffrey replied. "He might *try*, but I doubt there's a judge in the entire state who would ever grant that man custody. Visitation, however limited, might be approved."

Greg frowned. "I should've realized there was someone fanning the fires behind all the bad press."

"How could you have known?" Brad asked. "That jackass might have set a few dogs on us, but the reporters were the ones that turned it into a feeding frenzy."

"Brad is right," Geoffrey said. "Mr. Hart is claiming far too much credit." He put a gentle hand on her shoulder. "I do have to ask, Savannah, are you at all amenable to offering some kind of financial settlement simply to make this problem disappear?"

"You mean buy him off?" Brad asked.

"Unseemly as it sounds, that's exactly what I'm saying."

Greg said, "Would you even consider that, Savannah?"

When she took a while to answer, Brad had his say. "Don't forget what he stole from you—already." He turned to Geoffrey. "Why would you even suggest something like that?"

"Because it's my job to represent my client's best interests. In a perfect world, justice would be served and Mr. Hart would be forced to repay what he clearly owes Savannah. Unfortunately, this isn't a perfect world. Sometimes throwing some grease at a squeaking wheel is the easiest solution to a problem."

"Easiest," Savannah finally said. "But not necessarily best. The man has one big problem that a financial settlement wouldn't eliminate."

"And that is?" Geoffrey asked.

"He's never satisfied. Nothing is ever enough. If I toss some money at him just to make him go away, it would only ensure he'd be back wanting more in the future."

Greg nodded. "I have to agree. I might also add that

you're obviously in a much better financial state than you were before we began to work together, but you work hard for what you have. The man doesn't deserve your hard-earned money."

"*Again*," Brad added. "He's already stolen from you once. I wouldn't let him do it a second time."

Her forlorn sigh hit him like a punch in the gut. "I can't let him threaten my daughter."

Brad gave her hand a squeeze. "Geoffrey won't let him near Caroline." He shifted his gaze to the lawyer. "Will you?"

Surprisingly, Geoffrey shook his head. "Where it comes to child custody, I can't make promises like that. Should he follow through and try to sue for visitation rights or custody, all I can do is attempt to get the court to understand why that man would be a detrimental influence on Caroline's life."

Savannah paled. "You mean he'd have a chance to take her away?"

"Not a real chance," Brad replied. "No way."

"A *slim* chance," Geoffrey clarified. "Very, very slim, but in all honesty, he *would* have a chance. No one can ever predict what a judge will do when everything is said and done, and the man is, unfortunately, her biological father."

The change in her was so subtle that Brad doubted the other men saw it. Her lips pulled into a thin line as she tightened her jaw. He knew that look well—it was determination.

Good. That meant she was finally realizing that she could

fight Michael and win. Once she set her mind to something, she'd always get it done.

Geoffrey gathered the papers together, placed them in the folder, and closed it. "Might I suggest we meet again on Friday morning and talk about drawing up battle plans for how we can handle whatever Michael Hart throws our way?"

Greg checked the calendar on his phone. "Ten works for me. Savannah?"

"Fine." Her reply was curt. She didn't even check her calendar.

"It'll be fine, love," Brad said.

She didn't even wait for him to pull her chair out for her, jumping to her feet, grabbing her purse, and slinging it over her shoulder. "I need to go." Without another word, she left even as Brad tried to call her back.

Sometimes Savannah needed her space, and if he chased after her like a puppy, it might make things worse. He was left staring at the brothers. "Should I go after her?"

"Let her breathe," Greg replied. "She probably just needs a moment." He rolled his eyes. "What a waste of air that man is."

"Agreed," Geoffrey said.

"Money can bring out the worst in people," Greg added.

Brad let out a snort. "Worst is all that guy has to offer."

"Well, then..." Geoffrey pushed his chair back and rose. "It will be my job to make sure he stays as far away from Savannah and Caroline as possible."

CHAPTER TWENTY-NINE

Brad didn't officially hit panic mode until sixteen hours had passed.

He'd left Savannah's house around nine the night before. Not because he wanted to, but because she told him she was tired and really wanted some time alone to process everything that had happened in Geoffrey's office. Even though he thought she needed him more than she was willing to say, he'd reluctantly given her what she wanted.

Now he regretted it.

At first, he'd just been irritated with her. He'd texted when he got home to tell her he loved her and remind her that he was in her corner. After the confrontation with Michael, she'd been rattled. No wonder. The guy had tossed around threats like cheap confetti. So Brad had made a point of trying to encourage her about the situation, telling her repeatedly that things were going to turn out fine in the end. Something he believed to be true.

Each time he tried to reassure her, Savannah only seemed to grow more distant. And she didn't return his last text of the night, in which he told her again how much he loved her and how he would be there no matter what happened.

And then the weapon he'd been searching for had finally arrived. Just as Brad had suspected, Michael's business dealings with other clients had been every bit as deceitful as his representation of Savannah. His private investigators now had three separate sworn affidavits from performers Michael had defrauded and were wrapping up two more statements. Having those would give Savannah the upper hand.

But Brad hadn't even had a chance to tell her the news, because she'd disappeared. He hadn't been able to get in touch with her by any means. His texts went unanswered, as did his phone calls. When he dialed her number, his call went immediately to voice mail. The first messages he left were pleasant, but with each new message, he could hear his tone growing angrier and then becoming frantic.

Now, he sat in his office, staring at his cell as he willed Savannah to respond. He called her number one more time.

"This is Savannah Wolf. I'm not available—"

"Fuck this."

He dialed Joslynn.

She answered on the fourth ring. "Hi, Brad."

"Savannah's not answering her phone."

"Did she let her battery run out again?" She sounded sleepy.

He'd forgotten she was working night shifts at the hospital. "Sorry to wake you. I'm just really worried about her."

"Let me try to call her. Hold on."

The seconds ticked by slowly as he waited to see if Savannah was avoiding him and would talk to Joslynn.

She came back on the line. "Went right to voice mail. Want me to go to her place?"

"No," Brad replied. "I'll check with a couple of other people, then I'll head over there."

"Please text me when you find her. I'll never get back to sleep now."

"I'm sorry I bothered you," he said. His worries for Savannah were making his stomach churn. "I'll keep you posted, and please let me know if you hear from her."

His next call was to Greg, who answered on the second ring. "How are you this afternoon, Brad?"

"Have you talked to Savannah today?"

"I'm quite well, thanks for asking."

Not in the mood for another lesson in civility, Brad drummed his fingers on the desk. "I'm freaking out here, Greg. She won't take any of my calls, and she won't return my texts."

"Might I ask if you two are quarreling?"

"Why would you think that?" Brad asked.

Greg let out a sigh. "I could see some . . . tension between the two of you yesterday."

"Tension?" Sure, things were a bit rough at the meeting, but only because that jackass had been terrorizing Savannah. "There wasn't any tension."

"Look, I won't get involved in your quarrel—"

"We're not quarreling!"

"*But*...I will try her number again—"

"Again? She hasn't returned your calls, either?" The panic that was already flooding Brad's senses rose a notch higher.

"I've left her two messages," Greg replied. "Let me try again and call you right back."

Although Brad was tempted to give Greg a lesson in putting a call on hold, he let it slide. Teaching older people technology always made him feel as if he were banging his forehead against a wall. He texted Savannah again while he waited.

No response.

"Well?" Brad said the moment his phone signaled Greg's call.

"She didn't answer." The worried tone in Greg's voice and the fact he hadn't scolded Brad's bad manners spoke volumes. He was every bit as worried about her as Brad was. "I left another message to have her call me. I was rather insistent this time. Would you please contact me when you get in touch with her?"

"Yep. You do the same, okay?" Brad asked.

"I will. Try to relax. She's fine."

"I sure as hell hope so." Getting to his feet, he strode to the door and stuck his head into the hallway. "Russ!"

No one replied.

With an exasperated growl, he headed out to the restaurant to see if Russ had arrived for his shift. Lately, Brad had turned more of the responsibilities of running Words & Music to Russ so he could spend more time with Savannah and Caroline. Not only did that benefit Brad, but it kept Russ from going overboard on his "bouncer" role. Weekends could get a little crazy, and it seemed more and more that Russ enjoyed getting rough when a patron got out of hand.

Russ wasn't in the restaurant, so Brad kept hunting for him, finally finding him having a rather terse conversation with one of the new waitresses. He liked to teasingly complain that Brad had robbed him of one of the best members of the waitstaff when Savannah had become a performer.

Although he should've waited until Russ finished scolding the woman, Brad butted into their exchange. "I need you to take over for a while." On that, he turned to leave, figuring he'd start getting some of the answers to Savannah's disappearance at her new house.

Russ dragged him to a stop after only a few steps. "What in the hell is wrong with you?"

Brad stared at the restraining hand on his upper arm until Russ released him. "I need to talk to Savannah."

A goofy grin filled Russ's face. "There's this great new invention. It's called a cell phone. You can get in touch with people who aren't with you instead of hunting them down."

"Can it, smartass. She won't pick up."

The grin grew. "So what d'ya do to piss her off?"

Why did everyone seem to think he and Savannah were

fighting? "Nothing. Look, I gotta go." His tone sounded desperate, even to himself.

Any sign of amusement left Russ's expression. "What's wrong? Is our girl in trouble?"

"I don't know. I haven't talked to her since last night. She won't answer her phone."

"Did you text?" Russ asked.

While Brad wanted to blister his friend's ear with a heavy dose of sarcasm, he simply nodded. "I'm heading to her place."

"Want me to go with?"

Brad shook his head. "I need you here."

"Fine. Text me when you find her. And give her a bit of a lecture for making us worry."

Marching to the parking lot, Brad couldn't control his fear. Something was wrong, something beyond Savannah just being upset. He hadn't slept well because he'd been worried about how she would react when she had time to think. That was his mistake. He'd left her alone with her worries, and when she worried, logic escaped her. Now he had no idea what was flying through her busy mind.

Was she with Geoffrey, working on their strategy to take down Michael? That might explain why he couldn't get her to answer. She'd silenced her phone to talk to her lawyer.

A few voice commands completed a call to the law office.

"Jorgenson, MacKenzie, and Miller."

"Penelope?"

"Yes. May I help you?"

"It's Brad Maxwell. From the meeting yester—"

"I remember you, Mr. Maxwell. Please hold for Mr. Jorgenson."

"But—" Why was she having him talk to Geoffrey?

Unless Savannah's there...

"Brad?" Geoffrey's deep voice rumbled.

"Yeah, it's me. May I speak to Savannah? She's not answering her phone."

"She's not here. I can't get her to return any of my calls or Penelope's calls or texts, either. Do you know where she is? We had a meeting planned and—"

"She's not there?"

"I just said she's not," Geoffrey snapped. "I was about to call my brother. Frankly, I'm getting worried."

"You and me both."

"When was the last time you spoke to her?"

"I left her place at nine last night," Brad replied. "Nothing since. I'm heading back there now."

"Would you please let me know when you find her?" Geoffrey asked.

"Sure thing." Brad ended the call and pushed harder on the accelerator, deciding speed limits were more of a suggestion than a rule.

* * *

After letting himself into the townhouse, Brad tore through it. His frustration grew when he found no one home. He'd already searched through the new house, but

Savannah hadn't officially moved in yet. Most of her stuff there was still in boxes, and nothing appeared to be at all disturbed. So he'd headed to the town house.

For a moment, he considered busting the realtor's lockbox to get the key. What good would that do? She wasn't there.

So where the hell was she?

His chest tightened as he agonized over her safety. Had she and Caroline been in a car accident? Was she too incapacitated to contact him?

Since when did he become such a basket case?

Since he fell in love with Savannah. She was his whole world now. There wasn't anything he wouldn't do for her, nothing he wouldn't give up. No matter what the future brought, he would never leave her.

Unless she asked him to. He refused to be a weight around her neck.

But would she leave him?

God, he had to stop thinking like that.

His phone signaled a call from Ethan. Once it became apparent that Savannah was missing, Brad had asked Russ to contact everyone he could think of to try to track her down.

"Did you find her yet?" Ethan asked the moment Brad answered.

The question made Brad's stomach knot. He'd hoped a call meant new information. "Not yet. Nothing on your end, I take it?"

"I'm driving in to the restaurant now. Russ mobilized

Leah and Maggie, and with their connections, we'll find her by suppertime."

Yeah, right. Savannah was gone, and it was becoming more and more clear that she didn't want anyone to know where she was. "I checked both houses. They're empty."

"Did someone talk to Caroline's school?"

"They wouldn't give me any information about whether she's there or not. Privacy bullshit or something. I don't have the Wolfs' number, so I'm heading to their place now. Maybe she's there and just forgot her phone somewhere or something." That sounded lame even to him.

"Let me know when you find her," Ethan said. "Then I can give her a piece of my mind for worrying us."

"You're worried, too?" Ethan's concern—added to Geoffrey's and Greg's—made Brad feel less like a panicky fool. When he tried to apply rationality to the situation, he knew she hadn't been gone all that long. But his gut told him something was wrong, and he would do what he had to do to find her. If it turned out he'd overreacted, so be it.

Wouldn't be the first time.

* * *

A sigh of relief escaped when Brad saw the Wolfs' distinctive car in the driveway. The navy blue PT Cruiser had old-fashioned wood panels along the sides, making him think of the "woody" station wagons his parents had owned when he'd been a child.

He'd come to care deeply for Mary and Paul Wolf. He hadn't realized how much until it dawned on him that he was going to have to break the news of Savannah's disappearance to them. No doubt they'd be devastated.

The only reason he didn't hesitate was because he was desperate to get this over and done with so he could glean as much information from them as possible and then get back to the hunt for Savannah. With a hard swallow, he punched the doorbell.

A few moments later, Mary opened the door, a look of resignation on her face as though he'd been expected. "Please. Come in." She glanced back at her husband, who was walking into the foyer. "Do you have the letter, Paul?"

Shifting his gaze between Paul and Mary, Brad frowned. "You're not surprised I'm here."

"We were going to call you," Mary said, "but Savannah didn't give us your number before she left. I was going to call the restaurant soon if you didn't stop by."

"She gave us this letter for you before she left," Paul added, holding out a sealed envelope.

A little of the tightness in Brad's chest eased. "So you know where she is now?"

The Wolfs exchanged a glance that reeked of conspiracy.

Since they weren't going to betray whatever secret they were protecting for their daughter, Brad focused on the envelope. He ripped it open and took out a handwritten letter. In Savannah's distinctive feminine handwriting was the message she'd left for him.

My dearest Brad,

By the time you read this, I'll be gone. Please try to understand why I have to do this. I can't let Michael ruin Caroline's life. I just can't. So I'm taking her away.

I love you. I will always love you. But you can't leave the life you've made for yourself here in Nashville. Words & Music means everything to you, and you could never leave it behind.

I'm sorry for all I've put you through. I'm sorry if the horrible stories from the press made it hard for you. It seems that the moment your life got tangled up in mine, things went downhill for you. I love you too much to keep ruining your life. It's hard to love someone so much and know that you're hurting them. You're better off without me.

My life isn't my own anymore. I don't want to be someone who spends the rest of her days trying to protect her privacy and hide her child away from prying eyes.

I can't let Michael win again.

My heart is breaking, but I know you will be better off without me.

Love,
Savannah

Brad had to close his eyes for a moment to reclaim some kind of calm. While he was thrilled to know she was safe, he still had no idea where she'd run to. At least he took some solace in the fact she hadn't left him because of something he'd done. She'd fled to protect her daughter and to escape the press Michael had shoved into her path.

She was dead wrong to believe she'd ruined his life. Her love for him had saved him.

So now it was up to him to make this all right again.

He opened his eyes and stared hard at Mary. "You know where she is. Tell me."

Dread was plain in her eyes—blue eyes so like Savannah's. "Brad...I can't—"

"Oh, yes you can." He clenched the letter, crumpling it in his fist. "I need to find Savannah so I can help her get all this...this...*mess* straightened out."

Paul shook his head. "We're not letting Michael take Caroline."

"That jerk doesn't have a snowball's chance in hell of taking Caroline away from her mother," Brad couldn't help but point out. "Don't you see that she has to come back or she's going to make it worse?"

"What do you mean?" Mary asked.

"By running away, she's playing right into Michael's hands," Brad replied. "The moment he finds out she went into hiding with Caroline, he'll tell reporters that Savannah *kidnapped* his daughter. The paparazzi will go ape-shit over that kind of story. They'll crucify her. And worse, it might give Michael ammunition to take custody of Caroline. You don't want him using our girl like a pawn."

With a furtive frown at Paul, Mary said, "But she swore us to secrecy."

"Brad's right, Mary," Paul said, putting a gentle hand on

his wife's arm. "Savannah didn't think this through. I told her that. I told her this wasn't gonna bring her anything but trouble, but..." He shrugged as he caught Brad's gaze. "You know how she is once she gets something in her head."

"Where *is* she?" Brad asked again, trying not to shout. "I'll get her back before anyone even knows she's gone."

Unfortunately, Mary didn't still appear convinced. "I don't know...Savannah said—"

"Savannah's not thinking straight," Brad insisted. "She's just upset about Michael's threats. *Please.* Just tell me where she is, and I'll go bring her back."

Paul took Mary's hand. Then he said to Brad, "My sister has a cabin up in the Smokies. It's really hard to find, and Savannah figured no one would know about it. Come to the kitchen. I'll draw you a map."

CHAPTER THIRTY

Savannah took a sip of her chamomile tea as she leaned back against the kitchen island. After the long drive, a trip to stock up on food and supplies, and getting Caroline settled in the cabin, she was more than ready to get some sleep.

It was a chilly night, something she hadn't truly prepared for. Autumn-like weather had slammed into them the higher they went up the mountain. She'd forgotten how her Aunt Peggy had always warned her to "pack warm" when Savannah had been little and taking the same drive with her parents.

Had her parents given Brad the letter she'd agonized over? If he'd read it, had he accepted her decision to leave?

Leave?

"More like run away," she muttered to the empty room.

The trip had given her a lot of time to think. Part of her had wanted to turn around and drive straight home.

But whenever she began to feel courageous enough to face Michael, she'd glance in the rearview mirror and see her sleeping daughter. Every ounce of that bravery faded as the terror of losing Caroline smothered it.

When had she become such a coward?

I'm not a coward.

Her actions said otherwise.

Disgusted with herself and exhausted, she put the stoneware mug in the sink and flipped off the kitchen lights. It was a well after midnight, and she needed to turn off her stupid brain and get some rest. Caroline always rose with the dawn, so Savannah needed to be ready to answer the multitude of questions her daughter would surely toss at her. Savannah had done her best to push them aside on the long drive. That reprieve wouldn't last through breakfast.

She knew her way around the cabin well enough to get to the master suite without turning on any lights. The last thing she did before she went to the bed was to check the doors to be sure they were locked. As a child, she'd never realized exactly how isolated being all the way up the mountain could be. There had always been plenty of adults around, which made her feel safe and secure. Now it was only her and Caroline, and Savannah had watched far too many true crime shows. Her imagination was working overtime. Every shadow became sinister, every creak frightening.

How on earth was she going to stay up here for months on end?

Would it truly be *months?* Thank God that Caroline was only missing preschool. Savannah would've had a hard time explaining such an extended absence to a school had her daughter started kindergarten. As it was, she'd explained it was a family emergency that was taking her out of town. How long would that excuse hold up?

She wanted Brad there. Now. Being away from him for a day had been painful, and the future stretched out before her without him in her life, making tears sting her eyes. He'd never forgive her for leaving so abruptly. Even if he did, she wasn't about to make him commit to a life of running to keep her daughter safe.

What a nightmare...

The sudden realization that she'd just made a huge mistake nearly knocked the wind out of her.

She shouldn't have left. Not only was it a colossal error to spoil what she'd had with Brad, but she knew that by taking Caroline away, she was letting Michael win. Again.

Her father had tried to warn her, and now she wished she would have let his cautions sink in at the time. The panic had threatened to swallow her whole. All she could think about then was keeping her daughter safe. What she'd really done was give Michael enough ammunition to mow her down.

First thing in the morning, she'd gather their things and head straight back to Nashville.

After crawling into bed, she pulled the covers up and waited for her body heat to warm the freezing sheets. Exhaustion began to overtake her, and the first tendrils of sleep were curling through her mind when the sound of wheels crunching against gravel made her bolt upright.

Someone was here.

Trying to calm her racing heart, Savannah scrambled for an explanation as to why a car would be pulling into the cabin's driveway. Had her parents changed their minds and come to join her?

No, that couldn't be right. Her father had an important doctor's appointment the next day.

But no one else knew where she was.

Sweet heaven! Had Michael hired someone to follow her? Had someone in the press found out where she was?

A wash of headlights went through the kitchen window as she hurried to grab the baseball bat that always waited right inside the pantry door. Whoever it was, she'd be ready for them.

Holding the bat in both hands, ready to strike, she crept toward the door, not daring to peek outside to see the now silent car. Footsteps ground against the gravel, becoming mere whispers when the person hit the concrete walk to the kitchen door. A soft knock made her stomach lurch.

"Savannah? Are you there?"

She'd never heard anything sweeter than Brad's voice. Hurrying to the door, she saw he'd shielded his eyes and pressed his nose to the glass, trying to see inside. His eyes widened when he saw her.

Realizing how crazy she probably appeared wielding a

baseball bat, she set it on the island. "I'm so glad to see you!" she said after she threw the door open. She didn't even wait for an explanation before hurrying into his open arms.

* * *

Brad held Savannah close, closing his eyes as he breathed in the sweet scent of her hair.

The whole drive up the mountain, he'd worried about how she'd greet him. His biggest fear was that she might have wanted to leave him behind every bit as much as she wanted to protect her daughter. Her welcoming words and the way she trembled in his arms told him he'd done the right thing in going to her.

Now, he just needed to talk some sense into her. But he'd have to wait for her to calm down.

"You okay, love?" he whispered when she seemed to have composed herself.

She lifted her head to look him in the eye and nodded.

The urge to launch into a scolding lecture made it difficult for him to keep his silence.

"My parents told you I was here," she announced.

Since it wasn't a question, Brad didn't think it required an answer. He simply kept staring into her eyes.

"It wasn't you," Savannah said. Then she rose on tiptoes to brush a quick kiss over his mouth. "It was never you."

The repetition meant she'd seen his insecurity. "That's not what you said in the note."

"Yes, it is," she insisted. "I told you I left to keep Caroline away from Michael."

"You said you left because you thought you'd ruined my life."

"I did."

He kissed her so he wouldn't shout at her. Then a simple kiss wasn't enough. Forcing his tongue past her lips, he willed her to respond—and respond she did. The ferocity of her kiss was enough to make him put aside the discussion they should be having. Her tongue rubbed against his as she looped her arms around his neck. Although they had a lot to talk about, he suddenly thought it would be a great idea to make love to her.

Brad broke off the kiss long enough to ask, "Is Caroline asleep?"

"Yep."

"Thank God." He lifted her into his arms. "Which way's your bedroom?"

She pointed down the hallway. "Last door on the right. There aren't any condoms."

"I've got one."

Savannah cocked an eyebrow.

"Told you I'd be more careful in the future."

Encouraged that she wasn't protesting that they needed to talk first, he carried her to a large bedroom, having the passing thought that Paul had called this place a "cabin" when it was actually roomy and well-furnished. He nudged the door closed with his foot, taking care to do it gently so he wouldn't wake Caroline.

The bed was turned down, so Brad placed Savannah on the sheets and started undressing her. Not that there was much to take off—a thermal shirt and pajama pants. He had her stripped bare and was tugging at his own clothes when she rose on her knees to help him.

Once they were skin to skin and he'd rolled on a condom, he unleashed his hunger for her, a desire that had been fed with his fears that he might have lost her. The need to reclaim what was his was strong. He pushed her back against the mattress, spreading her thighs with his knee before settling against her core, loving the heat of her pressing against his cock. His tongue swept into her mouth, stroking hers as he drank in her sweetness and wondered yet again how she could have captured him so completely.

Breaking from the kiss, he licked and nibbled his way down her neck until he could feast on her breasts. Her nipples were always so responsive. He teased one into a tight bud with his tongue and teeth before pulling the hard nub deeply into his mouth and suckling. She let out a low moan and gripped his shoulders.

Already past wanting, Brad needed her to be ready for him. He continued his journey down her body until he could detect the scent of her arousal. He pressed a finger inside her, finding her wet with welcome, which nearly pushed him over the edge. Rising above her, he said, "Wrap those legs around me, love. I need to be inside you."

When Savannah obeyed with a sexy smile, he plunged

inside her, closing his eyes at how much pleasure she gave him. Being with her stripped him naked, robbed him of every bit of his self-control, and he knew this would be fast and rough.

Each time he pushed into her, she raised her hips to meet him, making those erotic little sounds from deep in her throat. Then she squeezed him hard with her legs before her body clenched around him, forcing his own surrender.

* * *

Savannah snuggled against Brad, draping a thigh over his legs while he texted all the people who'd been worried about her. Her guilt weighed heavily, but she knew they would all forgive her. They knew how afraid she'd been of losing Caroline.

The touch of desperation he'd shown when they'd made love had touched her heart. He'd been afraid of losing her. What he never realized was that even if she'd left, she would always belong to him.

"Guess what?" he asked as he set his phone on the nightstand.

"What?"

"We've finally got Michael where we want him, love."

Her heart skipped in her chest. "What do you mean?"

"By the time we meet with him, you'll be walking into that meeting with proof that he defrauded other clients the same why he ripped you off. You can use the affidavits we'll have to help open his eyes to the fact that he no longer controls you. No, now *you* control *him*."

Adrenaline racing through her, she couldn't contain her happiness. Thanks to Brad, everything was different now. Michael no longer held all the cards in this game.

In all the time she'd known him, the man had wanted one thing—to be Colonel Parker to some Elvis Presley. He wanted to be famous by making other people famous. With proof that Michael was nothing but a phony—a base thief—she could now hold his dream hostage in return for Caroline's safety.

She hugged Brad tightly, so full of gratitude and love. Through everything, Brad had been there, backing her up. Believing her. Believing *in* her. "Thank you. Thank you." She rubbed her nose against the crisp hairs on his chest.

"Did I tell you that I thought up another song on the drive up here—another one you inspired?"

"You did?" She was surprised to feel her eyes grow moist. Why she was such a muse for him, she'd never truly recognize. But she could think of no other way for him to express his love so effectively.

"I did. I'm calling it 'Don't Walk Away.'"

"I don't like that title," she teased. "It's not accurate."

"Not accurate? It's all I could think the whole damn drive." He kissed her temple. "I didn't want you to walk out of my life."

"It's still the wrong title, though."

"Why?"

"Because I'd already decided to come back first thing in the morning. Know why?"

"Why?"

"Because I can't walk away from you. Ever. So I think you should call it '*Can't* Walk Away.'"

He chuckled. "I'll give that some consideration." He rubbed her upper arm with his fingertips. "Are you ready to talk about things now?"

In his arms, her confidence had returned, as had her common sense—to the point she felt damned foolish. "I shouldn't have tried to run away. That was stupid."

"Glad you said it instead of me." The tease in his voice took away some of the sting, but she playfully pinched him anyway.

"If Michael finds out what I've done..." The thought made her shudder.

Brad squeezed her. "He hasn't, and he won't. This stays between us."

"And my parents," she couldn't help but point out.

He let out a little chuckle. "I doubt they'll rat you out."

"And Joslynn and Greg and..."

"Your secret is safe." He kissed the top of her head. "How can you possibly think you've ruined my life?"

"Not a very subtle segue there, Mr. Maxwell."

"Subtle isn't my thing."

"So I've noticed," she drawled. A heavy sigh escaped. "No, I don't think I ruined your life. But I did make it a hell of a lot more difficult."

"How?"

Since he asked as though he honestly didn't understand, she gave him the truth. "The stress. The stupid press. The whole ridiculous celebrity thing. I don't want to be a burden to you."

"How could you ever believe that you're a burden?" he asked.

"Oh, I don't know. Maybe because I had you running all the way up the Smoky Mountains chasing me?"

He let out a warm chuckle before he gave her another squeeze. "I love you, Savannah. I need you in my life."

She stroked his arm. "I need you in mine, and so does Caroline." A yawn slipped out that she didn't even try to smother.

"Get some rest, love," Brad said. "We'll be back in Nashville before lunch."

"It's after two already. If you want to get back by lunch, we might as well leave now."

"Let's get a few hours of sleep first," he suggested. "Have you thought of a game plan yet?"

"You mean for Michael?" she asked.

"Yeah."

"Not really. I'll be glad to take suggestions."

"I have a couple of ideas," he admitted. "Plus Geoffrey and Greg probably have some strategies. Oh, and Ethan wants to talk to you about handling the press."

"He would know," she said. "I can't imagine what it was like for him growing up with famous parents."

"That's why he thinks he can help you." After rolling to his side, he scooted down so he could face her and smiled.

"As for Michael—I think it's time we showed him that you're not the scared little girl he once knew."

She smiled back. "How exactly do you expect me to do that?"

"I think the time has come for you to turn the tables on him and make a few threats of your own."

CHAPTER THIRTY-ONE

Déjà vu," Brad whispered to Savannah.

She squeezed his hand, grateful he was trying to lighten the tension. For two days, they'd prepared for this confrontation. Her thoughts were focused entirely on the man waiting in the conference room.

Michael Hart.

If this plan was going to work, she needed to be strong—probably stronger than she'd ever been in her life. With Brad at her side and Caroline's future hanging in the balance, Savannah knew she had more than enough motivation to succeed. And thanks to the information he'd acquired, she also had plenty of ammunition.

"It's almost over, love," he reassured.

"I could lose Caroline," she reminded him.

Could, but *wouldn't*. Not only was Brad there for her, but she had two heavy-hitters in her corner. The Jorgenson brothers. They would never let Michael anywhere near

Caroline. As Brad and Savannah had driven back to Nashville, they'd hit the ground running and shared some conference calls with Greg and Geoffrey. Now there were plans in place to get Michael backed into a proverbial corner. Once there, they were going to do their best to keep his ass there.

Geoffrey came over to them where they waited right outside the double doors of the conference room. His brother followed behind, stopping to put a reassuring hand on Savannah's arm.

She gave him a grateful smile in return.

"Are you ready, Savannah?" Geoffrey asked.

"I am."

"And did you accomplish the task I requested?" His grin was infectious.

"I did. I've grown a pair of *cojones*," she announced.

"Well...then shall we show the esteemed Mr. Hart exactly how large those are?" He opened the doors and swept his hand out to allow her to enter first.

With all the confidence she could muster, Savannah strode inside. There were several things Geoffrey had coached her on before the meeting, and one important point was that she show nothing but utter composure and confidence. Michael was used to a woman who didn't question him, who didn't confront him.

He was about to meet the new Savannah Wolf.

Taking the chair at the head of the table, she acknowledged Michael and his lawyer with a curt nod. Then she waited for Geoffrey, Greg, and Brad to be seated.

Michael's face flushed as he pointed at Brad. "I thought I told you that I didn't want him—"

Savannah calmly held up her hand, bringing Michael to a sputtering halt. "He's here at my request. End. Of. Story."

At first, Michael's eyes widened before narrowing menacingly. He mumbled something to Tom.

Tom let out a resigned sigh. "Shall we begin? I understand you've come up with a proposal settlement to our suit and—"

She brought the man to a stop the same way she'd managed Michael. "If you don't mind," she said with a touch of condescension, "I'll run this meeting." Opening the file that Penelope had left on the table for her, she plucked out the first piece of paper, a summary to remind her of what she was going to "offer" to a man who deserved nothing. "To get you to drop your suit to have me pay you for your...*representation*..." She let the snidely spoken word hang there for a beat or two. "Here's what I'm offering. I—"

Michael knit his brows. "Shouldn't your lawyer—"

"I don't need my lawyer to speak for me," Savannah replied with as much rudeness as he'd just shown. She glanced at the three men lined up at her side. "I speak for all of us." Their nods were as brusque as hers had been, but she could see the pride reflected in their eyes.

Emboldened, she continued. "Here's what I'm offering. I'll pay you nothing."

Michael jumped to his feet. "Nothing?"

"Not a dime. *However*...I will give you three important promises."

"I don't want promises," Michael insisted. "I want what I'm owed."

Tom dragged Michael back into the seat with a tug on his shirt. "I think we should hear her out."

Anger written on his face, Michael said, "Whatever. Go ahead, Savannah. Have your stupid say. Then we'll see you in court."

She refused to rise to his bait. "When you withdraw this lawsuit, I will promise not to tell the story of what you did to me to anyone in the press."

"What's that supposed to mean?" he asked.

"That means you want new clients and to keep the few you've already got. If I tell the whole sordid tale of how you robbed me and left me alone, penniless, and pregnant, do you honestly think *anyone* will ever hire you again?"

His face blanched. "That's not what happened."

"Pardon me," she said, "but bullshit. And I'll milk it for everything it's worth. I have offers from three national shows, including *Wake Up, America*. I'm taping a segment for that show in two hours. If you don't agree with the proposal, well...I know *exactly* what I'll talk about. Trust me, the publicity will bury any chance you have of *ever* being a talent manager."

"You wouldn't dare."

"In addition," she said with conviction, "I won't release the information we've uncovered about the other clients you've defrauded."

Tom's brows knit as he glanced at Geoffrey. "Other clients?"

Geoffrey nodded, passing across copies of five different affidavits from former clients. "I do believe our private investigators will turn up plenty more before our quest ends."

After a quick shuffle through the papers, all the wind seemed to go right out of Michael's sails as he slumped in his chair.

"What's the third promise?" Tom asked while Michael sat in silence, throwing daggers at her with his eyes.

"I promise to waive any rights to child support," Savannah replied. "In return for these written promises, I want you to withdraw your lawsuit and relinquish parental rights to Caroline."

Michael always did show his emotions far too easily. He might be peeved that he wasn't going to walk out of there with a check, but he was at least considering the plan. "So to keep your trap shut, you want me to—"

"To sign away your parental rights to a child you never wanted. In return..." She plucked a thick packet from the file. "I will sign these papers. The first is a confidentiality agreement that states that I will never discuss anything about our personal or professional relationships in public and—"

"Oh, I get it," he said with a sneer. "You'll gossip to your friends, then they'll talk to some reporter and—"

"If you would please stop interrupting...What I was going to say was in public or with anyone outside of immediate family. Should I breach that agreement in any way, you have leave to refile your suit, and I will be more than happy to open up everything we've discovered with the press."

Michael stared at her with skeptical eyes, but he flipped his hand to get her to continue.

Despite his rudeness, Savannah pressed on. "The second agreement is that I will waive all rights to any child support—past, present, and future." She slid the papers to Michael's lawyer, who immediately began to leaf through them. "There's only one catch."

Michael flopped back into his chair. "I knew it! You want something else—something other than the kid. What is it?"

Tom was more patient. Still perusing through the papers, he said, "May I have a moment to review these and converse with my client?"

"Of course," Savannah coolly replied. Her heart was beating so fast she could barely breathe, but she'd never let them know exactly how afraid she was.

With a shake of his head, Michael said, "Not until she tells me the rest of it."

Tom gave a slight roll of his eyes and then focused on the papers.

"The rest," she said, "is that this deal is only good for the next ten minutes." She savored Michael's confused expression and how his attorney's head popped up.

Savannah pressed the point home. "The forms for signing your parental rights and another form waiving a family court hearing are in there. All you have to do is sign them, walk out of this office, and never look back."

Her ex settled back in his chair as Tom leaned closer and whispered as he pointed out things in the papers.

Then Tom said, "I need a few moments to confer with my client."

"Absolutely," Savannah replied. She made no move to leave when Geoffrey offered her a nearly imperceptible shake of his head.

After several moments of whispering, the lawyer glanced up to Geoffrey. "Who would notarize the hearing waiver?"

This point had been stressed by Geoffrey in their planning meeting. The only true error they could make in this process was giving Michael any chance to claim he'd been coerced into giving up his daughter. They were walking a fine line, and Geoffrey had gone to great lengths to create documents that would hold up in court.

"I believe you're a notary, Mr. Cummings," she replied. "We'd be happy if you could handle that chore to show these papers are being signed by your client with your consent and approval."

He nodded, said a few more things to Michael, and then set the papers on the table, opening the packet to the first of the pages requiring Michael's signature. He fished a pen and his notary stamp out of his briefcase and put them next to the papers.

Michael crossed his arms over his chest as he stared at Savannah. "I gotta say, *sweetheart*—"

A low growl rumbled from Brad's chest.

Tom slashed his hand down again, a gesture that was becoming quite familiar, a show to Michael that he should cool it, which made Brad settle down as well.

With an indignant huff, Michael continued, "I never thought you'd have the guts to stand up to anyone, let alone me."

Again, she drew on Geoffrey's coaching and her belief that this was all in Caroline's best interests. She might want to see him punished for the hell he put her through, but getting him out of their lives was the true goal. "I'm just trying to be fair—to both of us."

For the first time, Geoffrey jumped into the fray. "Tom, you need to stress to your client that this is an important offer. We're saving his future and asking for very little in return. Mr. Hart has had no contact with the minor, and all we're requesting is that he continue to do so."

Greg added his scripted piece of advice. "He can reinvigorate his management career."

Grateful to have Brad subtly rubbing her leg, Savannah kept her spine straight and her chin lifted. "So what do you say, Michael?"

* * *

The moment the office door shut behind Michael and Tom, Savannah's legs went weak. She sagged against Brad, who had quick enough reflexes to keep her from sprawling on the carpet.

Geoffrey patted her shoulder. "My dear Savannah, you

were amazing." He handed the file of signed paperwork to Penelope. "Please make sure Ms. Wolf and Tom Cummings receive copies of all of these after I personally go to Judge Hicks to obtain his signature."

"Congratulations," Greg added.

Brad held her tightly, which was exactly what she needed at that moment. Her courage had seen her through, but now she wanted to borrow some of his strength.

Penelope set the folder on her desk and disappeared into a small alcove. She came back a few moments later with a silver tray that bore five champagne flutes and a green bottle.

Once drinks were passed around, Geoffrey raised his glass. "To our Savannah, who was able to grow balls as big as any elephant."

After laughter and sips, Brad gave her a smile that reached deep inside her to touch her soul. "You were amazing," he said.

Her face flushed hot. "Thank you."

"Only one more hurdle left." Greg checked his watch. "Are you ready to tape your segment on *Wake Up, America*? We've only got an hour or so to get you ready."

"Oh, I'm ready," she announced. "After talking with Ethan last night, I feel good about this. Although...it's still really hard for me to trust any reporter."

"They're not all bad," Greg said. "You only need to win a few over to your side, and things will turn around."

"That's what Ethan told me, and growing up with cameras pointed at him all the time, he would know." She let out a sigh. "I guess if I can face down Michael, talking to a reporter shouldn't be too tough. After all, that's exactly what Ethan's parents did and it worked for them."

Geoffrey nodded. "The Duke and Duchess of Cambridge also asked the press to keep their distance from their kids—a trick I believe they borrowed from Princess Diana. That request is being honored."

Brad draped an arm over her shoulders. "Just be yourself, Savannah. Ask them to leave Caroline in privacy. I know you'll get through to them."

"Even if the paparazzi don't buy into your plan," Greg said, "your fans will. It never ceases to amaze me how much people can impact what the press does."

"Social media's influence," Geoffrey said before frowning. "That can be a double-edged sword."

"Which is why I'm going on television to win people over." Savannah glanced up at Brad. "I think I've got all my bases covered. Don't you?"

"I sure hope so," he replied. "I guess we'll just have to wait and see."

* * *

Savannah took a bracing breath as Brad parked in his usual spot close to Words & Music. She'd survived the taping for her appearance on *Wake Up, America*, and now she just wanted a glass of wine and a bite to eat.

He killed the engine. "How do you feel?"

She took his hand. "I feel fantastic."

"It went really well."

"It did. I can only hope it'll work."

He nodded. "You put the ball firmly in their court. If any of the paparazzi bother your daughter again, the good guy reporters will let them have it."

"And my fans?" It was still hard to trust in the people who only knew her through her music. "Do you think Ethan's right, that they'll support me in asking for Caroline's privacy?"

"You're starting a website, joining a bunch of social media—"

"When I hire an assistant," she reminded him. "No one has time for posting on all those sites."

"You're promising to be more available in return for giving your daughter some space. Of course they'll support you."

As Brad climbed out of the car, Savannah decided not to wait for him to come around and open her door. Today had been all about her striking out on her own, being a strong, independent woman. She might as well continue the trend.

Hand in hand, they walked into the restaurant, and when she saw Randy setting up the equipment, it dawned on her exactly what today was. An ironic laugh fell from her lips.

Brad knit his brows. "What?"

"I'm back where I started."

His perplexed expression didn't ease. "Pardon?"

She inclined her head toward the stage. "It's Indie Night. That's where all of this began."

A smile bowed his lips, and he raised her hand to kiss her knuckles. "So it is. I suppose that means we've come full circle."

"We really have."

Brad led her to a table, and after they were both seated, Cheyanne came over to take their order. Once they were alone, he gave her another smile. "Do you regret any of it?"

She shook her head. "Not a single thing."

"Well, then. I suppose this might be the right time to tell you that Ethan, Russ, and I want to sign you to a new contract."

"You do? But with Allied wanting me to do a few out-of-town shows and—"

"Let me explain the details before you get your back up." The teasing tone took the bite out of his words.

"Explain away," she said.

"You'll be a permanent headliner, but...we'll be flexible. You can take time when you need to record or if you need to tour, especially since you made Allied promise you'd never be away from home more than a few weeks a year." He shot her a grin. "There's only one requirement."

"Oh? And what's that?"

Brad winked. "You have to sleep with one of the partners."

"Ethan or Russ?" she teased.

When she glanced at the stage, she caught the first singer standing in the wings, looking terrified. Her heart went out to the young performer. "I think I'll sneak backstage for a minute."

"Why?"

"Because I see a very nervous singer who might benefit from a pep talk." On that, Savannah headed toward the stage door.

* * *

As Savannah walked away, Brad couldn't help but smile. So like her to want to help someone she didn't even know. It was one of the thousands of reasons he loved her.

If someone had told him a year ago that he'd be writing songs again and that he'd have a woman like Savannah Wolf in his life, he would've told them they were insane.

Not one to question his good luck, he watched as she took the singer's hand and started talking to her. He wondered if Savannah saw the wide-eyed admiration in that performer's eyes or if she knew how much her talk would help the girl face the large Words & Music crowd. Just before Randy went center stage to introduce the first act, Savannah gave the singer a quick hug, then she came striding back to the table.

Although everyone around him, including Savannah, was watching the performance, Brad watched her. One thought summed up the future that lay before him.

Damn, but I'm a lucky man.

EPILOGUE

Three months later...

Savannah opened the door to the mudroom and stepped inside her home, smiling when she saw Brad's boots resting next to Caroline's shoes. He'd promised to take Caroline for pizza tonight while Savannah sang a couple of songs with Tony Plunkett as he debuted at Black Mustang. Although she was sorry she was too late to read her daughter a bedtime story, she would sneak in and give Caroline a kiss.

When she stepped through the door into the kitchen, she stopped short. From where she stood, candlelight shimmered all around her. None of the lights were on, but it seemed as though candles were on every table, giving the kitchen and living room a soft glow.

Her gaze settled on Brad where he stood next to the fireplace. The gas logs were lit, adding more ambience to the setting. While she would've assumed he'd planned a seduction, Savannah had to rethink when she saw Caroline standing next to him, holding his hand.

Both were grinning.

"What's all this?" Savannah asked.

"We got surprises, Mama," Caroline answered, her voice loud with enthusiasm.

Arching an eyebrow, Savannah locked eyes with Brad. "Surprises, huh?"

He nodded as Caroline dropped his hand to skip over to her mother. Then she took Savannah's hand and led her to the couch. Two manila folders rested on the coffee table. As Savannah sat, Caroline crawled up to plop next to her on her right, and Brad took a seat on Savannah's left.

"So what are these?" She nodded at the folders.

"Those are the surprises!" Caroline announced.

Leaning forward, Brad picked up one of the folders. "Caroline and I have had a long discussion and we think there are some changes that we need to make."

"Oh, you do, do you?"

Since Caroline was nodding vigorously, Savannah couldn't help but smile. The two of them had obviously conspired for a common goal, and she was dying of curiosity to discover what they had in store for her.

Opening the folder, Brad plucked out a piece of paper and set it on Savannah's lap. "We think it's time."

She looked down to find a marriage license application that had been conveniently filled out with her name and Brad's. Before she could say anything, he was down on one knee, holding a small red velvet box. "You know how much

I love you and how much I love Caroline. There's nothing more in the world I want to do than make us a family. I'd be honored if you would marry me."

Her heart started slamming against her ribs. They'd talked about marriage a few times, but they'd pretty much abandoned the subject after she'd convinced Michael to relinquish his parental rights to Caroline. So she'd assumed Brad was content with the way they split their time between his mansion and her home without worrying about the two of them marrying.

But after all the time she'd spent with Brad, she'd learned the kind of man he was—a man who valued love, home, friends, and family.

This was a man Savannah could lean on, depend upon.

This was the man she loved beyond words.

"We asked Pop-pop if you should marry Brad!" Caroline announced. "Pop-pop said 'it's 'bout damn time'!"

That statement made a laugh bubble up, so she didn't scold her daughter for the direct quote. Knowing that Brad loved her enough not only to speak to her parents but to include Caroline in the decision made the answer easy. Placing her hand on Brad's arm, Savannah nodded. "Yes, I'll marry you."

A cheer erupted from Caroline, while Brad gave Savannah a smile and opened the box. Inside was the most beautiful ring. A teardrop sapphire was surrounded by small diamonds. As he slid the ring on her finger, he said, "It seemed like the right color." Then he touched the blue strands of her hair.

"It's perfect," she said, a bit breathless.

"It's my turn!" Caroline picked up the second folder. A paper slid out and fell to the floor. The girl picked it up and handed it to her mother. "Brad's gonna be my daddy!"

"He is?" This application was for adoption, and just as the marriage license application was already filled out, this one had all of its blanks completed—all except the line for Savannah to sign.

"If you agree to it," Brad said, sitting next to her once again. "When I asked Caroline if it was okay to marry you, I told her I wanted to be her father."

"And I said yes," Caroline announced with a decisive nod. "Can he, Mama? Can he be my daddy?"

Heart filled near to overflowing, Savannah had to fight the desire to weep. All she could do was nod.

Brad stood and then tugged her to her feet. A moment later he was kissing her.

Not to be excluded, Caroline jumped off the couch and tried to squeeze between them.

With a chuckle, he picked her up and kissed her cheek.

"We're a family now," Savannah said, unable to stop a few tears from spilling over her lashes.

With a broad grin, Brad gave Savannah a quick kiss. "'A family now.' That sounds like the perfect title for a new song."

Don't miss the next book in Sandy James's Nashville Dreams series!

Read on for a preview of
Can't Let Her Go.

Available in early 2018.

CHAPTER ONE

Holy shit. It's her. It's really her!"

Ethan Walker glanced up from the bar in response to his business partner Russ Green's words of awe. "What are you talking about?"

"Not what. *Who.* Chelsea Harris, that's who," Russ said. "She's here."

"Who's that?" Already annoyed at having to cover a Saturday night shift for one of the bartenders, Ethan didn't have the patience for Russ to be going gaga over some woman. The older he got, the more Ethan hated crowds, and Words & Music was packed tonight.

"*Chelsea Harris.*" Russ leaned against the bar and frowned. "Have you been living under a rock?"

"On a farm," Ethan grumbled as he set two drafts on a waitress's tray, wishing he'd been a little less sloppy with the foam. He wiped his wet fingers on a bar towel and moved on to the next order.

"Thanks, Ethan," she said with a saucy wink before whisking the booze away.

"Welcome," he mumbled in return. The last thing in the world he wanted to do was flirt with one of his staff. Sure, most of his waitresses were pretty damn cute. But as his daddy always cautioned him, he kept work and fun separate. He shifted his focus to Russ. "Okay. You've got my attention now. So what's with this chick?"

"Chick?" Russ let out a snort. "You're really clueless. The last thing I'd ever call someone like Chelsea Harris is a 'chick.'"

Well aware of exactly who Chelsea Harris was and that she'd breezed in with her entourage about fifteen minutes ago, Ethan had some fun jerking Russ's chain a little more. After all, teasing his two partners was one of his favorite pastimes. He shrugged. "Then tell me why I should know her."

"She's only the hottest thing to hit country music in the past five years." Russ's disgruntled tone and emphatic gestures made Ethan fight a grin. "Look over to high-top table eight, dipshit. You can't miss her. Hell, the woman can't seem to get a moment of peace."

Eyes already on the subject of their conversation, Ethan only shrugged again, despite the fact that nonchalant was the last thing he felt.

Chelsea Harris was gorgeous. A mane of long, wavy red hair. A curvy figure, the kind he preferred. But it was how she seemed entirely unfazed by the way the people around her buzzed with excitement and took her picture with their cells. Most celebrities ate that kind of attention up. Not her. She was chatting with the two other women sitting at her table, both of whom appeared to be friendly rather than celebrity suck-ups. A rather beefy security guard kept a close eye on her. Even though he wore dark clothes and was trying to blend into the wall, he was easy for Ethan to notice.

The woman clearly knew her own appeal, and she exuded confidence. Oh, she was quite aware of how many people were staring at her, talking about her, and she was fine with all of it. From the way she laughed and gave slight nods to anyone who was able to find the courage to make eye contact, she relished her celebrity status.

A queen on her bar stool throne.

Not all stars were that comfortable in their own skin. Many tried their best to hide from press and fans until they chose the time or place to make contact. A concert. An award show. A fundraiser. In all other aspects of their lives, they usually demanded privacy.

Not the eminent Ms. Harris. One of the reasons Ethan knew so much about her was because the woman lived her life in the open. His famous parents had been of that breed—acting as if every fan should be a best friend.

A person wanted to know where she was, what she thought, who she was with? All he had to do was pull up any social media account. *Bam.* Chelsea Harris was there. Hell, she was playing on her phone at that very moment, probably doing one of those tweety things.

Hopefully, she was telling everyone to get their asses

down to Words & Music. The business would always be welcome. If word got out that she'd stopped by and enjoyed the place, fans would be there waiting with hopes of seeing her the next night. Or the next.

As though reading his thoughts, Russ said, "She's great for business. Hope social media is eating this up." He let out a low whistle. "She sure is a looker."

Understatement of the year. Her thick hair caught the lights exactly right, making it appear like waves of fire rippling down her back and ending right above her shoulder blades. Her gaze swept the room, settling on the bar. When her eyes caught his, he sucked in a breath, unable to stop a physical reaction to the woman.

With a shake of his head at his own weakness, Ethan shrugged and drew another draft.

"Heard she's unattached again," Russ commented. "Kicked that pretty boy actor to the curb." He let out a chuckle. "Probably wrote a song about it. She has every other time she broke up with a guy, and they're always hits."

"Saw? Saw it where?"

Russ rubbed the back of his neck and glanced away. "On *Nashville Chat*."

"You watch that garbage?" The show was nothing but gossip pretending to be news. Ethan knew it as *Nashville Shat* since that's what he and his other partner Brad Maxwell called it.

"Sometimes..."

With a snort, Ethan turned his back and sliced an orange

to garnish one the foo-foo drinks women seemed to enjoy. Damn if he wasn't so preoccupied thinking about Chelsea Harris and that gorgeous hair that he nicked his finger when a feminine voice broke into his reverie.

"Ethan Walker?"

"Shit." He grabbed the bar towel again to hold against his sliced index finger. A quick check showed it wasn't serious, so he just kept a little pressure on it.

"You okay?"

The melodious voice made him glance up to find himself face-to-face with the object of his new and rather obsessive fixation. She leaned down, resting her forearms on the bar. Most of the patrons on the barstools were gawking at her.

He was dumbstruck. Her eyes were to blame. Such a sparkling green, but it wasn't the color that had him transfixed. It was the intensity he found in those depths, an intensity that put him immediately on his guard.

Despite all the people staring at her, this woman was on a mission.

"You're Ethan Walker," she said. "You own this place."

Since she hadn't asked a question, he saw no need to reply.

"I'm Chelsea Harris."

Several people laughed in response to the statement, as though she had stated something so obvious it became comical. He had to resist the urge to do the same.

"I know." Those were the only words he would spare until he figured out her angle.

Her gaze wandered slowly around the cavernous Words

& Music. "This place is amazing. I never saw it before—you know, when your parents ran it. But...wow. You've really done well."

"Thanks." Having no idea what was going on behind her mask of cordiality, he wouldn't say anything more. Better to let her lead so he could figure out exactly why she was chatting him up and plying him with compliments. While she seemed genuine, he didn't trust someone with her fame.

She gestured to the two women who waited at her high-top table. "We were all talking about how great sound carries in here. And you've got that fantastic dance floor..."

He took a quick look at the people learning a new line dance from one of the club's dance instructors. "Thanks."

Her lips drew into an annoyed line, but she quickly obliged a patron who'd worked up the guts to slide a pen and napkin her direction by signing an autograph. She even murmured her thanks for the way the lady was gushing over her songs.

The security guard took a few steps forward, but Chelsea stopped him with a quick flip of her hand and a shake of her head. Then she turned her attention back to Ethan. "You really should be proud of this place."

"I am." He pulled a new drink order up on the point-of-sale screen and went about filling it. His partners—his *friends*—often told him he had a way of irritating just about anyone he came across. At that moment, he couldn't help himself. Her increasingly exasperated reactions at his clipped answers were far too entertaining.

Chelsea put her elegant hand on the bar and began to drum her bright red nails against the wood. "Do you tend bar here a lot? Or is this just a one-night stand?"

He snorted. "Definitely not a one-night stand."

"So you're here a lot? Tell me this...do you hire the talent, or is that the Hitman's job?" she asked.

"Brad hates it when people call him that," Ethan cautioned.

"Everyone in the business calls him that."

"Not to his face."

Her fingers quickened their pace.

So there was a temper to go with that red hair.

Time to end the baiting game.

After setting a glass of white wine and a beer on an empty tray, he finally directed his full attention to her. "I'd really like to know something."

"And what is that?"

"What exactly do you want from me?"

* * *

The man couldn't be any ruder if he tried, and something in Chelsea told her that was exactly what Ethan Walker was doing. Trying to aggravate her.

Well, he'd succeeded. Problem was she couldn't show him what she truly felt. Not if she was going to get her way. No, she needed Ethan's cooperation. From what she'd been told, that cooperation would be a hard-earned prize.

She'd tried to learn as much as she could before setting

out to tackle her plan for her newest project. Although he was supportive of her plans, her manager had told her that she was crazy to even *try* to recruit Ethan Walker. His aversion to ever being a part of the country music world again was legendary.

From the moment she'd heard the duet he'd sung with Savannah Wolf, Chelsea had known that he needed to sing with her. God, but the man had the most amazing voice. Besides, she didn't understand why he should be different than any of the other people she was enlisting. So far, most of the offspring of former stars had been on board and rather enthusiastic about her plans.

Of course none of them had Ethan's reputation—a reputation that was two-fold. First, he hated being reminded that his parents were Nashville stars. Second, after walking away from a budding singing career years ago, he hated anything to do with performing or recording. Period.

And yet...he was friendly with Brad Maxwell's fiancée Savannah. She'd gotten her start at Words & Music, and Chelsea had been so mesmerized by the video of Ethan singing with her that she'd watched it too many times to count.

So he *would* perform.

But on what terms? Did he only pick up a guitar for a friend, or would a good cause—a great cause—be enough motivation?

He threw her a fierce frown. "Are you going to answer my question, or can I get back to work?"

The ill-mannered man didn't even wait for her reply and started tapping at the computer screen, all but dismissing her.

No one dismissed Chelsea Harris.

Sidling around the bar, she savored the surprised expressions of the people sitting close enough to watch her. She glanced at the drink order he'd been reading and then plucked two margarita glasses from the freezer under the counter. As Ethan gaped at her, she went about preparing the drinks, much to the amusement of the crowd. Muscle memory kicked in as she found the margarita mix and ice, blended the mixture, and then salted the rims of the glasses. After pouring the drinks, she garnished them with pineapple wedges and set them on an empty serving tray, earning herself a round of applause.

With a smug smile, she touched the screen to pull up the next order. While she wanted to see his startled expression—to savor it—she focused on the libations she needed to make.

"What in the hell are you doing?" Ethan demanded. Thankfully, his tone was more amused than irritated despite his choice of vocabulary.

"I would think it was obvious." She flashed a smile at a few people who laughed in response.

"I mean why are you pretending to be a bartender?"

Chelsea let out an indignant huff. "Pretending?" She nodded toward the drinks the waiter was carrying away, wondering if pictures of her acting as the bartender at Words & Music would've hit social media yet. "Those are damn good margaritas, if I do say so myself. You know what? Name a drink."

"What?"

"Name a drink. Any drink. I can mix it."

As he continued to gape at her, she pulled three draft beers, poured two glasses of different wines, and whipped up a screaming orgasm. After passing them off to a waitress, she folded her arms under her breasts and grinned at Ethan.

He grinned back, and damn if her stomach didn't plummet to her feet. The man was too appealing for her peace of mind. Her preference went toward long hair on guys, and his dark brown hair was pulled into a neat queue. If it were loose, it would probably brush his shoulders.

Sublime.

The first thing she'd noticed when she'd approached him were his eyes. Not only were they a warm mahogany, they sparkled with intelligence.

Even better than his obvious physical appeal.

She had no doubt that should the two of them match wits, she'd find herself with an adversary who rose to her level.

"Where'd you learn to bartend?" he asked.

"It's how I survived after college until I got my break in the business."

"You've still got the touch. You can work here if you ever need a job." He gave her another stomach-flipping smile.

"Thanks." She poured two more glasses wine and then whipped up a whiskey sour.

"Hey, Chelsea!" a guy shouted. "Hold up the tray with the drinks so I can take your picture."

With one of her practiced smiles, she obliged the man. "Be sure and say where I'm at! Words and Music, one of Nashville's best hotspots."

"Thanks for the plug," Ethan said, although his voice was devoid of true appreciation. A shame since the man had a smooth, seductive voice when he was sincere.

Always one to possess a wild and far-too-active imagination, Chelsea had to smile at the thought of how Nashville would react should she and Ethan ever hook up. The son of "Crawfish" and Dottie Walker—Nashville royalty—and the hottest female star in country music?

Reporters would be tripping over each other to get to them the same way people were now crowding around the bar to watch their exchange.

And the charity album would go platinum.

A chuckle slipped out.

Ethan's mouth fell to a frown. "Are you laughing at me?"

"Not at all," she assured him, absentmindedly signing a few more autographs. The action had become so perfunctory, she hardly thought about what she was doing anymore.

"Then what's so funny?"

He'd never understand how happy she was at the thought of her new album being a huge success, so she shook her head.

The frown became a scowl. "Why are you here?"

Knowing Ethan was in no frame of mind for her to

even broach the topic of his recording a song with her, she scrambled for something to say. She wished they had a bit of privacy, but that was in short supply whenever she was in public. "I . . . um . . . " She nibbled on her bottom lip, flustered that his gorgeous eyes and handsome face had erased every bit of information she'd gathered on the man, information she'd hoped would help her in this important quest. "Let's see . . . I—"

With a shake of his head, he gently pushed her aside so he could get to his computer.

She'd lost him before she'd even asked for his help. To rescue the situation, she was going to have to lay all her cards on the table at the start of the game. This man wasn't going to be charmed or cajoled, but maybe he could be convinced if she told him the real reason she was there.

The truth was that she needed him, she needed that rich baritone singing his parents' biggest hit with her.

"I came to ask for your help," Chelsea announced.

"Finally!" Ethan set a longneck he'd just opened on a tray. "She *can* answer a question."

The snickering around them made her sigh. Was nothing in her life private?

"All right," she said, a bit peeved at him and at the eavesdroppers. "I deserved that."

"Yep."

His superior tone grated on her. For a man everyone described as kind and helpful, he seemed to know exactly how to irritate her. "My father passed away last year." The memory still felt like a knife to the heart.

"I'm sorry for your loss." Those brilliant eyes found hers, and they were full of compassion. There was sincerity in his tone.

"Thank you."

"What does losing your father have to do with me?" he asked.

"He died of cancer," she replied. "I want to do something big to honor his memory."

Ethan encouraged her to continue with a flip of his hand.

After a bracing deep breath, Chelsea said, "I'm putting together an album to raise money for cancer research. I'm singing duets with the kids of former Nashville stars, and I'd like for you to cover one of your parents' songs with—"

"No. Way." Turning on his heel, he stalked away.

ABOUT THE AUTHOR

Sandy lives in a quiet suburb of Indianapolis and is a high school psychology teacher. She owns a small stable of harness racehorses and enjoys spending time at Hoosier Park racetrack. She has been an Amazon #1 bestseller multiple times and has won numerous awards, including two HOLT Medallions.

Learn more at:
sandyjames.com
Twitter @sandyjamesbooks
Facebook.com/sandyjamesbooks